LONDON
INCOGNITA

Gary Budden

First published in Great Britain in 2020 by Dead Ink, an imprint of
Cinder House Publishing Limited.
ISBN 9781911585725

Cover design by Luke Bird
lukebird.co.uk

Printed and bound in Great Britain by Clays Ltd, Elcograf S.p.A.

www.deadinkbooks.com

LONDON INCOGNITA

Gary Budden

[signature]

dead ink

To Nina, and the future

For if you think of it, there is a London cognita and a London incognita. We all know about Piccadilly and Oxford Street, London Bridge and the Strand. Olympia had made familiar with a little island in otherwise unknown Hammersmith; the Boat Race illuminates Putney, and the most inexperienced have ventured into High Street, Kensington. But where will you be, if I ask you about Clapton, about the inner parts of Barnsbury, about the delights of Edmonton?

– Arthur Machen, *The London Adventure*

There are certain memories that never really reach your brain. They stay in your blood like a dormant virus.

– Michael Moorcock, 'London Blood'

Contents

Contents

PROLOGUE

Sinker (a dark cadence)

You were talking about the past, and the things we had done before we knew what to do. I recalled how the sun died tired in our back garden, green that stretched out like a landing strip towards the cemetery. Over the wooden fence was where the dead lived and dreamed their dreams of London, trodden on by crackheads and alkies and the men seeking sex from other men. I felt the slower we went the better, easy-does-it over the fence boys, but a night of heavy drinking had impaired an already stiff and unagile body.

When I fell into the realm of the dead, my brittle collarbone snapped on a ruined grave and my head poured crimson. I blacked out, and when I came to, had lost my filter and spoke openly of the things that preoccupied me, but I felt too embarrassed to express in daylight. This troubled you, who ushered me through the dank and dripping tombs to the exit, where we had summoned a flashing ambulance. A man from the council was summoned to unlock the Victorian gates; all present advised that trying to scale the boundaries of the necropolis a second time was foolish. The paramedics took my heartbeat, asked if I'd taken something, my chest thudding fast and hard; the irony was that that night, I hadn't.

All I could think about was that night in the cemetery; the mossed statues didn't make for easy conversation. What we failed to speak of was how we got ourselves through the dark days and made it all make sense, how we tried to stop ourselves sinking.

Judderman

D.A. Northwood

From Daniel Eider's journal

Earlier this evening, while Mum washed up in the kitchen and dad sat in his chair nodding off in front of the latest news of bombs and missing children, I wrote the following phrase in my journal: 'This city is built on pain.'

That's far too simple. I know there is more to the city than just pain, suffering and trauma; but sometimes my vision is obscured and I can't see clear.

I am no anarchist, and I am not a communist, and I do not like limiting myself to the political categories people are so fond of in this time I find myself living in. The boxes we cram ourselves into trap us, and the lid locks, where we wait to explode like Jacks driven mad from our confinement. That should be obvious to anyone with eyes to see.

So, I would not say I was political. But I do care about people.

And I try to care about all people. It is the people that I love in this city. What is a city without its people? A city is *people*, and people are its corpus and its blood; its plasma and bone; its sinew and teeth. The people are its long, complex story and its fractured memory.

(Teratomas grow in the city. The teeth and hair and eyeballs all merged in a monstrous outgrowth. There is a teratoma swelling, here in London, in the year 1972.)

And this city, London, is the place of my birth. It is the place where my family's stories sprouted and grew strong and spread like vines colonising old red brickwork. One of these tendrils ended up bearing my name. One of those tendrils bears Gary's name also. My brother and I, we see the city in ways we know others do not. We try and see it for what it really is, and slowly, so slowly, but inexorably, we are succeeding. The hippies in their squats and on their communes out in the countryside talk about a third-eye opening, but I think this is something deeper, older and more hard-earned than that. Learning to see more than what the eye records.

Imagine an image swimming into focus through the eye of a telescope trained on a distant nineteen sixties tower-block; or the shock of third-world villager, her life spent with fuzzy and blurred vision, given lenses for the first time.

The important things to see are there and were always there, but you need the tools to see them. Whilst looking for the great god Pan, I may have found something else looking back at me.

Something that is able to coax overblown statements like, 'This city is built on pain' from my pen. Ha! I make myself laugh, even at times like this when everything feels too serious, too real.

And anyway, how could words, just scribbled symbols on a page, convey the true nausea and ecstasy of the physical world? Words fail me often, but what I am writing here, this is my attempt to get across the city that my brother and I can see. The place we know as London Incognita: our home.

It is true that London is built on blood. The blood of a bloody Empire and the countless thousands that Empire enslaved and exploited. I was schooled to be proud of that Empire, and a map distorted with pink-red tones, even as it was in its death throes.

And the city is built on the blood of London's own people too. The blood and sweat and struggle of everyone who came here, worked here, fell in love here, or was beaten up and died here.

At night, I walk by the River Lea near my family home and I imagine the darkness hides the truth of the river, and it is in fact a flow of warm crimson liquid, pumping towards the Limehouse Cut and into the Thames itself, then out into the estuary and beyond into the North Sea.

When not walking in the shadow hours, I struggle to sleep. I dose myself with alcohol on too many nights, but I make myself sound a victim or a figure worthy of pity and that isn't true. I like the drink, and it likes me. On the nights without alcohol, when sleep finally claims me I dream of scarred harlequins, idiot mastodons and leopard seals breaching the oily waters of the Thames. Unwanted dreams.

So, I drink with my brother and my crippled cousin in The Sovereign because there's a price to pay for seeing too clearly.

Why do you think the hippy dream is turning sour?

My days are spent plagued with images of Wat Tyler whipping up crowds on Blackheath, of the Gin Alley riots, of Spring-Heeled Jacked and the judderman, of hulking atlas bears on the Hackney marshes and the men who wear their skins. I have seen London Burrymen wearing outfits of nettle and buddleia along railway sidings.

I know of the terrible things that happen in the homes of wealthy men, to the defenceless and the voiceless. Each day I see the war in Ireland and its blowback here.

I have recurring visions of a blind creator god jerking its arms out towards me by a deserted stretch of the New River Path in the cold days of February; by the reservoirs of Woodberry Down estate; near the Adath Yisroel cemetery in Enfield. The location seems to change each time, but the creator is the same. Mantis arms, blindfold over its ruined eyes, receding gums and an idiot's smile.

There is too much of London for me to see now, a place constantly as busy as a work of Hogarth's, as terrifying as the violent and lonely nights the inmates of Bedlam endured.

I collect stories of the city, and have done for many years now. I feed on them. I am addicted, hungry all the time, unable to be sated. Drive and dissatisfaction are essentially the same, I realise. I need to learn all that I can, while I still can.

I have disturbed something in my searching; it has noticed me. Oh, to be seen.

So, I am writing down as much as I can about the Huguenots, the Jews, the Romans, the Irish, the Italians, the Indians, the West Indians, the gypsies. My own people too. Spivs and skinheads and mods and teds. Hippies and occultists. I have scribbled books containing the stories of coolies and lascars down on the docks. Native Americans in the Victorian Wild West shows, buried aboriginal cricketers in Hackney, accounts of the Maori who somehow made their way to London's docks from Aotearoa. Chinese Limehouse, opium smoke, ripper myths, the self-exiles hiding in Epping Forest.

I need to know their stories and so somehow understand my own.

I often wonder how long the true book of London would be? The thought terrifies me. I hope, in some way, these words I write in this cheap journal purchased from the local newsagent, as Mum clears the kitchen and Dad dozes, are part of the true book of London. The book of London Incognita.

I think about my own mongrel origins and the endless mix of people that make the city. It gives me strength. I am nothing pure, and happy with that.

There is London Cognita, and London Incognita, and I know where I belong. It won't be long now.

Gary

Danny was gone. Folded into the creases of the city. Vanished.

'Charlie, where the fuck is he?? I'm getting worried now.' Gary clicked his tongue in thought before sipping his beer. He wiped foam from his top lip and looked vacantly around the pub.

'Gary, he's probably just gone on a bender,' said Charlie, annoyed. 'You know what your brother's like. Out smashing it for a few days.' His cousin sucked roughly on a cigarette and massaged his damaged leg as he took a gulp of Guinness. Gary imagined the metal buried in Charlie's white flesh as sleeping grubs ready to awaken at a moment's notice and devour him. The damaged leg was a constant reminder of other realities. The limp forever grounding Charlie in the nineteen seventies.

'This feels different. He's never disappeared for this long before.' There was the thump of a dart connecting with a triple-twenty, and a beer-bellied man roared hoarsely in triumph. His team mate patted him hard on the back. 'It doesn't feel right.'

They were sat at the bar in The Sovereign, their local boozer and usual haunt. And today that felt apt; Gary felt lately as if he were a ghostly observer of his own life, a spectre among many in the backstreets and estates of north-east London. He was frightened of becoming a shade, a ghost with a hunger that couldn't be satisfied regardless of the number of pints he downed. It was a Wednesday night and the pub was half full. A fruit machine glowed and burbled in a corner. Old men, veterans like perennial regular Old Fen, sat at the bar not doing very much. Gary wondered if Fen and his mates had done anything other than sit and drink at that bar. Blue smoke from their endless cheap cigarettes coiled in the air. Fen coughed wetly with a sound like something was coming loose inside him, jerking him briefly into animation before resuming his static position. If you picked him up and shook him he'd rattle with all the loose bits inside. His geriatric black Labrador, a surly hound named the Barghest, dozed on the sticky floor by Fen's barstool. Fen and his comrades were comprised of damp coats, unwashed jumpers and stale cigarette smoke, fixtures as permanent as the beer pumps and the cold ceramic toilets. To Gary, they resembled fungal growths growing up from the pub's floor, fusing with and colonising the space of the bar. They reminded him of psychedelically patterned mushrooms he and Lisa had found last autumn kicking up leaves and holding hands in Epping forest. The old men were a form of ancient life springing stubbornly from the rot of the city, clinging on and surviving. The smoke from their cigarettes briefly assumed the loose shape of a wraith that grinned at Gary before it dispersed.

'He's been gone for five days and a night without a word and you think that's fine?' he continued. He rubbed his two-day stubble, the light brown fading to almost blonde in places. His hair was cropped short.

'He's probably met a bird, and good on him! Heaven knows he could use it, all the freaky shit he's into has got to get a guy a bit pent up. It's not healthy, all those books and long walks.' Charlie grinned under his long greasy hair. His face was lopsided and heavily freckled, but there was a sort of idiot toughness to it. Gary was still surprised his cousin had ever been in the army. Strangely, the limp suited him; not that Charlie wore it well, as such, but he looked the type.

'I should be so lucky,' Charlie added, his smile fading. And it was true, Charlie wasn't much of a hit with the women. He'd never had a proper girlfriend, and it was easy to see why the girls considered him a weirdo, a creep, a pervert. Gary thought his cousin may at least have been able to milk his injury, but so far, he'd had no luck, and it made Gary think that people never really change. Whatever happens to us, he thought, we stay fundamentally ourselves, only becoming more like who we really are as we age. Charlie had always seemed an odd kid to Gary, obsessed with guns and American cowboy stuff, John Wayne and the Vietnam War, and always wanted to be uniformed and booted fighting in a spurious war for a country that didn't give a shit about him. He got his wish, and was punished for it. But he survived, and Gary supposed he must be thankful for that.

Gary had different interests, like his brother. Guns and America, nor the Union Jack for that matter, ever really cut it for him. Now he was plagued with the suspicion that Danny had pursued those interests with too much vigour, straying out of the light and far into the bowels and subterranean levels of the city, stranding himself down in the darkness. They both knew dark things lurked down in the lost reaches of the underground; forgotten troglodytic peoples who'd taken shelter from the bombs who never came back up, whose tools and ephemera Jenny Duro and the other river larks claimed to find in London soil from time to time. Blind grey rats the size of terriers. A segmented and writhing carnivorous thing as thick as a man's arm, seen in the tunnels by workmen near Finsbury Park and dubbed the emperor worm.

Before Danny's disappearance, the brothers had been listening to and recording the tales of London's many street drinkers. They told stories of a figure that folded itself out of the shadows, flickering and juddering, before leading the susceptible, or the willing, away far into the darkness. It was a story whose meaning was not too hard to interpret, and Danny had started to become obsessed with this thing. A figure seen in the thin places of the city. A seductive danger.

'You worry too much,' said Lisa, leaning over the bar and poking Gary in the shoulder. His girlfriend, and resident barmaid at The Sovereign, who'd been listening in to the conversation in between serving Fen and his group. She gave Gary a wink and that cheered him up a bit, as he dredged up an image of her naked pale body, ash-black hair spread around her, stretching blearily and waking to another London day, half-covered in the duvet they were sharing with increasing frequency. He didn't really know what they were doing, but whatever it was, he liked it. Lisa claimed to be one of the black Irish, her skin like alabaster, like she was already half among the dead. Maybe that was true, but Gary wasn't sure how much any of that mattered. Too many men, long hairs and cropped skulls like himself, were talking of belonging and not-belonging right now. Pubs were turning the West Indians and the Irish alike away from their doors, signs splitting the city into further division.

'There's a lot to worry about,' Gary replied, slipping back into his mood. 'And mind your own Lisa, would you?' But he grinned as he said it, and she smiled back. He ordered more drinks, and they made plans to meet up the next day.

On leaving the pub, Charlie's shuffle disturbed the Barghest which barked the same way Fen coughed, mucoid and unpleasant. Its left eye was milky with blindness; it seemed to regard Gary as he exited the pub.

As the two young men walked slowly back to Gary's mum's in the hot summer evening, past the graffiti insulting their neighbours and telling them to go back home, a group of young children sat on a chipped wall singing a song.

Judder Judder Judder
All over now
Judder Judder Judder
You're all over now

Gary listened to the children's voices, repeating the verse over and over as they laughed and giggled and pointed at his limping cousin.

'Fucking spastic!' one of them shouted, shrill and impossibly young.

Charlie walked like that because of the shrapnel buried in his leg. A car bomb had gone off during his second tour of duty, taking out one of his mates and throwing him to the floor with blood leaking from his ruined leg, mixing with oil that shimmered like a metallic rainbow. Now every step he took, the bomb went off again. Gary could see it in his face.

The singing children tittered and laughed and pointed as he walked, cruel in an everyday and almost perfunctory way, like it was their duty and expected of them. They'd been taught that this is how people act. Difference was funny to them, there to be pointed out, a useful thing to demarcate the lines of belonging. Charlie was still a young man but had passed into some other realm in the eyes and minds of children. To them, only the old and the monstrous and the outcast walked like that. The city wasn't kind to people like Charlie. Charlie, for his part, did a good job of ignoring these things.

As the children's voices faded and distorted in the hot air of the city, mingling with the sounds of passing traffic, Gary thought he heard a little girl, her voice clear, piercing, and much more beautiful than the others, sing:

Your brother's with the Judder
He's all over now

But he was tired and drunk. He was angry, worried. His clothes smelled of sweat and were uncomfortable in this recent bout of hot weather. He was overdressed and underprepared, like all the English. It was one of the hottest summers on record. That's what they said on the telly and in the papers. Heat itself was news, rather than any of its effects. Ice cream vans were doing a roaring trade on street corners and people basked like prehistoric lizards in the city's parks, soaking up the rays they half-believed would never come again. As a people not used to warmth and light, Londoners went funny in the head when the temperature rose. They thawed out, only to realise they had suffered a form of freezer-burn and had been kept too long in storage. Now they were not fit for purpose. Their minds had turned to mush.

Bombs had been going off in this sweating city too frequently, all the time it seemed, in pubs, at football grounds, and in places where important men did their business. Blown out windows had an awful beauty to them, Gary thought, and the glass made fascinating patterns over the hard surfaces on which the city's inhabitants walked. There was something to read in the scattered fragments, an extreme and violent form of rune-casting. He didn't yet know the language but there was something crucial there to be deciphered. Danny could have helped him with that, and now Danny was gone.

Gary looked behind him, trying to identify the girl singing the haunting song. It could be any of them, and they didn't seem to notice him looking. Charlie with his loping gait and open weakness had ceased to interest them.

London was tired and stressed, and so were the people on which the city fed. Gary was still living with his mum and dad, carrying on with Lisa in the room above The Sovereign where she lived, and trying to take an interest in the things men were supposed to take an interest in, rather than the things that thrilled him. He wasn't succeeding at any of these things. He dreamed of other places and other ways of living, but having experienced nothing else but the dirt and pace of the city, the images were blurry and indistinct. It was more of a feeling than any concrete idea. But Danny's disappearance was now giving him a perverse purpose. He had someone to find, and something to achieve.

I'm imagining things, he kept telling himself, as Charlie and Lisa keep telling me. Danny would be alright. Gary's older brother knew how to handle himself, he was a top bloke, a sound geezer, a well-read and tough man, and all of that was true, but he still went missing didn't he? People disappeared all the time in this city. Just look at the news reports. Why did they all believe Danny was somehow immune? It was bullshit.

'Perhaps we're incapable of believing things can happen to us, even when they do. Things happen to other people. Whatever happens to you is just your life, and how could that be special or worthy of comment?' he said to Charlie, suddenly. Charlie looked at him.

'Things happened to me, Gary,' he said, studying his cousin's face carefully.

Gary knew the city could come and swallow any of its inhabitants at any time; especially those without the cushions of education, property and money. He and his brother had heard the dark rumours circulating, that had always circulated, the dirty undercurrents of narrative that were disturbing footnotes in the bright clean story that fuelled London. The book of London Incognita was not for the faint hearted.

Spirit of the Blitz and London can take it and swinging Carnaby Street and faded Beatlemania were all perfectly fine, and there was a kind of misdirected pride in that, but there were all the other stories to deal with and process.

There were mutterings in London Incognita about young children disappearing, their remains turning up in the undergrowth of London's parks or in patches of scrub growing from concrete. In the choked and dying canals. These kids were used for things you didn't want to think about too hard, by the men in power in the big buildings and the large houses on the tops of hills. So the stories said; so the street drinkers told them. These kids were always working class, often immigrants, and Gary had tried to listen seriously to the stories of missing little Irish girls, young black or brown boys swallowed up by the metropolis. All these people who weren't allowed to be a part of the story could be consumed by the people who formed the official realities. Who the fuck was going to listen if anyone complained? The London Met? What a laugh.

So, the burnt and chipped bones occasionally found in Victoria park were swiftly forgotten. Gary never found anything of use in the papers. Saw nothing on the telly beyond the first report of a disappearance. But the stories kept coming to those who could hear and were willing to listen.

'Don't ask, and you'll be happier. You can't forget the answers,' said Danny once.

And then there were the stories about the grinning men who were on telly every week introducing the latest pop songs. Gary knew something corrupt and rotten hid behind their smiles, smug smiles, like they were almost showing off the fact they were getting away with rape and murder. They knew they were monsters, they loved it, and so did their audiences.

As Gary and Charlie ate a tea of fish fingers, frozen peas and mash with dollops of vinegary red ketchup, Gary looked at the picture of his dad that hung in the kitchen, a young man of about nineteen somewhere out in North Africa in khakis and holding a gun he didn't know the name of. Gary looked at his cousin, another young man already injured by another stupid war. He remembered a time, the three of them – Gary, Charlie, Danny – on a family daytrip down to Margate. He couldn't work out if he was backfilling in the key details, but Danny was crunching through a stick of rock and his cousin and brother made fortifications from sand which were always breached and broken by the powerfully indifferent sea. Their young pink skins were mottled with dark sand. Gulls bobbed in the air above them, like they were suspended from a baby's mobile. Their parents watched them from deckchairs made from a blue and white canvas, frayed from use and bleached from sun and salt.

Was this image truth, or just based on a truth? He couldn't say. But the edited and embellished memory, filled with painful poignancy and nostalgia, was surely just as important. Here in London, as the seventies coalesced, Charlie was a cripple and Danny was missing. Gary realised that he was alive now, in this moment, and still had the chance to take control of his story.

As he thought of Margate and the damp sand and the past, he knew a new phase of his life was beginning.

Charlie shovelled in a spoonful of mash and hummed a tune.

Your brother's with the Judder. He's all over now.

The telly was on at low volume, interference on the aerial creating strange patterns and glitches that distorted the newsreader's face and words. Something grinned briefly through the static. In clipped BBC English, the newsreader talked about the heatwave, the war in Ireland, a flare up at the local football ground, and nothing about a disappeared Pakistani child Gary had heard about in Tower Hamlets. Same old same old, and all the worse for it.

Danny didn't come back that night.

In the end, he just didn't come back.

Danny never called. He never wrote. Though the pain of the loss was immense, a raw open wound turning septic, Gary admired his brother's ability to disappear. He could see the appeal, felt the desire to release himself from the quotidian, to dissolve into the bloodstream of the city and become one with its dark narrative. To follow that juddering man into the dark recesses of the city. What a pleasure that would be, a kind of ecstasy. Perhaps that had always been Danny's ambition, to truly disappear into the thing he loved. Perhaps Gary had always been destined to assume the role of detective, like the melancholy occultists in the books they'd devoured together as teenagers. He already had the surly demeanour and the fondness for the drink. His fingers stained yellow and burnt with old cigarettes. A clear eye for the realities of London Incognita. He had always wanted to participate in the London sketched out by Arthur Machen and C.L. Nolan, and he adored the Vincent Harrier stories by Michael Ashman. Part of him had always wanted the opportunity to hunt through the remains of a haunted, damaged city, tracking down ghosts and the shades of memory.

Well, now here was Gary's chance.

It took a long time for Gary's mum, Linda, to accept that such a thing could happen. She still made Danny's tea every night. Just in case, she said each evening, the words providing an insulating blanket for her. Gary never did accept it. Perhaps, growing up on the diet of novels and films he and his brother fed on, Gary still believed the world was something that could be solved. Even in the gloaming worlds of the occult detectives and the nebulous horrors they faced, there were things that could be beaten and explained, written down in books, pinned to pages and in that process somehow controlled. Words helped contain things and control them. Danny knew this. That was why he scribbled in his journal constantly.

Your brother's with the Judder. That's what the little girl on the wall sang.

In the first few months of Danny's absence, nothing felt real. Brick walls looked paper thin and painted by retarded children. London's iconic buildings looked as if they were made from papier-mâché at an amateur weeknight class in an outer London college. The pavements were doughy, the tarmac on the roads like black sponge.

There is nothing natural about pretending things are okay when they are not. Gary could not suggest to the world that he was not falling apart and wracked with the horror of not knowing. He could barely voice the fact that he loved his brother, but he did. He loved him, and he had lost him and didn't know why. Gary craved meaning in a world that he suspected may have none.

'You've got to accept the mystery sometimes,' said Lisa as they lay in bed at night, a worried look on her pale face. At times she looked translucent. Fading away from him.

As things deteriorated, Gary saw Danny in his Hawkwind T-shirt stepping aboard the Victoria line a few carriages away from him, and he would shout his brother's name loudly and with a tone of desperation. People would look at Gary like he was defective as they pushed past onto the train. Even Charlie began to find him embarrassing.

The few times Gary dragged himself to the football with Charlie and their dads he always saw Danny smiling, inexplicably kitted out in the colours of the away fans and comfortably stood in their end. He shouted his brother's name until his voice was hoarse and the other fans angrily told him to fucking shut up. He stopped being invited to the matches, and didn't care. His dad never tried to speak to him about the loss, but talked about Danny infrequently as if he were still in their lives.

Gary just missed his brother hopping flamboyantly onto a Routemaster and Danny waved cheerily as the bus pulled away in the direction of the West End.

Gary saw Danny drinking with other broken-down men and women by the rusting canals of the city, along the Lee Navigation, and under the bridges of London, cackling and coughing, warming himself around fires that flickered in metal drums as he and his companions swigged corrosive and blinding booze from plastic bottles.

Gary hunted through the stalls and bookstores and second-hand shops across London, and he'd see Danny browsing through a sack of fifties sci-fi paperbacks in Notting Hill Gate, or buying a Pan book of horror in Hackney, or sifting intensely through old wartime photographs in Spitalfields. He often saw his brother leaving Yaxley's shop, before disappearing into the crowds.

'It'll be alright, Gal,' said Charlie every night in the pub where they obliterated themselves. Fen coughed, the Barghest whined and watched the world through a milky eye. The summer sweated and ran its course.

Slowly the other parts of Gary's life began to fall away. Obsession took hold, and who could blame him? Lisa said it wasn't right and that he needed help from someone or he'd end up being locked up in the loony bin. A fucking psychopath, dressing like a fucking special-needs pikey, she said at the end. But she hadn't lost her brother and she didn't have to listen to the hopeless cheerfulness of a crippled cousin. She didn't see her brother pushing through the crowds at Ridley Road market, or working the docks at Wapping, or stepping out of a newsagent's in Turnpike Lane.

That's how it all started. Gary was just looking for his brother, and he found a nightmare.

He's all over now.

From Daniel Eider's journal

The judderman is a myth. A myth of a city that invents its inhabitants. A city whose inhabitants dream their environment into being on a daily basis. We made it and it makes us.

The judderman is a thing born from brick and fright. The judderman is the hate that bubbles up between the cracks in the tarmac and spills over into riot and spilled blood. He is the spent fluid dripping down walls after desperate back-alley passions. He is the dereliction and the decay of London.

Observe the shadows cast by the city's crippled buildings, designed sober and built drunk, and you'll find him crouching in twitching anticipation with the rats and needles and the abstract patterns of broken glass that one day I will decipher. The architecture of brick and stone rots in a metropolitan hangover and the judderman is your stale beer breath the morning after the night before, the blood flowing from your gums as you scrub hard to wash all the poison away, and the overflowing ashtray unemptied and stained with thick black residue. He is the rattle in your chest. The damp in your bones. He's that little old lady – you think you knew her somehow in childhood, was she a friend of your granny's? – who was found keeled over and her head cracked open like an over-boiled chicken egg. She slipped on ice in that bad winter a few years back. You remember the one. It was as cold then as it is hot now.

You think you can decode messages in the gum that sticks to the pavement, spongy braille for you to read with dead eyes, down on your knees and palms stretched lovingly over the pavement. You can see pyramids and temples and ziggurats form in the piles of crushed cigarette butts in the smoke-stained pubs. The dark stains left by spilled beer on threadbare carpets assume the aspects of faces, and it is there you see the judderman also. He is a rotten wooden windowsill that disintegrates into dust and flakes when you grasp it. He is the holes and tunnels dug by masonry bees that undermine and riddle our homes. He is the abandoned tube stations and their pale-skinned inhabitants who worship the old gods of London. He's that junkie girl you saw sprawled on a mattress that crawled with lice, sores around her mouth, dried vomit beside her cool body; you knew the other junkie lads were fucking her as they pleased. He is the black lad you went to school with found with his neck broken in Tottenham police station. He is the pile of children's clothing and burnt bone found in the bracken and nettle of Victoria Park, by the Regent's Canal. The judderman is the story of how those remains came to be.

What the underground mutters to itself, and that others treat as salacious rumour, it's true.

It is all true!

Those people, the ones in power, the ones who lives on the tops of the hills of London and who sit in the seats of government, who run our police force, they are feeding on the forgotten and the unwanted. Worse: on the children of the forgotten. They know who people care about, and who they treat as something unworthy of seeing. They are feasting on the unseen. Is this what the judderman is? Does he do their work for them, these men and women in suits and sly smiles? I think I see him now lurking in crowds on kids' TV shows.

The judderman is the pigeon with rotten stumps for legs, hopping around in decreasing spirals for the amusement of braindead tourists in Trafalgar Square. He is in the glass fragments of a pint glass pulled from a man's face in A&E on a Saturday night. He is the bootboy's steel capped boot as it connects with bone. He is the policeman's baton and the grey-brown dust encrusted on a black maria with CLEAN ME thumbed in the dirt.

Once you know about the judderman, you see him everywhere. I see him everywhere.

I do not know how to tell people the things I know, other than, perhaps, through these words I write. I have seen too much and no one will believe me, not even my brother. How could I explain what lives in the shadows?

I will say it again: the judderman is a London thing. A myth of my city, born from grim necessity. I do not yet know its motivation or its reason for taking an interest in me. This trauma that we live through needs a form for us to understand. It needs a face; it needs grasping arms and pointed fingers and sharp teeth. It needs a voice like ink and velvet. And now the city has what it needs. Perhaps I am perverse in my thinking, but I daydream of how, in some obscure way, the judderman could be the city's saviour. How I will find myself again if I can find and prove his existence.

I have seen him, but that isn't enough.

I saw him peel himself out of the shadows of the Woodberry Down estate by the reservoirs and grin right at me. Like he was taking the piss. Woodberry Down, that was where I'd heard he was, and the stories were true.

The stories are true!

The judderman's grin replicates the flashed smiles given by Top of the Pops *presenters. The smiling men who entertain us, who entertain the children. The judderman was leering, displaying openly the fact it was a thing of darkness.*

The judderman is open knowledge no one goes on record about. We are all messengers not willing to be shot.

When I saw him, he was tall and slender with a BBC smile, onyx, inky like the night-time waters of the Lea, with a smell like the Thames at low tide. He had a violent grace, I admit. A terrible beauty, the beauty of the bombed-out building, the abandoned school, the dried-up aqueduct in the stony ruins of a forgotten desert culture.

He moved like something out of old stop-motion animation. A British version of something Russian or East European. He had the melancholy quality of Bagpuss, and the tension of an unexploded WWII bomb.

I must trust what my eyes tell me: and I see that the judderman is the 'pakis go home' graffiti in white paint on the brickwork down my street. He's the uneven lettering of 'Keep Britain White' daubed large on a doorway, and he is the look on my Bajan neighbour's face. He is the worry I see in Gary's face every day.

The judderman is the broken bottle at Millwall that scarred a friend's face, the uneven line that connect his eye-socket to his chin. This city feels like it's carpeted with broken glass, violent confetti left after a crimson wedding.

The judderman is the car-bomb that left shrapnel in Charlie's leg out in Belfast, and it's the way Charlie now limps to the pub for his nightly session of ale and reminiscence, despite the fact he's only just pushing thirty. He was a squaddie, and I feel sorry for him. But he's much more cheerful than my brother and me. Do not ask me why – he has no right to be.

The judderman is the unions on strike, he is a reimbursed thalidomide, he is my fear and loss, he is the dirty streets and he is a swastika inked indelibly in raw pink skin.

That night I saw him, he melted back into the shadows of Woodberry Down. More rumours came from Stoke Newington, Stamford Hill, Clapton, Seven Sisters, Tottenham, Enfield Chase, Turnpike Lane, the Hackney marshes. Where the stories went, I followed.

The Malachite Press

The Malachite Press was formed back in 1955. Founded by a breakaway editor from a large and respected publishing house, they began with reprints of some of the greats: Algernon Blackwood, Arthur Machen, C.L. Nolan and Hecate Shrike, before moving into publishing the dark imaginings and twisted fever-dreams of contemporary writers who had crawled out of the counter-cultural explosion that would come, erroneously, to define that decade. These books affected Gary and Danny greatly; they were not sure if they were allowed, or supposed, to be reading such things but the brothers had a knack for words and loved the shapes the symbols made on the pages, and the strange meanings those symbols communicated. The Malachite books were available in affordable paperback editions and so the books helped the brothers open their eyes to the wonders of the city that was their home. And once they could see what there was to see, they could also see the blinkers so many people wore. Or perhaps the people they considered blinkered just didn't care that much. Gary became fascinated – obsessed, Lisa would say – by how two people could be looking at the very same thing and have totally different experiences. If that was the case, what was reality?

The Malachite covers became more lurid but the content did not. The press moved into publishing a form of hard-edged

Albionic literature, dealing with myths both ancient and contemporary, rural, urban, and suburban. The stories at first were from a hippy utopian perspective (something that would turn sour; the authoritarian tendencies lurking beneath the skin were obvious if you looked), before branching out into stuff that married their traditional focus with the burgeoning youth cults that appeared across the violent streets of Britain. They moved with the times without ever changing their core. They were commended and respected for that.

The two brothers read stories of skinhead gangs ripped apart and reconstituted by urban demons, creating patchwork monsters of Spurs and West Ham fans. The leering bootboys were stitched together into lumbering beasts that terrorised the towpaths of the Lea Valley and the back alleys of the darker parts of the city. The absurdity was the constituent parts always attempted to war with each other, a monster that was as angry at itself as the rest of the world.

They read tales of bikers who rode literally out of hell, to engage in punch-ups with lads on scooters down on the shingle of the south coast. The devil wore leather.

Danny was taken by psychedelic and drug-strafed narratives of hippy communes that slowly but inexorably morphed into weed-stinking prisons of the mind. *The Days of Family Wild* stuck with him; perhaps unfairly presenting a deeply pessimistic view of the communal living that had taken root in parts of Scotland, Leeds, and right here in London in four-story Victorian terraces in Hackney.

The Malachite Press had an occult-detective series that Gary especially loved, following the adventures of a grim and war-damaged investigator named Vincent Harrier. A returning soldier who had served during the war and then in the British Mandate in Palestine during the formation of Israel, Harrier had a knack for navigating London Incognita and a bone-deep cynicism born from the things he had seen.

Taking place almost exclusively in the bombed out remains of late-forties and early-fifties London, the Harrier books were in the tradition of John Silence and Carnacki, but there was something different about them that really grabbed readers and set the books apart. They were set in a world Gary and Danny recognised – they were born in the late forties and though of course they'd never experienced it first-hand, they had seen some of the damage that remained from the war, both in the scarred architecture of the city and the damaged psyches of the adults around them. Many of the men of their father's generation had a sense of having been somewhere far away and never fully come back. Part of them had gone astray, or been left behind, in another land. Their father was a prime example of that. Now he spent his free time sat in a fraying chair, shovelling in the food made by Gary's mum, and laughing at suited comedians on the telly making fun of Pakistanis and West Indians and the Irish. Woolly patriotism replaced memories of a world ripping itself asunder. There must be comfort in that, Gary assumed; the world reduced to a simple place of us and them.

Gary didn't want to single the Second World War out for special treatment – when he saw Charlie hobbling to The Sovereign, and thought about the scraps of metal embedded like maggots in his flesh, it seemed unfair to suggest their seniors were somehow exceptional, that their experience was more noteworthy than the victims of other wars. Gary thought of his hero, Vincent Harrier, witnessing the explosion ripping through the King David hotel and finding his comrades and mates strung up from olive trees by the Irgun. Because something was less-remembered, more troubling to the stories we tell ourselves, did it make it less worthwhile? Gary realised that without a collective recollection people could start to doubt their own memories. The memories of the horror they experienced morphed into what they believed were nightmares. Lived experience became remembered experience. That then became fiction and myth. Gary and Danny also knew ideas of simple good and bad were unhelpful, dangerous. This is why the brothers collected the literature of London Incognita, and the true stories of the people who had endured the war. *Saxifraga Urbium, From the City, From the Plough, The Human Kind* and *The Lonely Soldier Returns to Finsbury Park* were all favourites.

The brothers tried to imagine what it was like to be an adult in this city of theirs, knowing that the people of another nation were dropping bombs on you with the express purpose of causing damage, mayhem, violence, terror. Or worse: they were just doing their job. In some real way, they wanted to kill you. Not *you* specifically, it wasn't quite personal, but it was getting close. Knowing what the allies did to the Germans gave the brothers pause for thought. Gary wondered what words like 'deserve' meant.

Near a favourite pub in N16, Gary often stopped to look at the plaque on Coronation Avenue that dedicated itself to the 160 people who died in a single German blast; a bomb that somehow took out the shelter families were hiding in. Sometimes he visited the victims' graves in Abney Park Cemetery.

Gary wondered who put these plaques up; he had never seen anyone in the act, but there they were, screwed into the brickwork. Worse things happened abroad, worse things were happening in Ireland you could argue, but still. It made Gary realise that even London had its moments of weakness. The city that he had thought of as invulnerable was not. The place he and his brother mythologised in their long rambles through the city and their constant hunt for the hidden literatures and lexicons of the metropolis was capable of being compromised. A bomb could drill through a shelter and obliterate all you ever knew. There were enemies without, and enemies within, and the worst thing was that those enemies believed they were doing the right thing.

Via the stories of their family, and the films and shows on television, Gary felt like he had experienced the war himself. He always had the belief, never fully fleshed out but more felt as an instinctive truth, that London had an ancestral memory that percolated in the blood of all who were born, lived, worked, or died here. It was something to do with the history of the place; and Gary was keenly aware that he made the place and the place made him. This was true of all places, of course; a snake devouring its own tail. London, though, was a huge world-spanning serpent, a Jörmungandr, something Bibilical like the Behemoth, an emperor worm, and the way it cannibalised itself was terrifying.

The Vincent Harrier books from Malachite Press, with their distinctive black and white covers of urban decay and occult imagery seamlessly merged, understood all of this. The writer of the series, Michael Ashman (rumoured to be a pseudonym, a rumour never proven), waded through the genres of crime and the fantastic, ended up creating unique and essential under-appreciated works that, Gary felt, were vital to the city. His very favourite of the series was titled *Saxifraga Urbium,* the third book to feature Harrier. The cover showed blitz rubble colonised with the London Pride of the book's title, with the figure of a woman and toddler, hand-in-hand in eerie silhouette, their faces hidden in a choking haze as they walked away from the scene into the dust of the city. The book concerned Harrier's investigations into apparitions seen on the bomb sites in the years after the war. Returning Tommies, reduced to boozing and self-housing (now, in the seventies, they called this squatting), were seeing spectral bears on the marshes and sabre toothed cats in the shadows cast by the rubble piles. Strange children in gas masks were reported to be running and giggling over dense clusters of fireweed and through the streets singing *judder judder judder, you're all over now*. In the novel, Harrier speaks to floriographers, the flourishing swell of self-housers, occult booksellers, the gangs of kids stripping copper from the damaged buildings, all of whom know something is not right with the city. Harrier is drinking heavily of course, damaged by the sights he saw in Palestine, and listening to the talk of the old men in the war-damaged pubs all over the city. The narrative comes to a climax on July 27th, the day of London Pride, suggesting a city itself can suffer psychic trauma and project those nightmares onto its populace. It remained one of Gary's favourite London fictions.

Gary was at home, upstairs in his brother's bedroom, perched on his bed beneath a creased poster of Hawkwind's *In Search of Space* tacked to the wall. The bottom left edge was ripped off and frayed. He was poring over the books Danny had left behind.

From Daniel Eider's Journal
Canadian Gaelic

I have been reading lately. Spending hours in the libraries.

There is a story that has taken my interest. There was a group of hunters that spoke the language of their grandfathers who had fled Caledonia in the wake of the Highland clearances. Perhaps they had fought and lost at Culloden, maintained crofts, endured cold rain and black winters. These hunters padded slowly along the brutal and beautiful coastlines of Nova Scotia, Cape Breton and Newfoundland. Their quarry was the sea mink, a mustelid with fur valued highly by the traders who slowly moved the dead pelts of the animal across the North American continent, pelts twice the size of its cousins that we may be familiar with; this led to its ultimate demise.

What makes a thing desirable kills it.

The same applies to a place. To geography. To a postcode.

The native peoples of North America hunted the animal also. Remnants of its pelt were found in the shell-heaps that litter the island coasts off Maine; but it is highly doubtful that these peoples pushed it to extinction. The European fur trade is what extinguished the sea mink.

Now, I hunt for any remnant of the animal in the second-hand shops of London, where a habit is made of consuming history and its fauna in equal measure. I have found nothing, yet, yet I am sure I would know the animal's fur should I see it.

Do I have to point out the irony to you? The mink hunters were themselves threatened with extinction. The fate of the native peoples is well known and little cared for, their hearts buried at Wounded Knee for generations now. The Gaelic speakers of the North American continent present a deeper and more troubling problem to me. The very words 'Highland Clearances' are merely a sanitised, English version of a bitter truth. In their language it is referred to as Fuadach nan Gàidheal. *Literally, 'the expulsion of the Gael'. A clearance is what you do to a patch of wasteland, rooting out stubborn buddleia and knotweed. This was something different.*

A people and a culture, told that it was no longer of any value. Fled, were pushed, across the Atlantic. Here, they helped hunt the sea mink to extinction, allowing it to become one of the many forgotten fauna that form a supporting caste of history. So, a threatened culture aided the extinction of another species.

In the mid-nineteenth century, behind those imperial languages of French and English, the Scottish Gaelic and its close relative, Irish, were the most widely spoken in Canada. Now it resides merely on Cape Breton island, and other isolated pockets. A few still speak it in cities, but the memory dwindles. A language must be lived. Does language need the landscape that formed it? What happens to the London accent when the city dies, and what did people sound like here generations ago?

Those of us who traverse London Incognita know the diasporas of the world took their myths with them. So now selkies can be sometimes seen off the coasts of Boston, kelpies in murky ponds on Cape Breton Island, and spriggans in the Canadian forests now jostling for attention with the wendigo. In a similar way, the Jews brought their golems to the streets of London, the Arabs their djinn, and the South Africans their tokoloshes. And something of the loss and pain remained, or came and mated with the native suffering, I am not sure, but whatever happened, something new was formed and that thing is the judderman. This thing that lives in shadow, the bacterial presence in the bloodstream of London, the secret history of the city ready to take the unwary or the too-aware.

I have no proof of this, of course. No photograph to offer as evidence. But I know for certain that he walks the half-forgotten alleyways of my city. This is not speculation. I have seen him. I am creating a map of sightings of the judderman.

But why am I bothering to write about the fate of Scottish Canadians? Well, I am interested in the forgotten tributaries of history. I can acknowledge that the British Empire formed us, and formed the city I love. It created me. That Empire threw our myths and histories into the air like dandelion spores for them to land on distant shores, and mutate in the backstreets at home.

There is an imagined path I call 'the wolf walk'. It leads into the centre of the sickness, the swelling teratoma that is forming on the banks of the Thames where a mangled form of the city is growing in random spurts, its component parts jumbled and mashed, no past or future now. So, you may see a limb-like tree from Tyburn bearing its hanging fruit, aspects of Newgate prison, Bedlam ejecting its howling inmates as they clamber *over a wreckage of red telephone boxes, paddy wagons, penny farthings, crumpled pornographic magazines, Roman coins and penny dreadfuls.*

I can feel the teratoma swelling, the reappearance of the judderman and the sickness in the city. I have a choice. I know there is no way back to the innocent and naïve world I knew as a child. The choice is to remain here or move on to yet another new world.

The people who belong to London Cognita, who cannot see what is amiss, they live in the teratoma. They peruse the shelves in the aisles of its supermarkets, and they buy, they consume, they eat, sleep, shit, fuck, and they watch their flickering screens at home in living rooms, they laugh at the racist comedians and they laugh at the men who grin on our televisions and hide their dark secrets. They cheer at the football, and trade blows outside the stadiums. The wealthier ones who live on the hills of London pursue other entertainments, explore a world of art and literature that occasionally intersects with my world, but they delude themselves that their arbitrary position in society elevates them, and their choice of what to spend their money on makes them superior somehow – but culture consumers, thinking themselves removed from the consumer culture, are sad tragedies with delusions of grandeur. The people of London Cognita exist and they believe, by and large, that they are happy.

None of this can last.

Jenny Duro

Three months had elapsed since Danny's disappearance. Autumn was coming in and All Hallows' Eve was on the approach.

'It's a thin time of year, Gary, you know what I mean?' Danny had said, just over a year ago, as the two brothers watched fireworks burst and scream over Alexandra Park. Gary remembered the tongues of flickering bonfire flame in their family garden. 'A thin time of year, when you can find the thin places.' Gary remembered how his brother had then thrown his cigarette into the bonfire, how as a toddler he had thought it was called a 'bomb fire', and the way the orange light had twisted and illuminated his parents' faces.

Gary felt that he now, when it was almost too late, understood. If he were to find his brother and find the judderman, it would be in a thin place. This was the thin time of year where the fictions of London became all too visible. Now was the time.

The leaves were turning, rusting, reddening and yellowing, and the mornings were misty and indefinite. Gary was standing on the South Bank of the river Thames, opposite the Embankment, watching the river larks. As always now, he had risen before most of the commuters were on the move, pulled on his walking boots, made a thermos of strong sugary tea, and set off through the city from his parents' home in north-east London. He was enjoying the encroaching chill in the mornings and the rapidly darkening days. Jays and chattering magpies flitted in the trees of the green spaces he passed through, darting grey squirrels perched on the rims of dustbins watching him with dead black eyes. In these morning rambles through the city, he saw lucid foxes with eyes like deep yellow stars, plump rats plopping into the water of the overgrown canals, and people awake when they really should not be. Gary knew the appeal of the amphetamines that powered these living ghosts; he was starting to rely on them himself. London, at dawn in the minutes before it roused itself, was a place of wonder. A place of dream and possibility. It was through this dreaming city that he made his way down to the sacred river, walking for miles as the city awoke.

The Thames, when he arrived, was at low tide, as he knew it would be. The river larks he had come to see sifted through the mud and detritus with a patience and determination that Gary admired. There were three men, what appeared to be a child or a dwarf, and a woman; the woman he had come to see. One of the men inserted his hand into the soft mud of the Thames shore, searching for something his equipment had alerted him to. To Gary it looked like he was performing an obscene gynaecological examination on the naked river. He shook away the thought as he lit a cigarette and swigged from his thermos.

'Do not think of the city as gendered, as man or woman, Gary. It's way too easy. Lazy. A cliché. We need to think harder and deeper than that.' The words his brother had spoken on one of their long evenings together, discussing the hidden knowledge of London.

'I know, Danny. It is both and it is neither. Woman and man. The first and the last. The emperor worm that devours itself.'

Gary thought the mud of London must be polluted, toxic with age, but the larks were there regardless. They were addicts, turning up bits of pot, animal remains from old abattoirs, clay pipes, auroch thighbones, medieval combs, the occasional human knuckle, old and corroded coinage depicting dead monarchs. Gary had read many novels that romanticised the river larks of London Incognita; *Through This Mud We Find Ourselves* and *Poor Jack* were his favourites, and he idealised the larks against his own better judgement. To Gary, they stood on the edge of criminality, slathered in London's sludge and grime and muck, sorting the forgotten histories of the city and making a profit into the bargain. It was irresistible, mythic. Whereas he wandered geographically, they journeyed through the layers of time in the city, mining history. They understood the idea of city-as-palimpsest better than most.

Over the last few years, Gary and Danny had made the effort to get friendly and swap knowledge with the river larks. Their interests intersected and intertwined (like a rat king, or a coil of emperor worms, thought Gary), and pooling the right information helped them all feed their obsessive addictions.

'Together we are all stronger, and nobody has the final say,' said Danny, frequently.

Since Danny disappeared, Gary was targeting anyone he knew with a competent working knowledge of London Incognita, asking them for signs of his brother, of course, but also about this thing called the judderman that was making whispered ripples through London. The larks, surely, would know something.

Leaning on the metal railings, lighting another cigarette and briefly examining a coiled fish sculpted in the metalwork of the lampposts, he shouted and waved down the river lark he'd come to see. Jenny Duro was one of the few female larks that he'd encountered in his years spent exploring with Danny. He didn't know much about her life outside of her activities down here on the shore, nothing about her past or her future, but he liked the very fact she existed. Knowing more about her would only ever spoil things. The anomalous attracted him; he was an anomaly himself, he realised, and the knowledge that there was a solidarity among the freaks and weirdos, subtle but real, cheered him up at even the bleakest of times.

It took Jenny a while to notice him waving, her ears muffled, listening to the beeping frequencies from her detector. Jenny's light brown hair was ragged, blown about by a rough wind gusting up the estuary, and she was dressed in shapeless and practical grey clothing. Gary had no idea if she had a job, or if this was it. Finally, she noticed him, removing her earmuffs and beckoning him over.

He took the stairs by the Oxo tower down onto the shore. Some teenagers had scrawled their love for each other into the damp sands, soon to be swept away with the incoming tide. That felt appropriate. Lisa was barely speaking to Gary now. He was too far gone, she said, a fucking nutjob. She didn't understand when he told her he had to become London, to enter its arteries and dissolve into the bloodstream of the city. This, surely, was what Danny had done?

'Alright Gary,' said Jenny. She had a distinctly south London accent, from Bermondsey way. It suited her. 'Up early aren't we?'

'Alright Jenny. I could say the same to you. Early bird, worm, and all that. Dug up anything decent lately?' Gary flicked his spent cigarette onto the sand. Out on the grey waters of the river a tug chugged along, a slow churning wake behind it. Herring gulls followed.

'Nothing much to write home about today Gal, if I'm honest with you. It's swings and roundabouts, this game, you know? I hunt for fucking ages and nothing turns up, then I'll find something that blows my mind. But I *did* dig this up the other day, something you might like. You're a morbid bastard.' Her face creased into a beaming grin and she laughed as she dug into her trouser pocket, fishing out a worn piece of dark metal.

'I found this coin, a bit further east, out Wapping way. I'm not sure what it is, but I'm sure it's the kind of thing you and Danny are into; Yaxley and his lot too.' He looked at her intently for a second as she said that name. Yaxley, the mad bookseller in Notting Hill Gate, corrupt chronicler of London Incognita, charlatan and expert.

'Have a look at this.' She dropped the coin into Gary's outstretched palm.

He held the coin up to the light. It was made from a kind of alloy, blackened and smoothed by the waters and the corrosion of years. A monstrous pastiche of a British monarch grinned on one side of the coin – a crowned being with the body of a fat worm and the head of a lion. The other side was imprinted with the image of a malevolent stick-figure man that also resembled a candelabra or menorah. The words that rimmed the circumference were indecipherable, not through erosion as he had expected, but because they were written in a language he could not understand. There was nothing too strange about that, this was London after all, but Gary couldn't place this. It wasn't anything he recognised as European. Not Cyrillic and not Hebrew. Not Latin. The worm-monarch's feline face had teeth like knife-points. Gary shivered in the autumn air.

'What the hell is this, Jenny?' he asked her. A huge herring gull landed nearby, hunting for scraps of dropped food.

'Not sure, Gal. You know I turn up a lot of weird shit here, and I'll admit this is one of the weirdest. I stopped passing this sort of stuff onto the museums and the professionals a while back, you know? It never seemed to surface in the exhibitions. This kind of stuff just vanished. The stuff they can't categorise... well they don't categorise it. It disappears into archives, for a few dusty Oxbridge types to look at occasionally and shake their heads over. So, if the stuff is going to disappear anyway, I figured I'd sell it onto the dealers. Keep a few choice bits for myself. You know the faces, Gary, you know who's selling right now. But I figured I'd give it to you and you could show it to Yaxley? That thing on the back, that looks like the judderman thing the alkies are going on about? That's what Danny was looking for and I know he'd gone to Yaxley for help. And you're after it too, right?'

Yaxley. Dealer, chronicler of, and self-declared expert on London Incognita, a fucking hairy weirdo holed up in that pit he called a shop in Notting Hill Gate. You wouldn't be surprised to find out he was a nonce. Yaxley gave Gary the creeps. For a man who spent his life seeking out the weird and the outré, this was saying a lot.

'Fuck Yaxley,' Gary hissed.

'Yeah, well, the guy knows his stuff. And you're still looking for Danny, right?' Jenny looked at Gary intently, like she was noticing him properly for the first time in the conversation. She saw his bloodshot eyes. The bags beneath them. He smelled of old sweat, too many cigarettes, boozy, eyes wired from three months of amphetamine use.

Gary nodded, looking out at the waters of the Thames. He lit another cigarette, and offered one from his pack to her. She took it and he sparked her up.

'Yeah. Three months now. A quarter of a year.'

'I'm sorry mate,' she said. And she was. 'But it does look like the—'

'I know what it looks like, Jenny. The judderman.'

'Yeah. And your brother was researching it right?' Smoke leaked ragged from her mouth, gusting over the river.

'Yeah. Yeah he was.' Gary kicked away the herring gull that was getting uncomfortably close to them.

'I've seen the graffiti too. I've read the same books as you two, you know. Us river larks and you lot, we're not that different. Ashman was writing about it in the Harrier books. The old boozers and druggies have seen it. The acid heads and space cadets and speed freaks in the squats. Those sad burned-out hippies, all those guys hanging out in Ladbroke Grove listening to their Trees and Fairport and Shirley Collins records. Isn't there one of those old folk songs called "The Jaddar Men of Camden Town"?'

'There is, yes. It's a London song going back centuries they reckon.'

'Well now we can assume Ashman was putting something real into his stories, something really here in London. What do you call it again?'

'London Incognita. Where you and I live.' Gary grimaced and coughed.

'Yeah that's the one. The city we choose to live in. I like that.' Jenny Duro crushed her cigarette beneath a mud-caked boot. 'Take the thing to Yaxley.'

'Fuck. Alright. Yaxley it is.'

And then Jenny Duro shook Gary's hand, picked up her detector, and walked back towards the lapping waters of the great river. Gary saw her trade words with a few of the other larks as he headed back up the steps and onto the South Bank.

A few couples, arm-in-arm, strolled along the South Bank. Already, tourists with Polaroid cameras hung round their necks were out, urging family members to stand in position with the Thames in shot behind them. The brutalist concrete of the National Film Theatre seemed to shine obscenely in the bright morning light. It was showing a film called *Savage Messiah*. Something to do with Ken Russell and Christopher Logue; facts able to interest Gary despite his addled mental state.

The day was still just beginning. He had Jenny Duro's coin to take to Yaxley. He decided he would walk to Notting Hill Gate. Walking was the only way to map the streets of London Incognita.

From Daniel Eider's Journal

I dreamed a dream last night.

I had been drinking in The Sovereign with Gary and my cousin. Too much lager and stout as I petted the Barghest and listened to the old men and their long meandering stories. My lungs were scorched with tar and nicotine and my stomach was an empty ocean of alcohol.

As I fell asleep to the sounds of London, I saw alien creatures that resembled polar bears, and these things perched motionless on the stomachs of prostrate little girls. They were made of smooth lines, and had the quality of myths half-remembered and badly translated into a new language.

Then I stood on an icy plain with my friends and family, though they chatted amicably among themselves and seemed unable to see what I could see or hear my pleas for them to look. Gary was there and Lisa too, Mum and Dad, my limping cousin Charlie, and the river lark Jenny Duro. Why wouldn't they look? I figured if they chose to truly see, then they may have to do something. To act, and to change.

And then I saw another figure conversing with them, a figure who was neither friend nor family and he seemed terribly familiar to me, a jagged figure composed of thin lines and deep shadows. I knew him. He had infiltrated, found his way even into the wintry landscapes of my dreams. There was a strange comfort in that.

I realised I was somewhere on Doggerland, standing on the frozen earth that filled in the gaps between what would one day be Britain and Norway. My friends and my family murmured obliviously, the soft trickle of their conversation indecipherable. We all wore modern clothing even though I knew that Doggerland had sunk beneath the waves long before the arrival of the nineteen seventies.

I had read about the lost landmass, of course I had, the land that connected us to the rest of the continent. In second-hand books I'd found on the stalls and waste markets of London I read about the sunken country. Yaxley, who I could now see chatting amicably with my mother, had pressed a Malachite Press novel concerning Doggerland on me. What I Found in the Drowned Land *by Michael Ashman, a barbed pair of Irish elk antlers, like the ones dredged from the North Sea, its cover.*

Through binoculars normally reserved for birdwatching on the marshes of north-east London, I observed a herd of mammoth, their fur resembling expensive, soiled rugs. The herd were out on the tundra, rooting the earth beneath with the tusks that would be the envy of any poacher. One of the animals stood apart and loomed larger than its fellows.

I couldn't take my eyes from this mammoth. It was a distended child's rendering of a furred elephant; a grotesque mastodon. Its proportions were all wrong, the features bent and out of shape, like a drunken Picasso had interpreted the face of an ancient elephant. The deformed mastodon noticed my gaze and as I looked through my binoculars into its idiot eyes

I knew, somehow, that this thing was a destroyer, a destroyer of worlds, though it would do its job without any malice or even forethought and anyway, destruction is just another form of change, isn't it?

My friends and family, close to me but oblivious, crowded around the man of shadow, the juddering man who haunts my city, listening to one of his anecdotes. They laughed without constraint, hysterically, as the snow began to come down heavily. They refused to notice the destroyer.

This idiot crippled mastodon began to shuffle towards us, the shuffle breaking into a trot, and the trot into a charge, and I could see this thing, the destroyer of worlds with its innocent child eyes and twisted features, approaching fast and I shouted and shouted to my family and friends to move, get out of the way, can you not see this thing, this destroyer, in front of you?

But they couldn't hear me. The snow muted my screams.

The judderman laughed, his teeth like junkies' needles, like torturers' knives, and I woke drenched in an alcoholic sweat. My bed was a swamp, my heart thudded painfully, and I knew then that even sleep would give me no solace.

Yaxley

The streets of west London were becoming crowded, the city's veins thickening as the orange sun hauled itself into the sky. Gary walked, remembering the Norse myths and stories he and his brother had loved as kids; the orb's endless movement as it ran from a cosmic wolf that would one day swallow the sun and plunge us all into darkness. The wolf was taking its time, Gary thought.

He had left Jenny Duro sifting through the mud on the exposed shore of the Thames. He wondered if she viewed the encroaching high tide sweeping up the estuary with a sense of disappointment or took joy in the continual ebb and flow of London's waters; there were always new histories with a chance of being disturbed among the silt.

He drifted towards the stalls and junk shops where he felt he might find some answers; to the second-hand stores of Notting Hill Gate and Ladbroke Grove. London was a city adept at recycling itself and at profiting from its own past. Gary thought of the city as a feedback loop of self-mythologising. Or, like Jörmungandr in the tales he and Danny had thrilled at as children. A serpent devouring its own tail.

The past itself was of value, a commodity of sorts, to be bought and sold like anything else. Gary considered that the things he took for granted now, right now in the banal and terrifying year of 1972, could one day be fetishised, recontextualised into the backward-looking fashions of a future generation. Or perhaps they would be forgotten except by the few, and hoarded by collectors, searched for at the bottom of dusty boxes and crates in shops in these very streets decades from now. Gary knew this because he did something similar himself. Already the magazines and fag-ends of the nineteen sixties hippy culture was becoming the stuff of history, collectible, tradable, forgettable. He pored over mouldering papers from the nineteenth century, thrilled at the Malachite first editions he had managed to secure, and salivated at the stack of London novels from the twenties and thirties he'd found in the Spastics Society. Paper decayed in a way the Roman coins fished from the Thames by Jenny Duro did not.

Danny had liked to come and visit the markets on Portobello Road. He collected old photographs; anything that featured London's architecture and preferably the posed smiles of families long gone or dissolved by time. Mouldy or water damaged Polaroids, or sepia-toned and slightly out of focus prints, these were the qualities Danny craved. His journals, ordered into a semblance of order, began each 'chapter' with one of these inscrutable photographs from London's past. They were stuck to the page with a strong adhesive. As he walked, Gary imagined his brother himself in the act of imagining, picturing one of these salvaged photographs used as part of a cover for a book that would now never be completed. You could almost see the Malachite edition, thought Gary with a smile. *London Incognita*, he would call it.

In the months since Danny's disappearance, Gary had spent many evenings sifting through his brother's possessions, rifling through his boxes of accumulated London photographs and poring over his journal. The night previous, Gary had plucked out an undated picture that he assumed must have been taken during the war, or very shortly after. It reminded him of a scene from one of his beloved Vincent Harrier novels, with piles of blitz rubble and figures indistinct in a murky haze. There were small children in the background, and a large silhouette of a tall and slender man. Another photo showed a couple dressed in the clothing of the fifities, on the South Bank during the Festival of Britain, posing in front of a huge sculpture titled *The Islanders*.

Journal entries had scribbled titles like 'Blitz cats', 'The bear', 'On what I found at Enfield Lock', 'Of ruine or some blazing starre', 'A London Tamblin', and 'Beggar stories of the juddar men'.

As Gary walked into west London, he went over in his head the journal entries he had been reading. Danny had this idea of a 'supporting caste', all the forgotten life and sacrifice that went into the foundations of our societies. The animals ground into history that were slaughtered, or simply tipped accidentally into extinction, by earlier generations. It was hard not to think, then, about the auroch herds that had padded patiently through Kent and Sussex, Middlesex and

London, and Doggerland too; their skulls were fished from the Thames to this day and were a mighty sight. Gary liked to imagine Jenny Duro hanging one of these majestic skulls on the wall of her Bermondsey flat, before standing back in satisfaction, regarding the size and the epic sweep of the animal's horns. She deserved such a thing.

He thought about Irish elk immortalised in pigment at the Lascaux caves. Atlas bears, cats with fearsome teeth. Furred and icy elephants, destroyers, with the minds of children.

And human beings too. Those gaelic speakers in Nova Scotia and Cape Breton, hunting the sea mink, that his brother had written about. The animal's extinction some obscure fault of the English. And how could he not think of all the immigrants and refugees and people desiring something else who landed somehow in the city. Jews fleeing pogroms. Huguenots running from Catholics. The West Indians still refused housing by racist landlords, spat on by old ladies on the bus, terrorised by boys with shaved heads. The children disappeared for the sexual pleasure of sadistic Conservatives. Working class girls of every colour servicing the depravities and lusts of the men who ran things; the men who beat them and sometimes killed them without ceremony. The supporting caste.

Gary had a favourite bird of his, something called the great auk (also known as spearbird, littlewing, gairfowl; names in Inuit and Basque and old Norse), a flightless and penguin-like cousin of the guillemot and the razorbill. As a child, he had loved the illustrations of the bird in his books of natural history. No photographs, of course – it was gone too soon for that. He knew how its last egg was smashed and the final pair murdered in Iceland. And Gary understood that what makes a thing desirable is what will kill it. Could this happen to his London, to the places he loved? Could a place, a real physical space, become like the spearbird, or the sea-mink? Loved, romanticised, idealised, then forgotten. Gone.

Strange to think about the forgotten fauna accompanying forgotten human lives, all their fates jumbled up and intertwined. Gary realised the destroyer, that his brother had imagined as an idiot furred mastodon and was somehow linked to the judderman, would eventually invalidate himself once his enemy was annihilated. That was something Danny had not considered: the destroyer was on Doggerland, and was therefore doomed to sink beneath the waves.

And as Gary walked, he ran through all the stories he and Danny had gathered over the years, of the fearsome golem of Stamford Hill and the Wandering Jew Ahasuerus; of Spring-Heeled Jack bouncing over Victorian terraces; the mischievous and malevolent water sprites that inhabited the River Lea ever-ready to drag down the unfortunate. All of Danny's clippings and transcriptions of the accounts of bear sightings and the prehistoric crocodiles on the Hackney Marshes. The rumours of the judderman, a story transferred around the city via the guttural mutterings of drunks. The children lost to the obscene rituals of the powerful.

There were suggestions, gleaned from all the explorers of London Incognita, that there were weak spots in the outer areas of London, by the New River Path in Enfield and Turkey Brook where it cut through Forty Hall. A crossing point where at times you'd find changelings, things not quite human.

All these stories. The days and weeks and huge chunks of his life spent searching for the hidden. It all had to mean something. Otherwise his life would be a total waste. Otherwise he was a sad drunk in the making like his cousin, ready to fuse with the bar in The Sovereign like Fen. Otherwise he was set to disappear, be forgotten, like his brother.

He was on his way to Yaxley and the men who traded obscure stories, forgotten nuggets of history, lost narratives they were desperate to resurrect. Gary's hunger for meaning was inflamed by a chemical cocktail, all the more real for it and accompanied by an unspecified sense of loss.

He had spent hours talking with the men with long grey beards and twinkling eyes who sat decrepit behind stalls selling the junk and detritus of the city's collective past. Yaxley, though, was something different.

Gary wandered the city, with a burning desire to know it from the inside out. At a parlour in the West End, he had had the tube map tattooed onto his left arm, thick lines of colour and evocative names that often didn't match the broken-down realities of the streets he'd exit onto. Gary liked to imagine himself being skinned and spread out, his veins, arteries and capillaries forming a complete map of London's streets, roads, and dark alleyways.

At the boot fairs and jumble sales and the markets in Ladbroke Grove, Gary would stop and sift through boxes of ephemera and the remains of other people's lives, buying old photographs, postcards with personal inscriptions written in dead ink describing other times. Anything with a personal inscription or a dedication to Londoners long deceased caught his attention. Anything that could clue him in to what led to his brother's disappearance. Anything that would lead him to the judderman.

It was in the land of the second-hand that Gary fattened his collection of books, buying everything he could find from Malachite Press and the New English Library, but also books of ornithology, London architecture, old books of folk tales, fairy tales, dead mythologies, obscure biographies. In a city so old, the past available to root through was almost endless. There was a thrill in that, and something sad too. He could never shake the nagging feeling that perhaps London's best days were behind it. But his researches also told him that people had always felt that way. The world, for somebody, somewhere, was always ending.

So, he spent some pleasant time imagining the city in various previous incarnations, peopled by long-dead inhabitants:

Londinium. Romano-British. The place was razed to the ground by irate Celts, evidence of that act to be found in a burnt layer of subsoil. Coins and eagles were still plucked from the mud to this day – Jenny Duro had a good stash. The London Mithraeum is still there on Walbrook, they found it back in the fifties. (Side note: there's a Mithraic shrine in a church on the Romney Marsh)

Lundenwic. Anglo-Saxons, the people who would become, basically, us, before the Normans arrived. They understood the concept of wyrd, and the interconnectedness of all things, before Christianity was brought to these shores.

Lundenburh. Was this not the same place as Lundenwic? The size of the city in the nineteen seventies distorted Gary's perspective on distance and geography.

The London frost fair, held on the thick ice of the Thames. What a celebration that must have been! Only possible during a miniature ice-age, in a climate that mammoths would enjoy.

Spring-Heeled Jack, bounding over the rooftops of the Imperial city, nicking ladies' knickers, the dirty bastard.

Whitechapel, 1888. The Juwes will not be blamed for nothing, etc. Surgeon's knives and an unending mystery that obviously was fascinating, it was not to denigrate the people who died or turn suffering into lurid entertainment, but how could you not be interested in such a thing?

Jimi Hendrix unleashing green parakeets into the air. Their screech would become so memorable in the plane trees of London. What a twat.

The Blitz, a city on fire, the reflection of flame seen in the eyes of a young girl watching her local school burn to the ground. Was she happy as well as scared?

58

The shrieking, gibbering, salivating inmates of Bedlam. Illness as entertainment. Imagine what they endured at the hands of the guards, it's bad enough now. Hell indeed.

A petty crook swinging from a noose at Tyburn. People would turn out to watch the hangings. Gary presumes he would have attended, possibly jeered, along with the rest of them.

Suffragettes, bombing the orchid house at Kew – the symbolism is clear, and potent. Posh girls slicing up paintings in the National Portrait Gallery. You had to have some respect for that especially when you knew about the torture and the force-feeding in Holloway Prison, like they were fattening up geese for foie gras.

Gary loved the Malachite Press books when he could find them. The more lurid and trashy the cover the better, acting as a smokescreen for some of the heavyweight and esoteric ideas inside. Gary stockpiled his Malachite novels next to his Richard Allens and other New English Library stuff and it looked okay to his mates, to his old man and his mum. Not that they would have minded, or cared, but he wanted to keep certain things to himself. He didn't want people to think he was getting ideas above his station; or maybe he was just scared of being thought of as effeminate, an oddball, one of the freaks. Either way, it was generally better to not advertise your interests on the streets of London; as the saying went, it was hard to keep your chin up and your head down.

*

He entered Yaxley's shop. A tinkly metal thing sprang into action as Gary pushed open the door, leaving the bustle of Notting Hill Gate behind him. A few faces snapped up to look at the newcomer, peering at Gary in the dusty gloom, before gradually resuming their browsing positions. The place stank with a mingled reek of white sage incense, old books, joss sticks, sweet marijuana, yellowing paper, and old body odour long dried and never washed away. These were Yaxley's smells, the smell of London's lonely and obsessed underground. Gary found it comforting.

A few other men, serious and scruffy like himself, were flicking through piles of old occult and topographic magazines, browsing the rows of paperbacks and hardbacks, sifting through the arcane ephemera and pop-cultural detritus that Yaxley had made his speciality. He quickly scanned the shelf of books – Maureen Duffy's *Wounds,* a book about the West Indians called *The Lonely Londoners,* some Pan editions of Alexander Baron's novels. All piqued his interest, but he wasn't here to shop for new reading material.

Stacks of back issues of short-lived zines like *Magnesium Burns, Forgotten Fauna* and *Thunder Perfect Mind* dotted the shop unevenly. Gary picked up a crumpled copy of a magazine that promised, 'Fear not, for you are now entering Gandalf's Garden'. Adrian Mitchell was one of the contributors, he noted. But Gary wasn't really into that weirdy-beardy wizard stuff. He felt that something harder-edged was needed and must be coming. He would help will it into existence if he could.

'Gary, my lad! I thought you'd be making an appearance sooner or later. Good to see you sunshine.'

Yaxley. He was standing behind the counter, for all the world the image of a London desert ascetic, a self-styled mystic, a wise-man, a hippy guru, a raconteur, a word spiv. You could imagine him trying to wow young university girls at Ladbroke Grove parties with his knowledge of Mary Butts's mystical fiction and Arthur Machen's uncollected London journalism. He could expound on the virtues of Sarban's more obscure works, claimed to know Michael Ashman and the poet Hecate Shrike, and could talk in a way that was compelling even as it made you feel grubby, sexualised in a way you couldn't quite grasp. He could talk about the theories of London Incognita, French situationism, Gnosticism, the myriad sects and belief systems spawned by the English Civil War. It was from Yaxley that Danny had learned about the Muggletonians, the Jezereel sect in Gillingham and their strange tower, patripassianism – he imagined Danny, alone on Earth and suffering in oblivion for eternity – and so much more.

Yaxley fished for a pouch of loose tobacco from somewhere inside his baggy clothing. Gary watched his yellow fingers with the tips bitten as he rolled. He fished his own pack from his jacket pocket. He lit Yaxley up with a cheap lighter he'd bought from one of the tourist shops on Oxford Street a few weeks back. The lighter's image of Tower Bridge was slowly fading, eroding in his pocket.

Gary considered the strange solidarity between smokers, even the ones who disliked and distrusted each other. The shop filled with tobacco smoke.

'I saw Jenny Duro this morning. She's dug something up and told me you might be able to help explain what it is. I think it's to do with my brother. Something to do with what he was looking for.'

Yaxley clicked his tongue. 'Your brother, yes, yes, hmmm. Daniel Eider, strange boy, bit like yourself, but a smart one. Smelled of alcohol. I was sorry to hear about him. His disappearance. He had come to see me a lot before he went, you know?'

'I know,' said Gary. He handed the coin to Yaxley.

Yaxley held it up to what light filtered through into the shop, closing one eye as he examined it. 'Where did the lark find this?'

'Out Wapping way.'

'Well as you most likely already know, or have at least guessed, this is something that shouldn't exist. And yet here it is. Quite the conundrum, wouldn't you say?'

Yaxley dragged on his cigarette and continued. 'This coin is a coin of the true god of London. The blind creator, the mad god that thought it was all powerful but, in the end, was just a failed experiment itself. We are the failed creation of a failed experiment. I hope you know that?'

'Of course. You're not that smart Yaxley. It is the only explanation,' said Gary flatly. 'For all of this.' And at that he waved his hand vaguely around his head as if to indicate all of London, all the world, all that ever was or would be. 'And the judderman?'

'Again: you know already. But I'll tell you, if you need to hear it, and I think you do. When the city's subconscious weakens, becomes stressed or ill or corrupted, Londoners, or at least some of us, will start to see what you call the judderman. The stories of London Incognita, all the dark narratives we suppress, they come back and coalesce in his form. A revenant of sorts. A symptom. Clearly, right now, the city is sick again. You don't have to be a fucking genius to work that one out though, do you Gary?'

'And it took Danny?'

'It doesn't *take* anyone. Those who want him find him, and they go to him willingly. They lust after the shadows and want to live in London Incognita permanently. "A permanent vacation" as the yanks say, right? They want to join the troglodytes down in the tunnels. They don't want to change the story of London – they just want to revel in the obscure and nasty parts of it. Wallow in the filth. I'm sorry to say, that is what your brother wanted. It makes sense now, him disappearing. He couldn't hack it could he; this dreary reality, these cracked streets and the grey skies. That darkness is so much sweeter, isn't it? Daniel Eider, the cop-out.'

'Fuck you, Yaxley.'

'You wanted my opinions, right? Well there they are.'

He flicked the coin back to Gary, who left the shop without a word.

Harlequin

That night, Gary slept badly.

He sat in the garden of his childhood home. A garden where he and Danny came of age and ran in circles shouting and played their early games of London Incognita. But in this garden, whispering reeds grow from the boggy earth, and honking v-shapes of Canada geese fly overhead en route to Scandinavia. It is winter; as cold as the winter a decade ago when he was young and the lakes and rivers of England froze, in the nineteen sixties when London felt it may become something other than the grey and bomb-scarred place it is now. Yes, it is the winter of 1962 and that feels correct; he knows he is in an altered past, mining his own history. Memory is a raw material here.

He can hear the lap of the sea. Impossible of course, here in London, but he gets up and follows the sound, through the garden of his mother's house along a path leading directly down to the water's edge, winding through a lawn that gives way to reed and marsh and finally a shore. He crunches through snow and over freezing pebbles, down to lapping waves that sigh and mutter like the alcoholics under the railway bridge.

And he knows that this is not the sea, not an ocean, but it is the Thames from aeons ago when it was wider, thicker, stronger than it is now. In the distance, out on the river, are icebergs. Glaucous gulls and arctic terns float in the air. The river's surface breached by leopard seals that bark and hiss in laughter.

There is a narwhal pod out in the open water of the Thames. He sees them, their tusks breaking the surface, and fine mist gusting through their blowholes. Their backs are shiny with brine and glisten in the bright winter sunlight. Gary feels an unspecified sense of loss, then indescribable joy.

His mother calls him, come back to the house, she has made tea, come out of the cold Son, come out of the cold. I've made tea for you and brother.

But my brother is gone, Mum.

He turns back to look at the house, that building that contains and constrains his childhood. But it is invisible, obscured by encroaching Thames mists that gallop in at frightening speed, a freezing fog in which the judderman himself can be spotted enticing the souls of the city's damned. Damn, it's cold.

He notices another figure on the shingle. Looking out toward the narwhal pod is a harlequin. His pale face is marred by scar tissue and his right eye weeps continually from old injuries that never fully healed. His multi-coloured clothing is ragged and threadbare. He is old but familiar, his eyes betraying a wisdom that stretches back decades if not centuries. He sits upon a mound of albino bones.

They share poitin from the harlequin's rusted hip-flask. It burns Gary's throat. The narwhal pod swims in an endless loop out at sea, like a serpent devouring its own tail, their tusks harpooning the surface as they spar with the laughing leopard seals. An arctic tern dives into the river hunting for sprats; a sound like a freshly minted coin dropped in clear water.

Squalls form and clouds gather over the river. The mists thicken.

Gary sits with the harlequin by the banks of the prehistoric Thames, as freezing droplets begin to fall from the sky. Poitín burns their throats.

'Magnesium burns,' says the harlequin, pointing at the scars that ruin his face, as if explanation were required.

Boys, your tea is ready. His mother's voice, floating out there in the mist.

Suddenly, there is commotion out at sea, a leopard seal taking down a narwhal in a burst of blood. Then the screech of a glaucous gull.

Gary wishes he were a winged navigator, flying high over the ancient river, gazing down on the proto-settlements that would one day become London, the herds of auroch, the seal people, Jenny Duro sifting the mud for trinkets and bone. He needs a boat, not a crippled and sad jester who drowns himself in bootleg liquor.

He turns to find his way back to his mother, away from the fogged banks of the river.

But the mist is everywhere. He can't get back.

The harlequin laughs. His breath is carcinogenic.

The harlequin Gary now recognises as a man of darkness and angles; the judderman.

'Your brother's with the judder,' the harlequin states flatly.

In the mist, he hears the bellow of a crippled mastodon, idiot mammoth, the great destroyer.

'It's all over now?' asks Gary.

'It's all over now,' replies the harlequin, not without kindness, and sips his liquor.

The mammoth screams.

An extract from *Your Architect is Degenerate* (The Malachite Press, 1964), by Michael Ashman

Harrier chased his quarry down, weaving between the piles of rubble and coughing on the dust that seemed everywhere in the heat of this London night. His chest was heaving and he was sweating hard.

He was running through an old industrial district, blown to smithereens and never fully rebuilt. The ruins of factories, where city larks would strip the copper and any other salvage to sell to those who needed it. Warehouses with gaping windows, the smashed glass like the grinning teeth of the thing Harrier had glimpsed last night. What had Vincent Harrier seen in a back alley in Mile End? A being of shadow and lines, its eyes weeping blue pits. He was not a man frightened of the world; and this thing had frightened him.

This part of the city, east London, was still a raw wound. Harrier grimaced, feeling the ghostly ache of the bullet wound in his leg. Healed long ago, the result of an Irgun sniper whose comrades had hung up his friend Trev like a piece of overripe fruit from an olive tree. For a second, he stumbled, his mind full of exploding hotels, the endless blue skies in the lonely desert, a Palestinian olive grove on fire and the air rippling in a greasy heat haze.

But that was then. He was still alive, and this was now.

Harrier had to catch this man who ran from him; this thief, this abductor of children, provider of victims for the wealthy elites. Elites that had hidden in luxury while the working people of London were bombed, their homes obliterated, their city ablaze. The people who now denied the returning soldiers a home, who forced them to self-house, to squat the margins of the city. The rich in their homes on the hills looking down on the rest of London.

The war, Harrier reflected, had made something of a Marxist of him.

He had taken this job on for nothing. He had heard the whispers of course, but had never had conclusive proof, until now. The streets of post-war London kept him busy as it was, dealing with the terrors of the damaged and shell-shocked city. But then a wife and husband came to him, his name now carrying weight in the underground currents of the city. Vincent Harrier, a man who could get things done – but not at any price. He had to believe what you asked of him was right, that it would in some small way make this unbearable world more tolerable. This husband and wife from Stepney Green, they clutched each other and attempted to look stoic, but revealed their son was gone. Taken. Disappeared. They had heard rumours of children disappearing, and worse rumours as to why, and now the unthinkable had happened. Their little baby boy (well, he's a toddler now, said the husband) swallowed up by the darkness.

'The night they took my Bobby,' said the wife, choking back her emotion, 'I saw the strangest thing. I was bringing the washing in from the garden – I say garden, it's a strip of grass basically, but it's ours – and I see this thing at the back, where our fence meets the alley, where the cats and foxes screech all night. It looked like a man, but it weren't. Like a shadow, too thin to be a person. It looked like it was grinning at me. Taking the mickey, almost.

'But then I looked again. It was gone, and I thought I'd imagined it. Not enough sleep, too much work, you know. But then Bobby disappeared that night.'

Harrier's quarry accelerated, and tried to duck across the road and down a side street running next to an abandoned textile factory. Harrier already had his pistol in his hand, fired his weapon with precision, clipped the guy on the back of his left Achilles tendon. He screamed. Harrier noticed pigeons shooting up into the air, and a wary tortoiseshell cat bolt into the shadows at the shrieking noise.

The few other people on the street silently melted away. They knew not to get involved.

The man, this abductor of the lonely and unloved, sobbed and whimpered and tried to haul himself to safety as Harrier approached, calm and collected.

What must this man see, thought Harrier. An ageing man, scarred, stubbled, grim. A man who once had a sense of humour and now has none. A man who has seen too much.

A man who never needed the stories of the judderman, never needed to see those spectral cats the squatters were babbling about. You cannot unsee, and you cannot forget.

But you can end things.

He would provide this sobbing man with a kind of ending.

The man, gritting his teeth in pain, pulled a knife and brandished it at Harrier as he approached. Harrier paused, almost smiled, shot the man in the wrist. More screaming. Blood flowed, thick like syrup. Harrier could see through the hole he had made, flaps of shredded flesh, splinters of bone and tendon. He'd seen worse.

'You're all over now,' said Harrier, pointing the gun at his victim's head.

One shot, a crack like a leviathan's spine breaking.

Blood pooled around the man's shattered skull. Grey matter formed a filthy paste in the dust of the city. Harrier looked at this mess that had once been human, and felt nothing.

He rooted around inside the man's pockets, locating the piece of paper he knew he would be carrying. Now he could find Bobby. Now he could bring him back, bring some light back with him to the streets of Stepney Green.

He looked around him, at the skeletal remains of a once thriving part of his city.

'London, your architect is degenerate,' he growled, and spat on the asphalt.

He lit a cigarette.

From Daniel Eider's journal

The weather was strange last night. The skies over the reservoirs of Woodberry Down were the colour of a bruise, yellow and purple with a sense of faded injury. I could smell stagnant water, the kind that wriggles with larval life and turns the stomach. You could feel that autumn was coming and with it a storm. I hoped for a storm strong enough to scour all that was ill in the city away; I knew it would not.

I walked home past families of orthodox Jews in Stamford Hill, the men with plastic shopping bags stretched over their furred hats to stave off the coming rain.

I stared at the swollen sky, and I grinned as the first drops of rain splashed on my dirty skin. I felt the drops trickle down my face and gather in my beard.

The city could be so beautiful. A Routemaster passed me slowly as I made my way along Amhurst Park and the sight of the passengers on the bus making their journeys that would always be unknown to me made my heart feel fit to burst. My people.

A beggar begged at the Stamford Hill Broadway. I saw fruit and vegetables from one of the many grocery shops spilled and ruined on the ground we all walked. An Indian man swept up the detritus and it was beautiful. I flipped a few coins into the beggar's hat. He replied in an accent I couldn't place. Irish or cockney, perhaps.

The rain intensified, making London a city of water, a drowned land, deluging it and trying to wash away its dirt and sins. But the problems were too ingrained. We didn't believe in baptisms.

I entered Springfield Park as the downpour continued, a man alone now, and I sat on the sodden grass and watched the oak leaves bend under the weight of water, and it was in that park that looked out over the Lea valley and north-east London that I felt at peace and knew what I had to do. There were Canada geese floating on the Lee navigation, and a blackbird braved the rain to take advantage of worms summoned to the surface by the water's insistent tattoo.

I hope these words make sense. I once hoped I would turn all of this into a book but I see that is no longer possible, that the thing of shadow I pursue is now ready to meet me on my own terms, so these scraps of writing that form my journal and diaries will have to suffice. And I hope someone can one day make sense of them. My brother Gary, perhaps, or even Yaxley and his lunatic followers. I no longer dream of the Malachite Press.

I fear the book will never see the light of day. At least I hope these words convey my feelings towards this city that I love and fear, even if what I have seen can never truly be pinned down on paper.

In the end, Gary never found his brother. Danny Eider was gone and all that was left were the scraps of his journals for the freaks and occultists and hippies like Yaxley to pore over. Perhaps that is what Danny had wanted, never to be truly known, but to be one of those whispered undercurrents of London's alternative and subterranean cultures. A passing reference and a sly in-joke for Jenny Duro and her crew. A phantom, as insubstantial as the spectral cats that had terrorised the blitz victims, as mythic as the black bears faced down by Vincent Harrier. A cult figure for the cult of London Incognita.

But Gary did find the judderman. The jagged figure of lines stared back at him with eyes like leaking, stagnant rockpools, from a cracked and smeared mirror in a cold public toilet on Finsbury Park, a place where deals were made and men came for quick handjobs in the cubicles.

Gary didn't know what had led him to this spot; he had been wandering for hours, drunk on a bottle of cheap vodka, his clothes stinking and people avoiding eye contact with him, or spitting on him, telling him he was a fucking disgrace, pull yourself together mate, get a fucking job, there's kids around here, you stink you cunt, and so on. He must have been ranting, raving, saying the following things:

London Incognita (can't you see it?)

the mammoth is our destroyer or maybe it was once

an emperor worm will rise as the emperor of Nematoda!

Danny where are you mate? You left me

the tunnel-tribes they're down there and they're real and

they're alright actually, little child-sized things, they hand
poke tattoos and speak to me in their lost London dialect
Lisa's alabaster skin God I miss it
Jenny Duro I always liked Jenny Duro she's as sound as a
pound – what a lark!
the Barghest and its milky white eye what does it see?
there are disappeared children and tortured innocents and
grinning men on the television do not trust them what hides
behind the smiles will destroy us
Irish bombs will it ever end will there be peace in our time,
though I do see the Republicans' point (don't hit me)
swastika tattoos are inked deep in your shitty pink skins and
you have nothing to be proud of
shrapnel embedded in flesh sleeps like the grubs of a vile parasite
disfigured harlequins sip their liquor on a hollow shore but
for what reason
creased sepia photographs what did Danny want with them all?
skinned sea mink, sea mink pelts, a stuffed sea mink sitting
somewhere unloved maybe the Horniman museum down
south near Forest Hill
gairfowl, littlewing, great auk, my parallel penguin of the deep
north, one of the forgotten fauna and part of the supporting
caste, you know what I mean or maybe you don't
old paperbacks, their spines are broken, and paper decays
Malachite is a green deep green stone

who is Ashman???

Vincent fucking Harrier.

This would explain why his nose was dribbling blood, clotting in his beard. A group of sharply dressed skins on the Holloway Road had found his shambling form worthy of violence, and who could blame them? They'd put the boot in hard. Bruises were blooming like approaching stormclouds across his skin. There was a lump like a snooker ball coming up on the back of his head, throbbing and sharp. He limped a little from where his ankle had been kicked hard by a steel toe-capped boot. Gary imagined his own body as shattered architecture, a derelict building falling apart, a relic to be torn down and moved out of the way in the name of progress.

Gary was all over, a walking ruin. His limping cousin now said he couldn't stand to be around him (you stink mate, you're mental) and they no longer went to The Sovereign together. His mum and dad, wilfully oblivious as they were, withdrew even further into themselves and let their last living son slip into oblivion. Lisa was long gone, and good for her. Sometimes Gary would sit on a wall near his house, watching Fen and the Barghest pass him on their way to the pub.

He spent nights awake on coffee and amphetamine reading over his brother's papers, flicking through his boxes of ancient photographs, trying to find clues in the Vincent Harrier novels. His days he spent floating on a sea of vodka and whiskey and occasionally the white spirit handed to him as he stood warming himself by a fire on a patch of waste ground. He spent more time now with the old men and the destitute drinkers under the bridges and railways. He enjoyed it. Felt a solidarity with them. They had so many varied, colourful stories, of the judderman and the emperor worm and so much more; and he was more than willing to listen. His favourite spots with his drinkers were around Manor House, Stamford Hill, and the Tottenham marshes where he liked to watch the kestrels hover as they hunted rodents in the long grasses.

But how he came to be in this bloodied state in this piss-stinking building in Finsbury Park he didn't know. He must have been walking, shouting his obsessions to the people he passed in the street, his blood a cocktail of alcohol and amphetamines, chain smoking unfiltered cigarettes as he tottered along canal towpaths, staggered through the estates of Woodberry Down, harassed the commuters at Arsenal tube, insulted the skinheads in Holloway.

He listened to the drip of water in the cisterns. The soothing low hum of the traffic on Seven Sisters Road.

He recalled a fond memory of him and his brother together. It was the day Gary and Daniel Eider finally mustered up their courage and descended into the tunnels beneath the city and found the abandoned underground station they were seeking. The lost tunnels and forgotten connections that snaked and wormed beneath the city.

Gary recalled how Danny held his torch and the look on his brother's face when that beam of light landed on the beings that they had come down here to seek but never truly believed existed. The troglodyte tribes down in the tunnels were real living breathing beings. They existed. Wrinkled, pale skinned, and child-sized, something amphibian to their movements and appearance. Salvagers, with their own salvage songs sung in an obscure London dialect, shanties built from the rubbish of the city above. The tunnel tribes' world was built with the discontinued styles of the world above. An eclectic, retro style, Danny said, and laughed at his own comment.

In a way, Danny said later, they were larks like Jenny and her crew. Gary remembered the troglodytes' inquisitive features and their frog-like eyes, their hand-poked tattoos of the emperor worm and the giant bear, and how his brother squatted on his haunches, supplicating himself in a way, offering them things he believed might endear them to him. Silver jewellery, a Marathon bar, a bottle of strong West Indian stout. The encounter with the tunnel tribes affirmed the power and reality of London Incognita, and the brothers realised that all the stories, it seemed, were true. Things were never really the same after that. In the months after Danny's disappearance, Gary had enjoyed looking at the sketches, taken from life, his brother had made of the tunnel-tribes. Danny gave each sketch a title – Gary's favourite was *The Chthonic Tribes of the Tunnels that Wind and Writhe Beneath our Feet*.

It had been a good day.

But now, in a cold, wet, dripping public toilet, the walls beaded with moisture, Gary looked into a cracked mirror and saw the judderman staring back at him and Gary dissolved into the bloodstream of the city, merging with its pain and its psychosis, and he became a thing of shadow, a man of lines and harsh edges, a story for all the lost and scared of London to talk about through the cold dark nights of the winter that was gripping the city.

I hope it never lets go, Gary thought.

You're all over now.

The Scorched Music of
The Emperor Worm

'There is a writhing worm in all of us, waiting to be freed.'
From *The Salvage Song of the Larks, and Other Stories,*
by Michael Ashman

The first time I heard the scorched music of the emperor
worm coincided with my first sighting of the place that lay
behind the city I had inhabited for fifteen years. The city I
lived and worked in was London, a place I had always felt to
be lacking in reality, with its tarmac roads, grimy pavements
and corporate spaces merely a flimsy stage set.

As the set was torn down and replaced at an ever-
increasing rate, and as the actors became increasingly
unconvincing and the plots more boring and nonsensical,
I began to catch glimpses of another city. It was then that I
heard the first rough cacophonies of the scorched music of
the emperor worm.

This other city I christened Nematoda, and it was a hellish
and parasitic place, but also possessed an honesty I felt my

London was lacking, and that drew me to it. I went willingly, is what I'm saying.

I remember distinctly the first time I glimpsed Nematoda. I was coming into Blackfriars station on one of the smooth Thameslink trains that connects the city to the commuter towns of Bedforshire and Hertfordshire; I did this most weekday mornings as part of my commute, changing from tube to Thameslink at St Pancras station.

It was a gorgeous spring morning in late April, and the river sparkled like it had been scattered with expensive coruscant jewellery. I could see the river larks on the muddy shore, singing their salvage songs with gusto, a few detectorists out early, and a lonely man with an ancient dog that barked at the murky river.

My fellow commuters seemed happier than usual after the weeks of rain, dark skies and slushy snow that had beleaguered the city. The Thames at Blackfriars is a wonderful sight, enough to spark the heart of a jaded Londoner, and that day was no different. I can remember clear, specific details from those moments before my first sight of the hidden city where the emperor worm held sway: the strange crease in an office worker's shirt sleeve; the way a young woman bobbed her head arrhythmically to an internal soundtrack; a nervous looking Galician couple on their way to Gatwick, half-hidden by monstrous plastic red suitcases. And I remember the story I was reading at the time: 'A Life Constricted, or, These Serpentine Coils Will Crush Us Both', by the legendary

London chronicler of the arcane, Michael Ashman. It was from a collection published by the Malachite Press but now out-of-print. It was a nice, manageably sized hardback edition, with a glowing endorsement from the writer D.A. Northwood on the front cover.

As I looked over the river before taking the steps down to the South Bank, the salvage songs of the larks increasing in volume, the horizon of buildings – walkie talkie, shard, gherkin, etc. – warped and dissolved, and the sky, just seconds before the swirling blue of a larimar gem, became a dark and brooding green, reminiscent of the briny waters of the Thames estuary. Other, more ramshackle, buildings took their position on the skyline and it was then I heard that glorious scorched music. Monstrous, some would call it, but I enjoyed its brutal and experimental nature, its wilful tunelessness and insistence on repetition and brutality to make its point. It brought to my mind burnt earth, the acrid smell of marijuana smoke confined in a small space, brittle grass in waterless desert plains, the toxicity of melting plastic. The dissonance was gorgeous, the impurity true, honest.

The vision of this other city was brief, perhaps ten seconds at most, but behind the ramshackle and decaying buildings of Nematoda's skyline I saw the contortions and writhing of the thing I understood to be the emperor worm. And I knew, as I stood at Blackfriars station, that the emperor worm, with its segmented body and fearful mandibles, was the source of the scorched music bleeding into my world and bringing me joy. I was happy for the stage set and its ever-changing cast of actors to be proven false.

As the years went by and my life in London continued, I would see Nematoda and hear the brutal music of the emperor worm occasionally. In the depths of winter by the New River Path as it approached Alexandra Park, the water iced over and frosty, I saw a writhing mass of eel-like creatures beneath the ice, and I heard the caustic refrains of the worm's music.

I once thought I heard the scorched music at a decadent and hedonistic party held in an old warehouse somewhere out beyond North Acton; but when I pressed who I thought was the DJ, he claimed to have no knowledge of the emperor worm, despite the T-shirt he wore clearly depicting a squirming limbless beast: a wyrm, serpent or hagfish, perhaps.

Standing at the platform of Pimlico underground station, an announcement came over the tannoy informing those who were waiting that the next train would not be not stopping. It was a common enough occurrence in London. But as the train passed through the station, I could see it was no train at all, but the fast moving and segmented body of the emperor worm. At that moment the scorched music surged, powerful and raw, through me. The other travellers at the platform seemed not to notice.

I glimpsed the city of Nematoda many times in those years, but it was always distant and hazy, and I could never find a way to access that ramshackle metropolis. I tried, enlisting the aid of urbexers, lonely psychogeographers, brutal hardcore bands, urban birders, the alkies who knew about the judderman, obscure sound artists, and troubled writers of grim poetry who idolised the writer Hecate Shrike. All people, I should say, who had some awareness of Nematoda and its inhabitant, but none with a passion that I felt matched my own. Through these people – I considered them allies, really – I discovered many wondrous things, broke bread with the frog-eyed tunnel-tribes who lived in the disused parts of the underground, danced long into the night in party caverns, and learned so much about the secrets of London Incognita. But Nematoda remained out of reach, enigmatic.

I tattooed my thin and wasting body with images of bobbit worms, lampreys, deep-sea eels, coiled Celtic serpents, ouroboros, Jörmungandr, and my own artist's impression of the emperor worm, in the dim hope that I would somehow entice the worm into revealing Nematoda, into showing itself fully. It was an act of devotion that in the end was futile; perhaps all such acts are. I never found the entrance to the city.

And now, as my time in London is nearly over, I doubt I will ever find the entrance to Nematoda, and the source of that beautiful scorched music. I had so many questions that I never found answers to in the years since that beautiful day at Blackfriars. What was the emperor worm? Was it benevolent, malicious or indifferent? Why could only some of us hear what it seemed to offer us?

I will never know. But then, I will tell myself as I jump in the car to drive off to a new life in the west of England, it is important for the world to still contain mystery.

I Precede Myself

Camden is PK's first stop. Already he can see himself arriving, Trev's welcome face as it creases up into a goofy smile; he can smell the vinyl records and their plastic sheaths, categorised and sub-categorised, documenting over four decades of a spiderweb of subculture. And, as always, he pictures himself glimpsing Cerise as she boards a shining new hybrid-engine Routemaster; as she hops onto the tube carriage two-along from him at Edgware station; as she disembarks into the crowd at Chalk Farm before running up the steep stairwell and into the light. He pictures his sister sitting silently on a bench next to the sunglass-wearing wire-mesh men who guard the platform at Golders Green. She is all over the city, now. Always with him, just ahead of him, slightly out of reach.

PK is on the hunt for a record, a cherished thing he once had but then lost, a rarity now the years have slipped away. Scarp's second LP, *Your Degenerate Architect*.

In a recent interview looking back at their legacy and looking forward to what the reformation would mean, Scarp's lead vocalist, Andrew Eider, revealed he had taken the title from an old London novel by the writer Michael Ashman, a story of panic and Blitz rubble popular, apparently, in the nineteen fifties. PK has never read it.

Scarp were allegedly named after the North Middlesex/South Hertfordshire tertiary escarpment, to reflect the band's interest in the landscapes and deep topographies of Greater London and its surrounding counties; or, it has been suggested, it was a contraction of 'scarper' i.e. the British slang meaning 'to run away'. Andrew Eider never gave a definitive answer on the subject.

Only five hundred copies of the album were ever pressed on vinyl. There's a CD edition that can be picked up for a few quid second-hand, but no one cares about that, certainly not PK. Three hundred copies pressed on marbled 'London grey', two hundred on a deep 'Middlesex green', put out by the now-defunct Positive Records, who went under in 2010, taking a decade and a half of the underground with them. The funny thing is, PK *owned* that Scarp record, on Middlesex green; he had the damn thing in his possession, and he sold it in 2009 when he was down on his arse. He'd like to say he sold the majority of his physical possessions due to the calling of some higher spiritual purpose, an Eastern spiritual thing like some of his hardcore heroes, a rejection of the consumerist world he knew was poisoning all of us. But no. He just needed the money.

For a while, he liked to blame the economic crash of 2008 and its ripple effect through the next decade for those miserable days and his constant struggle to support himself, but the truth is he was lazy, putting half the money he had up his nose. Nights in the crumbling architecture of the city, buildings soon to be bulldozed and replaced with luxury apartments, better people, sour coffee. PK thought it radical to work cash-in-hand whilst still claiming housing. Believed it was punk rock to swamp his brain with booze and sneer at the nine-to-fivers as he spent his mornings with stinging stomach acid and stale ash and *The Wright Stuff* for company. The good old days, eh? Well somewhere in those days his girlfriend, Jenny, took off. Who could blame her?

PK sold most of his records soon after Jenny jumped ship. He kept the party going with Melissa and Billy for as long as they could all manage it. And somewhere in that mess, as he floundered in an empty black ocean, he lost his sister. Cerise, who had tried to help him, who acted as the medium between PK and their mum and dad, the one who set him up with work he never followed through on, the sister he let down again and again.

She was caught in the attacks a few years back, the vans and ceramic knives down London Bridge way. Drinking with mates at a new craft ale place near Borough Market. Bad luck, nothing more, proof there was no logic to any of this. PK was fucked at the time, dribbling in a squat in Deptford, and it took a while for the news to filter through to him. He didn't even know she was gone for two days after it happened.

And so, PK strolls to Edgware underground station, leaving his small flat out at the suburban edge of London, sucking on an electronic cigarette and missing the ashy bite of the past. A beggar stops him, asks him for change. The guy is wrecked on Spice, synthetic stuff that's decimating London's homeless community, a population that swells despite the damage the drugs do. PK can see it in the man's eyes as he presses a few coppers into a chapped and flaky palm. The signs are obvious to those who can read them.

Pathetic wreckhead.

You despise what you recognise in yourself, right?

PK is at the station now. Two Jehovah's Witnesses stand by the taxi rank; today the leaflets and pamphlets they offer are in Polish. They stand out here, dead smiles on their faces, in all weathers, multilingual and dedicated. They stand among cigarette butts, chocolate wrappers, the dust of the city.

A small child's glove, dirty blue, lies on the edge of the pavement where it meets the gutter. PK kicks it into the road, grimacing.

He feels contempt for the Jehovahs; bites the feeling down, sucks on his vape, exhales, tries to be more understanding.

These fucking God-botherers. The nerve.

Cerise always said he should try to be less judgemental. Who was he, after all? Nobody, that's right.

His sister gives him more guidance, now she is one with the city and gone from him, than she ever did in the days when she would grasp his hand and give it a concerned squeeze, slap his face in desperation, pound the top of an old wooden table as tears streamed down her cheeks.

These promises of false salvation.

Calm it down, PK.

He half-jogs down a wide staircase to the platform, passing a row of recently updated advertisements: a coppery orangutan promoting audiobooks; a new mindfulness app dedicated to inner peace and exploration of the self; and an album titled *Keep Going* from a popular television celebrity, in collaboration with the bassist from a defunct indie band. PK stops briefly to examine the advert. It looks like it's for a self-help memoir, those books that are so popular now, aimed to combat the spread of depression and anxiety that PK sees colonising society like creeping black and choking mould. The celebrity uses the modern communication channels – social media and digital personality – adroitly, and has a legion of devotees.

There is no authority but yourself.

PK tries to quieten the outraged voice inside him, the one that's been raging his whole life. Without the liquids and powders he once used to drown it with, the gorgeous swamp he used to wallow in, ignoring the constant running commentary in his head is a daily battle. The voice, always two steps ahead of him, gets in there first.

Monetising spirituality. Charlatan. Another way to rinse the lost and lonely. Bunch of mugs.

Please be quiet.

Whatever helps people, he reasons.

That's bollocks and you know it.

Whatever helps, that doesn't hurt others. That's what Cerise would have said. The problem is, PK does not believe it, but he wants to. Maybe that's good enough.

Whatever works? Like Spice and the bottles of supermarket voddy and the pills and powders?

Shhh. That *did* hurt people, didn't it?

PK reasons that the Jehovahs have their judgement day that will never come, he has his landscape punk and his posi-hardcore records, and the celebrity has his platitudes that help people… if not swim, then at least stay afloat. This city is awash with anxiety; it's knackered, overly caffeinated and depressed. People need to cope somehow.

That's all it is. Coping. No solutions.

PK can swallow this argument, with gritted teeth if necessary, that the Aldi-brand spirituality can help, the packaged salvation is a welcome ointment. He can accept it; if he finds it narcissistic, gauche, what does that matter? He is after Scarp's second record on Middlesex green. That music, that scene, that gave him a way to get through the days and nights and now it does again. How is what the celebrity peddles, what the apps sell, any different?

The album has just been released on a major record label, one arm of a global and wealthy corporation.

PK hops onto the tube. Two orthodox men engage in a vigorous conversation in Yiddish; they are noisy, bellowing at each other as the rattle and hum of the train increases, so he rams his headphones into his ears as the train departs. Thumbing and fumbling at his cracked phone, he locates *Break Down the Walls,* and sticks it on. 'Make a Change' kicks into life like a violently revving engine.

I can't turn my back anymore.

He's been listening to a load of the old straight edge and youth crew stuff of late – Bold, Judge, Gorilla Biscuits, Youth of Today, Shelter, you know the stuff. Since he lost Cerise in one of London's nightmares. It felt to him an imported ideology, but always inspired him despite the fact that PK was a fixture in the pubs of the dirty city for fifteen years; despite the many years attempting to outrun himself. PK sucked down smoke with a religious fervour for a decade and can recount twenty-pint sessions and then the rest. This is London and the edge thing never fully fit, but PK understood what it was all about: it was the same thing we all believed in our scene, and this was global anyway, right? Right. Believe in yourself, stick together, maintain a bit of human compassion in a world gone mad, etc.

Change.

PK is sober now; he could never outrun himself, regardless of the speeds he travelled at. He's down to a few fags a week.

*

Your Degenerate Architect can, of course, be listened to on online streaming services, and it is downloadable and yeah you can find the whole record on YouTube with pictures of the original sleeve and liner notes and the Middlesex green vinyl; Christ, the band have just started playing a few reunion shows, to the joy of those who followed them between the years 1999 and 2006, so no doubt there's a reissue in the works; vinyl sales are on the up and up. PK can see it now: a boutique label, new liner notes from a fashionably underground writer, deluxe packaging, 180gsm. Maybe an anniversary piece in *Vice* or *The Quietus*.

He has tickets to see the reformed Scarp play at the Boston Music Room in Tufnell Park later that summer; he's going with Melissa and Billy, just like the old days before they turned into the dark days. PK can already see the three of them there, as if they've already arrived. Bill fighting his way back from the bar clutching frothy plastic pints. Mel rolling loose Golden Virginia into a cigarette.

That's the past.

So it is. Coke Zero and a vape, maybe one of those no-alcohol blue Becks, then.

PK skips on from *Break Down the Walls*. Something heavier, darker; 'Take Me Away'. It sounds like black clouds coming in, a storm about to break on an unprepared and depopulated coastline.

I have to stay clean.

He sold his copy of *Your Degenerate Architect* to a sniffy record-dealer prick in one of the exchange stores in Notting Hill Gate. PK is certain now he was ripped off, but the guy fluttered a few notes in his face and that was enough for him; he could see what the paper would buy, how the notes could be coiled tightly into tubes.

The dealer was the kind of guy who'd claim the live version on the unofficial bootleg from the ill-fated Japanese tour was the best representation of a song. A joyless twat, more Victorian entomologist than modern music fan.

PK is flooded with memory as he travels to Camden and the tube thickens with people. Further down the carriage, he watches Cerise hanging slackly from the metal bar the standing travellers cling to, moving with the currents and eddies of the underground, thumbing her phone and laughing silently to herself.

He writes her letters sometimes, little text messages, emails that can't be sent. Passing thoughts about loneliness and self-improvement and how perverse it is that we can all imagine better worlds but never reach them.

He looks up from his phone and notices there's another advert for *Keep Going* on his carriage. He sighs.

Self-improvement is being presented as saleable commodity. Mental illness is the fault of the individual. Get confident, stupid!

Calm it PK. It's helping people.

It's your *fault you're unhappy, not society's. Burrow further into yourself. Dig in.*

He could murder a drink at times like this.

No.

Change the track again. 'Start Today'.

Today, on his way to Camden, he might be able to put something right; if he is to rebuild, to make a change, reconstruct himself into a new form with a chance of surviving this life, then he needs to reconnect with the things he loved and cared about. It seems small, but he needs to find this record. It's something to build on. They say if you can't love yourself, how can you be expected to love anyone else? Treat yourself. Go on, PK, you've deserved it mate.

Narcissist nonsense, capitalist mantra, a lullaby of the atomised society.

Magnesium Records might have a copy – today's the day Trev sticks the new stock that's come in out on the shelves, labelled and stuck in those plastic sleeves with the pleasant chemical smell. Magnesium specialises in the kind of music PK thrills to, the stuff he once loved and is helping him fight his way to the surface again: punk, hardcore, Oi, post-hardcore, crust, youth crew, that sort of thing.

He owns the other Scarp records, still; they managed to survive the purge. One he particularly cherishes is the split EP, *The Between Places*, they recorded with the Finnish hardcore band, Etiäinen. A record in support of the joint tour the two bands took across Europe in 2004. That was a time: PK is lost to memory again. He is right there again, bilocated. The cheap, long coach ride nipping whiskey from the hipflask with Mel and Bill, over to Amsterdam to get blazed and catch the beginning of the tour, following them on to Berlin to see them play at the Kopi, a punk rock jolly out of London before returning a week later for the hometown show at The Underworld, right here in Camden.

Do you remember, Cerise?

She was with him at that gig, she was part of the scene at the time. Nomadic Tribe and Dead Industrial Atmosphere in support at the hometown show. What a lineup! You could almost call it definitive; capture it in amber and you'd have preserved a perfect day when the landscape punk scene was really a scene and PK and Cerise, and Melissa and Billy were right there in the middle of it, documenting it, living it, drinking it, breathing it. It was around then that Melissa stepped up what she was doing with the *Magnesium Burns* zine. When Cerise had her hair red and the lip piercing and the bull ring, the happy years before the junk took over PK and whatever he thought he was.

Nomadic Tribe released only one album, the critically regarded *Concrete Palimpsest*. It's rumoured they may be making some new music soon. PK is a big fan. Dead Industrial Atmosphere are still going strong, with albums like *City of Worms* and *Miracle at New Cross Gate* considered staples of any discerning underground music fan's collection.

In his worst days, his sister said it was like talking to a drunken doppelgänger, a pathetic, weaselly clone, a coked-up facsimile of her brother.

'You think you're a bar room philosopher, some kind of visionary, but you're just a selfish cunt.'

Some wounds never heal with the passing of time.

But all that came after. That tour, those years, they were genuine, they meant something. It must have been how stoned he was at the time – a joint before breakfast and another for a chaser after his cornflakes – but each venue felt like a homecoming, as if they'd all been there many times before. That was one of the very good, one of the best things about the scene, the sense you could travel the world and still be right at home in basements, clubs, squats and pubs that had the right symbols and the right people, like the multilocation Scarp sang about. It wasn't going nowhere; it was being everywhere.

The Between Places had three songs from each band on ten-inch, marble pink vinyl: a gorgeous thing that's worth a fair bit now. It was going for a hundred quid the last time PK checked on Discogs. *The Between Places* has one of his favourite Scarp songs on it, 'Bilocation', later collected onto a B-sides, EPs and rarities CD given the name *What Never Was* and that – as is often the way in the scene – became one of their best loved songs, and frequently the track they'd encore with.

If Trev doesn't have *Your Degenerate Architect* in stock, he may have a lead on the record. PK knows he's a fan of the band, they know each other from the London scene back in those days. That's how PK knows Mel, through Trev; he's aiming to pick up her book there too. It's had a few good reviews in the alternative music press and on the punk and hardcore sites. *Magnesium Burns: Two Decades in the Underground Capital*

1999-2019 (Positive Press) is a collection of the long running zine-cum-mag that Melissa ran, now all collected together into a heavy, fat book printed on thick paper with new essays from Mel putting the whole thing in context. She even got Andy from Scarp, her brother, to give an endorsement on the cover. It's a must-buy; he supposes he could have cadged a freebie off Mel, but it's important to support those close to you. He knows that now.

And it's more than that. PK needs to redocument himself, pin down what he loved and why. Otherwise the past is just fog and smoke; it's just Cerise bleeding out beneath a fruit and veg stall in Borough Market as sirens and people scream and shots are fired as the Thames flows oblivious.

The scene was adept at documenting itself, perhaps aware that no one else cared. It was like they could see ahead, could see themselves in the very near-future and that gave them the ability to realise that they were going to have to document what they were doing, or so PK reckons.

Hence the proliferation of the zine culture, both online and still in print – he has his old piles of the original *Magnesium Burns* zines, *Fracture, Punk Positive* of course, and even the zine he wrote for and produced for a couple of years, that he gave the unbearably pretentious title of *Through This Mud We Find Ourselves*; forgive PK, he was just really into the whole landscape punk thing back then. He was passionate.

Mel's an interesting woman and a good mate to have. Get

her on a few vodka and oranges and talking about her family and she'll tell you about her great uncles, Danny and Gary. The Eider family have a colourful history. Gary got filled in by a bunch of skinheads; a homophobic attack it's reckoned. Found dead in the gents on Finsbury Park back in the winter of '72/'73. The story always makes PK think of when he lived round that way, near Manor House station, in the warehouse. The barmaid found on Boxing Day, strangled and dumped in the park's undergrowth. She'd been pulling pints at The World's End in Camden for a few months. Italian, if he remembers right.

He is, he supposes, glad to be alive.

Anyway, if all else fails, he can always buy something else from Trev; in fact, he knows he will. There's a new Youth of Today reissue he has his eye on; he once owned that record, and he will again.

*

PK enters Magnesium, the door making a tinny tinkling sound as he pushes it open. The walls are plastered with gig posters, old ads for new records. A plastic leaflet holder overflows with fliers, black and white and cheaply Xeroxed.

'Alright Trev?'

'Easy, PK. You forgotten something?' Trev has vinyl stacked thickly against his chest; he reminds PK of a waiter teetering with dirty plates through a busy restaurant. His slight beer gut is visible, a black Cro-Mags T-shirt rucked up.

And PK laughs, unsure. 'What are you going on about?'

'You were just here, weren't you? I was out the back sorting out the stock, but Gemma says you came in, bought the Scarp record I'd just got in. I knew you were after it. Said you barely said a word. I thought it was unlike you, you gobshite.'

Gemma is Trev's wife and helps him run the shop. PK thinks Trev is on the wind up, making one of his obscure cockney jokes he only ever half-understands.

'Pull the other one, Trevor.'

'Swear down. I sold it this morning. She must've got her wires crossed; I mean, here you are, right?'

And Trev makes a kind of 'her indoors' face. PK doesn't laugh. Gemma has sold the record, the idiot.

'You're fucking kidding me.'

Trev shrugs.

And so it goes, PK traipsing London's record stores, finding that someone else has been in before him, preceding him, asking after the same record, before they finally struck gold at Magnesium.

Adverts for *Keep Going* and the mindfulness apps are everywhere; the orangutan too. But what does PK expect? This is central London, consumer ground zero. Perhaps he thought he'd find peace in the eye of the storm, but no such luck.

Around Oxford Circus, on his way to Berwick Street, he finds himself surrounded by a flock of Hare Krishnas: saffron robes, funny haircuts, tinkly bells like the door opening to Magnesium. They're just saying 'Hare Krishna' over and over.

Do they not get bored of their mantra?

What like
You can't love if you don't love yourself
Haha.

*

PK returns home, defeated. He sees Cerise, headphones in, her hair a Middlesex green, on the top deck of a 73 bus as it passes him near Euston, and he smiles. He has a copy of *Magnesium Burns: Two Decades in the Underground Capital 1999-2019*, that he picked up from Trev, and he'll get Mel to sign it when he sees her next. Maybe they can grab a coffee somewhere; one of those new healthy vegan places, full of punters that remind PK of all those people over the years who took his dietary choice as an affront. Things change. Everything is up for sale.

And he can see the days and weeks ahead before the Scarp reunion gig, sober days that he intends to spend trying to reconnect with the people in his life.

Give Mum and Dad a call.

Check in with Bill.

Think about the apology he'd give to Jenny if it wasn't all way too late.

Keep writing those notes to Cerise, the messages he will never send.

Think about others, and how he fits in with them, and how they all fit into this insane and polluted city.

But give him a bit of time. He's getting ahead of himself.

We Pass Under

In the shadows under the concrete walkway I am something trollish, sister of Grendel, daughter of Cain. I am a thing best forgotten.

A heavy goods lorry thunders and rattles above, ferrying products to the Brent Cross shopping centre. I spent much of my life there. It was in the shopping centre that I first encountered the Commare, as she smiled at me across a crowded coffee outlet.

I imagine the lorry carries the foundations and concealers and lipsticks I once used, that I demonstrated to middle-aged Greek wives, brittle north London mums, and shy young Persian women. Perhaps the lorry contains the brands the traveller girls tried to steal that time; I remember how Tricia laughed hard when I told her the story.

My time on counter was a life of endless harsh light that revealed, I believed then, all. Now I am a thing of shadows, something hidden and purgatorial. I wonder if they miss me there. Many girls come and go, as is the way of things in north-west London. I suppose to outsiders – people in offices or hot desk co-working spaces in more fashionable parts of the city – we all look the same. But I believe the Commare saw us for who we really were.

A rusted can of lemonade trembles as it's swept past by rainwater flowing freely through the underpass and along the walkways. The can clanks against metal railings that resemble incarcerating bars, a strange polluted comb, a dented plant grown from cracked concrete. Further down in the murk of the underpass, Aliyah is weeping. I listen to her choking sobs as her emotions peak, before she sniffles, then laughs a sad little laugh that might be an attempt at bravery before the crying resumes. I wish she would stop, pull herself together, but I do understand. She has had a tough time of things. I wish I had helped her in some way, whilst I could, when we were both on counter. There were things we shared that we couldn't ever bring ourselves to discuss; and now we are both here. Perhaps this is a lesson of the Commare. Perhaps it just is what it is.

*

There are rats down here, skittering along the walkways and under the traffic. Big things that stink of refuse and the rot of London; however long I have been down here, I have retained my sense of smell. The rats ignore me as they twitch and squeak and scrabble in the darkness.

I used to see rats in the alleyway by mine and Tricia's flat, and I think of the old joke: in London, you're never more than fifty feet from an estate agent. I chuckle to myself, despite the incessant rain and the grey gloom.

I saw a vixen down here, just the once, a greasy and ill-looking thing with glowing green eyes that padded along the walkway in the small hours of the morning. I observed it crouch, freeze, as a pair of alcoholics, their faces covered in scabby sores and bruises, shambled by. I have seen sad people indulging in sticky sex acts down here; wide-eyed men in need of care shouting and gesticulating at invisible enemies; a group of teens, knives out and setting about a rival before one of them tripped and banged his head into the railings. Grim sights but with their own kind of humour. You've got to laugh or all of this would just crush you, wouldn't it?

*

I remember a time in Canning Town with Tricia, before we passed onto Bow Creek. We were exploring east London with the end destination of Leamouth; we had foolish, never-realised dreams of moving to another part of the city. There was an exhibition by the river there that we wanted to see, something that would fit in with our hoped-for life. The traffic thundered along Newham Way, where it meets East India Dock Road. Under a hard-to-reach section of the raised A-road, the cars elevating up and over the River Lea in a smooth curve, we saw homeless men and women sleeping on a kind of sheltered concrete island, a place where they would barely be noticed and not be disturbed by the authorities. The traffic passed over them and they slept underneath. I could barely breathe in that place, the exhaust in the air was so bad, and my skull was all vibrating dissonance. I remember the filthy blackened tissues after we blew our noses. Something was wrong in the air. The place was corrupt. I thought of the noise, the smell, of scarred lungs. Those people lived there.

And I now live here, with the roar of traffic ever present. I can smell it, but the pollution does not bother me, however, and I blacken no tissues.

*

I wish I were truly a monster, waiting to devour the unwary or the unlucky, hiding under my bridge. That would give me purpose, a clear identity, a reason for lurking in shadow beneath the walkways.

Understand that I was dehumanised in my other life, before I came to the underpasses and walkways. All the girls down here were. Online, I was told I needed a real man to sort me out. My cuck of a boyfriend couldn't satisfy me (I had no boyfriend); I was a whining snowflake. But I was never political, and never fully understood what the accusation meant; I don't think my accusers did either. I survived these attempts to make me into something monstrous, shrill, a hag, a Jenny Greenteeth lurking in the waters of the River Brent, Peg Powler sloshing in stagnant duckweed in the Roding, a nag like a kelpie, a rabid bitch but certainly no green-eyed vixen, a shambling saggy-breasted mother of Grendel. As reward for views I expressed publicly, things I believed in, I was sent pictures of pornographic actresses, stuffed full, with my face cheaply grafted onto theirs. I received death threats, of course, but also my mother in her semi-detached house in Borehamwood was threatened with murder. These things clogged up my inbox.

I just needed the right man to set me straight.

I had said, before I came here to the walkways and underpasses of Brent Cross shopping centre, that I believed in equality, that the women I respected should be paid the same as their male counterparts. They did the same job, did they not? It had been in the news, hotly debated. All I did was agree.

I did things like tweet pictures of a trip to the Suffragettes exhibition at the London Museum with Tricia; selfies of us beaming in the brutalist architecture of the Barbican complex. It was inspiring, how could you not at least respect those women, feel a joy in their contribution to history? And then I read a couple of articles and then a few books and I then had the nerve to suggest there were poisonous aspects of masculinity; it was damaging all of us and we could all be better, so much better. I could see the problem everywhere.

I had to believe in a future better than this present. I pointed out all those lonely young men hanging from nooses of their own construction. Bleeding out in bathtubs in isolated bedsits, a final futile Tinder message left unsent. Slipping into oblivion on a dirty mattress in their mother's home as a bottle of vodka and a pile of pills did its job.

I pointed out all those women sent to early graves by partners who claimed to love them. The girls I knew with scarred arms, bad self-esteem, their endless encounters with men on London's public transport network.

Some people – men mainly, of course, but some women too – saw something monstrous in that. The Commare, giving me the slightest of acknowledgements as we passed each other on the escalators at Brent Cross shopping centre, gave me the strength to weather those storms.

*

It wasn't always like this. I wasn't always here. But for how long I have been listening to the roar of the traffic and watching the passers-by who scuttle along laden with heavy plastic bags, I can't tell you. I am waiting for the Commare, but as each lonely day goes by, I wonder if she will ever come, as she seemed to promise us in the bright lights of Brent Cross. I saw her, quixotic and elegant, among the clothing racks of Zara. I saw her looking older, tired but determined, behind the perfume counters of John Lewis. She stood flickering in the distance as I worked the makeup stalls of Fenwick, thick-waisted, busty, oozing sex.

In these places I glimpsed her, and realised she was a thing born of them. I once hoped she was there for us, for me, for Aliyah, for Tricia and Siobhan and Rebecca.

I never knew her real name, if she had one.

As I beeped my car open in the grey car park before the drive home to Hendon, I would see the Commare standing amongst a patch of polluted hedge that flanked the car park, a knowing look on her face. She held a beautiful male blackbird in her hand, its beak banana yellow, feathers like onyx. I felt she understood an issue I was yet to fully articulate to myself, issues that got me in trouble when I discussed them.

How the Commare looked is hard to describe. She wasn't viewed through or idealised by a man's gaze. I think she was recognisable only to us. The men, and the boys, even the ones I loved and respected, wouldn't understand. They would never see her; she was not for them, even though they had worshipped wide-hipped and big-titted idols since time immemorial.

*

Aliyah is still crying. I look down at the rain-slicked paving slabs, where there are hard wads of gum. They form a braille code to be deciphered. This is something Tricia wanted, to know our city fully, to try and decode it together. I hope the Commare allows her to achieve that goal. I hope Tricia still thinks of me.

Lights from the passing traffic illuminate me, then disappear, strobing the bridges and walkways.

Now I live with my sisters. Not my blood relatives, but we are bonded nonetheless, a shared suffering perhaps, but I prefer to just think of it as shared experience. We are all survivors.

There's Siobhan, her neck oddly bruised, who wanders the walkways and the flyovers and the underpasses, and sometimes hangs off the grey incarcerating railings like a schoolgirl and sings the Irish songs of her parents or, more likely, her grandparents. She could never recall these songs when we were out in the clubs of Kilburn, or in that awful pub in Hendon we all went to regardless, but I guess experience and the songs live in the blood, or what remains of the blood: what I'm trying to say is we possess all the experiences of our ancestors, it's just a question of accessing them. But perhaps we are frightened by what we might find there. What did our mothers, grandmothers, our ancient matriarchs experience? I imagine busy fists, the crunch of knuckles, things left out of sight and kept behind closed doors. Hopefully there was love, companionship, too. I do believe those things existed and do exist.

Sometimes I see Rebecca – from Golders Green, as she always tells me when we meet on the walkways. "I know, Rebecca, you've told me," I say. Rebecca looks constantly surprised, blinking, like she's just waking up. Her face is a mess of bruises, like a burst bag of over-ripe plums. However long we have been here, Rebecca never heals.

I look down at the sloshing water of the grey River Brent. Where I like to stand is below the roaring traffic but above the water, where the river is dead, just polluted black liquid like something bursting from a clogged outflow pipe. There is no life, only the occasional bloated bodies of rats, foxes and failed pets.

Back in the days of artificial light, when I contoured the faces of bored housewives and jittery young women, there was a thing called the Brent Cross beach. It is still there I believe, but I cannot go and check; I cannot leave until the Commare comes. London's biggest urban beach, funfair rides, amusement stalls, deckchairs. 'The Costa del Staples Corner' it was dubbed. Ha. I found it all unbearably sad. I understood that families and kids in this area found it hard to escape the tangle of London, that getting to the coast was a challenge for some, especially for the single mums and those on tight budgets. But just breathe in the air there, listen to the roar of not waves but articulated lorries and four-by-fours. Think of those people sleeping in the toxic air of Canning Town. I picture toddlers drinking from the black waters of the Brent, the sludgy wetness dribbling down their chins as they grin in satisfaction.

Maybe I am a snob, but it is a terminal beach, a place not right.

I have seen life on other stretches of the Brent. A few years ago, Tricia and I walked a route to Horsenden Hill, crossing roads choked with traffic, to part of the river flanked by shabby green. A few Polish alcoholics sat by the water and muttered dull sexual threats and laughed in the gurgling sort of way Tricia and I were used to. We ignored them. Those male mutters were like the roar of the traffic above, echoing all around me; just so much background noise. Unpleasant, damaging to your health, but what are you going to do?

*

It is raining hard over north-west London. Out there, in the open, where the traffic thunders, all is water. The rain is thick with pollutants, punishing the tarmac and all who walk on it. I can see now, perhaps twenty feet from me, Aliyah, translucent in the half-light, weeping still amongst a patch of stubborn grass and nettle that has pushed up through the concrete and formed a sort of life in the underpass, as my sisters and I have.

Aliyah was a counter girl like me. I thought she had disappeared years ago, but here she is. There had been talk of something to do with her dad or maybe a boyfriend from Pakistan, and then one of the John Lewis managers had used a phrase unknown to me, honour killing she had said, but I didn't believe it, I tried not to believe it, but of course I knew these things happened, they happened in London, dreadful things happened in London, but we thought we were a civilised city in a civilised country. What a joke.

I am from an Italian Roman Catholic background but my friends and work colleagues – my sisters now, all waiting now for the Commare to come lead us from this dark place – were Bangladeshi Muslims and they were Ashkenazi Jews and they were from the Ivory Coast, Trinidad and the Republic of Ireland, and of course England too. We all ended up here.

Aliyah, though, she always was a weepy one, a bit melodramatic. You know the type. Here come the waterworks. She would cry at an advert or a cheaply made soap opera and we always gave her a good-natured piss-take for that. If I'm honest, I felt sorry for her, as bad as that sounds. She looked like a victim. She had the mannerisms of one.

When I attempt to speak with Aliyah, she doesn't notice me, or she ignores me for my past sins. Sod her then. She weeps in the grass and nettles and dead buddleia and lets the rainwater flow around her, soaking her knees, her thin skirt, her sad little trainers. Cigarette butts, beer cans and old magpie feathers pile up behind her.

'Aliyah!' I see Siobhan at the other end of the walkway, shouting in an accent I feel she is putting on, as she was born in Galway but grew up in Cricklewood. 'Aliyah stop your grizzling!' She does this at least twice a day. Aliyah's weeping never ceases and neither does the rain.

Occasionally, very occasionally, Aliyah will notice Siobhan and I, and shriek something about a child. 'Where is she?' Aliyah asks. But if there ever was a child, it is long gone. Perhaps I am wrong, and she is asking after the Commare.

I am aware I should feel frightened, angry, alone. But I feel no real pleasure or distress, under here, in the tangled paths leading to Brent Cross. Just a yearning to see the Commare one final time. And as much as I like them, to get away from Rebecca and Siobhan and Aliyah would be bliss.

The traffic above, below, and beside us is endless and the air chokes with fumes and exhaust. It is a world stained grey. There are houses so close to the traffic, surely pre-dating this mess of flyovers and tarmac. Do people live, if such a word is accurate, in those buildings? I see blackened tissues, hear terrible racking coughs.

I am used to the illumination of the makeup counters. My eyes are not accustomed to this gloom in which I now lurk. I miss, in a way I never thought possible, the bright shining lights of the stores. The perfume counters at John Lewis and Fenwick. The eager customers and the irritating, entitled, rude women. The lunatics and the sleazy men.

Aliyah is the colour of an asphodel flower. Translucent like an undiscovered deep-sea creature, something lonely and forgotten floating in the darkness. Siobhan seems more substantial today, though at times her bruised neck is the only thing in focus, the rest of her blurry and indistinct.

I always hoped Tricia would arrive here and be with me. We looked so good together, her darker skin against my Mediterranean tone, and if that sounds superficial I don't really care because we looked great and it felt great. With her, for the first time, I felt like myself. My grandparents didn't understand of course, but they never gave us grief either. Dad was out of the picture; he was a bastard anyway, he knocked Mum around and I'm glad he walked out the door. Mum was embarrassingly supportive.

My life with Tricia comes to me as an impressionist slideshow.

The time the snow hit London so hard we had to walk the three miles from Golders Green to Mill Hill through a blizzard. Crossing Henlys Corner as traffic swerved and skidded, a giant menorah at the crossroads dripping with wet icy slush.

Lying together, dappled by green light, under the trees of Regent's Park.

A picnic at Forty Hall where I drank too much scrumpy and slept in the sun to awaken lobster red and livid; Tricia's hands as she applied cooling ointment, trying not to take the mickey. 'I thought you were Italian,' she said.

All these moments the Commare allowed to be taken from me.

*

It was Danny, a boy who called himself a man, whose heart he said I had broken. That wasn't true, but I'd shredded his pride – I didn't mean to though, Dan. It's just I was living a lie. That was what caused the grief.

Ah, that's it.

That's why I'm here.

I remember now.

Tricia and me were out in Kilburn. Drinking at the North London Tavern, celebrating a recent promotion of mine. Bad luck, Danny and his mates were there. I was never one to back away from a situation and neither was Tricia, it was a matter of pride; I had seen what my mum had gone through when I was small, and I had heard about, via whispered hints over the years, what our grandmothers had experienced, and I'd had so many of those threats and grotesque pictures and condescending messages sent my way. Sometimes you have to stand up for yourself.

We were outside vaping. Gorgeous green clouds of nicotine mist enshrouded Tricia's face. She was a smoke demon, a being of clouds, something spectral and kin to the Commare.

I said alright to Danny and things were looking okay but, as they left, one of his mates, a loutish Essex-boy called Phil with a thick neck and a thicker mind, shouted out fucking lezzers, and goes ha-ha-ha and then belched wetly. Then Tricia has a go, and so do I and all of a sudden, I'm arguing with Danny, who is red-faced, but was it with embarrassment or was it anger? Did he push me, or did I trip? I like to think that I tripped – I was steaming, after all, so I'll accept some of the blame. Either way, my head cracked on the kerb like a cheap ceramic vase dropped from a third-floor balcony. And I remember Trish screaming and Danny shouting and sirens howling in the distance and then I woke up here, in the shadows of Brent Cross.

'Siobhan, what am I doing here,' I'd said as I got up groggily. 'And what is Aliyah crying about?'

I noticed a woman I didn't recognise, her face like dark split fruit, anxious as she peered at me from the shadows.

And it struck me that I hadn't seen Siobhan in years, not since we were girls at sixth form college, and why was she here anyway? I noticed bruises and handprints around her neck. Choke marks. That was it; it was in the papers, wasn't it? Big news in Brent. An Irish girl strangled by her partner, a man with a long history of abuse. The Old Bill didn't do much. The papers said her boyfriend had been through care, and we all knew what that meant. But that didn't excuse him; it didn't make any of this right, even if he was a victim himself. And then it struck me that those stories about Aliyah were true, of course they were, and she *was* a victim, and the shame I felt at laughing at her in the past was vivid and intense and it crippled me.

We were not survivors.

*

Siobhan says this is just temporary, we are waiting for the Commare to come from the shopping centre to fetch us, and she will take our hands and lead us from the walkways and out of the underpass. That day we will pass under, under all this, into a happier world.

But for now it rains, and the traffic thunders.

Where No Shadows Fall

Alex ducked down Chapel Stones. The alley was sprinkled with broken green glass that spiralled around crumpled cans of Polish lager. The day was blazing and arid, making the usual smell of piss formidable and engulfing. He held his breath. An abandoned microwave sat by the railings, ancient brown grease spread in avant-garde patterns over a smashed door that hung like a crippled limb from one hinge. Fly-tippers were never prosecuted, let alone seen.

On the wall to his right was a mash-up of graffiti: *Judder Judder Judder, game over now* next to an image of a sharp and inky-looking figure; N17 BOYS ARE A BUNCH OF CUNTS; *I Saw the Gollem*; gang tags he couldn't decipher; a painted image of a woman that resembled a cheeky Virgin Mary crossed with one of those wide-hipped earth goddesses on display in the British Museum; the usual Spurs rubbish, and Antifa slogans he presumed had been sprayed on the brick by the local crusty punks. It all looked sad in the harsh sunlight.

The church on the other side of the railings hummed with life. Women in colourful outfits and men in tight suits and children in their weekend best spilled out onto the street as the service ended. A booming and crackling voice bled from the church's PA across the carpark and through the railings into Chapel Stones. It was something about God and praise and salvation, but so distorted the message was entirely open to interpretation. Alex knew the god they worshipped was just one of many in the city.

Continuing down the alley, the pair of crackheads he often saw thieving in Sainsbury's scurried by in the opposite direction. They were all bones and juddering movements and they paid him no attention, shouting loudly about something, but at each other or to the Chapel Stones or to something else entirely, he couldn't tell. Alex imagined their shouts as the language of an ancient and degenerate sect, loaded with meaning, just waiting to be decoded and shed light on a wider mystery. But they were probably just off their heads, heading to the park to sink tins of corrosive booze on the benches by the Holocaust memorial, near the travellers and their mobile homes that materialised overnight last week, or to the cemetery where no shadows fell. If it were me, Alex thought, I'd head to the cemetery; a good place to sit and drink and think. He'd seen a greater spotted woodpecker there, back in the spring, flitting between the trees above downy goslings and tufted ducks. You could find a bit of peace there, still in sight of the cranes and the stadium. In the cemetery were quiet graves and sleeping foxes and the soft trickle of the River Moselle. It was a place he liked to walk with Sally; one of those places that never changed and never really got boring.

Alex hit the High Road. The stadium that defined this postcode was being ripped apart by monolithic machinery that creaked and moaned like idiot beasts of burden. The stadium was being rebuilt only a few metres away, but for now the fans were away in Wembley and, as such, the area was much quieter at weekends. No fuckups where he'd roll out of bed not checking the fixtures, walking straight into a punch-up between Spurs and Millwall. Alex liked it when the fans were absent and tied himself in knots worrying if this was the attitude of a gentrifier armed with an avocado and a bag of bitter coffee beans.

Construction dust choked the air and he saw whirling, svelte figures coiling in the haze above the slowly moving traffic; curious sylphs and mischievous djinn and the other polluted spirits of London's poisoned air. Tottenham High Road was a cacophony of sirens, honking horns, the low rumble of engines and the whisper of spirits.

He figured he would walk down to Chances. The buses were going nowhere, deadlocked and shaking with frustration. It was not a scenic route; it was dirty, there was exhaust in the air; grime and grot was embedded in the concrete. Broken glass everywhere, and broken people too – fractured people, splintered people, people who'd come undone or been stitched up. Still, Alex got a pleasure from the place, enjoyed the fractal patterns of glass and the incomprehensible braille of gum stuck hard to the pavements.

He wondered what a gollem was, what the cheeky earth goddess painted on the brickwork meant, why someone was taking the time to graffiti these images in these parts of the city. Dust devils swirled around him as an ambulance shrieked up the high road, pushing traffic up onto the pavement. More horns honked and someone shouted from their car at another motorist, seemingly believing it would help the situation.

He approached Chances, passing the police station. He was meeting Jamie to sort some stuff out with his van, the van that no longer ran, the van with its suspension shot, the van smothered in street art and graffiti and slogans. The usual punk and activist stuff, but some other, weirder iconography too, the stuff Alex and Sally liked and that left Jamie perplexed, the kind of stuff that was appearing all over the city with the culprits not even tagging themselves. Jamie was practical, he always had a scheme for a benefit show or campaign he was roping Alex into without fully explaining it to him, or anyone but himself. But he kept himself, and by proxy Alex, busy, and he was a good drinking companion.

A broken woman sat on the pavement by the police station, out of it on a substance stronger and more effective than alcohol. Lipstick was smeared around her face, like she was a derelict clown, or performing an extreme satire about the expectations of female beauty. She was here most days but Alex didn't know her name. He never gave her money as she never asked for any. Alex wondered why the coppers never bothered to try and move her on, and he wondered too where she went at night and what she had for dinner. She smoked long thin cigarettes and often barked to herself, more fox than dog.

She barked at Alex.

Alex turned to look at her, and now she hissed at him, a sound like a knifed lorry tyre, foamy white spittle flecking her lips. The sibilance coincided with another swirl of hot dust as a rumbling HGV roared past.

*

Lately, things had been bad.

Tower blocks blazed like overwrought metaphors. Ceramic knives slashed and stabbed the necks of Friday night revellers in Borough Market, tourists and the people of London running and screaming over artisan foods flung all over the pavement, trampled underfoot to mush. Smashed and broken bodies were retrieved from the murk of the Thames where they'd met their end. Alex thought about bloat and rot and sinking bodies as he clicked his mouse and answered emails at work and tried to have opinions about new Netflix shows. Sub-letters were torched in the shitty flats they paid way too much for, their unregistered names forgotten even before they died in the crematorium tower. Alex lived through elections that only proved there was no confidence anywhere; from Edgware down to Morden, Cockfosters to

Uxbridge, Brixton to Tottenham, there was no fucking clue. Attacks came in retaliation to attacks, then more attacks, and on it went for eternity. He knew it was a violent city and always had been, he'd been in punch-ups himself, but this felt different, nastier, more personal somehow.

Old imams died of heart failure. White men screamed 'please kill me' as they were dragged from vans by the police into other vans. British nationalists were herded like cattle into Whitehall Wetherspoons, to enjoy cheap beer and protection from the police. Boys on mopeds chucked acid in their enemies' faces, giving Alex visions of blind teenagers riding buzzing bikes into the heavy traffic of the Old Street roundabout, skin smoking as it bubbled away, their features erased to leave only scarred and skeletal smiles. The bridges that crossed the river had erected barriers to stop drivers targeting pedestrians; as if it couldn't happen on any street anywhere and anytime in London. Alex remembered the whale that once tried to make headway up the river, making headlines before dying. Now they said you could see seals in its waters.

The worst thing was, even as he tried to fight it, Alex could taste the fear. It was gripping the city and old fearful energies were being unleashed. The demons and writhing gods of London were back on the streets; Alex knew they'd always been there, lurking in the shadows and temporary spaces, but they were emboldened now and happy to show themselves. In a world lacking facts, where every bit of reality was up for debate, the nightmare life of London, contributed to by all the communities who populated it. The nightmare was thriving. Sally always said, 'This is city is a monster,' and she was right.

So:

Alex jumped a little too hard when a tube train lurched for no identifiable reason.

A shout in a strange place made Alex flinch.

A bag on a bench at Liverpool Street, or a bang at Euston, or a young man running in Kings Cross made Alex want to run and run too until he was safe back in the streets of Tottenham, sat safe in the park by the Holocaust memorial drinking super-strength cans, safe in All Hallows cemetery by the ornamental lake, safe with the dead in Haringey Mortuary.

He yearned to jack in his job, to dance forever in Chances with Jamie and Sally and Hank and Roberta, with the people he counted as allies. To hold the world at bay with loud music and tins of Red Stripe.

He tried to fight the bad atmosphere, but he couldn't help it. On his commutes on the packed trains in the sweaty mornings he could see himself trapped and hear the future screams and taste the panic. He watched fellow commuters and imagined how they would react when the nightmares of London were unleashed in confined spaces. Worst of all, he could read these thoughts in the faces of his fellow commuters.

He was becoming pathetic, he knew that, a jittery and curtain-twitching *Metro* reader, consuming, commuting and working and little else. Black misanthropy, that Alex always pictured unimaginatively as a huge onyx city-fox padding the towpaths of the Lee Navigation, crept in at these times.

He tried talking about these feelings to Jamie, to Sally, but it was always when he'd had too many, or when he was having a good time, when the fear and the blackness seemed further away and had been successfully dampened down with a chemical and alcoholic reprieve.

In the cloying heatwave of the city's summer, he had dreams bedevilled by enough imagery to populate an entire bestiary. Alex saw creaking clay men with paper in their mouths pound the pavements of Stamford Hill and Hendon and Golders Green. They knew a threat was coming, that old ideologies that had been fought for decades had to be fought again.

Alex saw a monkey god and monkeys too overrunning the temple that sat in the grey dirt of Neasden. He dreamt of pile-ups in the Neasden underpass and all of Harlesden consumed by an inferno.

Tokoloshes ran gibbering along the trickle of the River Moselle cutting through the cemetery as jackdaws and jays and magpies sat in the tree branches like dark fruit, cawing and laughing.

Alex jumped awake at night, dripping with sweat after visions of a screaming woman with many arms and a severed head hanging from one of eight hands; her skin was cerulean or jet, depending on what night it was. Beautiful women in shimmering saris danced as she screamed, and they screamed too but with a smile on their faces.

He dreamed of a predatory bird that grasped its own tail, giant and silently sleeping on the rooftops of Peckham Rye.

He dreamed of a giant worm writhing and thrashing in the Thames at Blackfriars.

In the dusty haze of the city's pollution he saw ifrits, coiling through the choking exhaust of the endless vehicles that ferried goods and people, and other mischievous djinn too, things that would promise you the earth and then fuck you up. These Alex saw along the Edgware Road, in the backstreets of Finsbury Park, in the estates of Shadwell. But they were everywhere, really, integrated and woven into the fabric of the city.

He saw Jamie on his boat by the River Lea taken down and ripped apart by grindylow and his bones sucked clean of marrow by Jenny Greenteeth and gangs of vodyanoy and his remains left to float in the oily waters of the navigation.

In his dreams there was Sally, his partner he said he'd die for, running through Tottenham cemetery, through the picnic tables by the Holocaust memorial, and around those picnic tables sat horrible acid-scarred harlequins and pierrots and pulcinellas that drank cans of White Ace from the local off-licence, and hissing women in gaudy makeup, derelict clowns the lot of them, who laughed at Sally as she passed through this place where no shadows fell.

He dreamed of leaf-faced women and wooden men dancing in the Wick Woods, more out of duty than desire. They bent branches and left offerings as bait to urban photographers. They were the last of their kind and already someone had put an offer in for their image rights.

These were the dreams Alex dreamed that summer.

*

Jamie was waiting for him at Chances. He was scowling at his van. Someone had covered it with similar slogans to those Alex had seen up Chapel Stones. You could see where the paint had run, hardened trickles now, a sloppy job all told. There was a grinning inky-devil, the Mary-thing, clay men. Neither Alex nor Jamie were particularly surprised.

'To be honest, it's to be expected, leaving this here mate,' Alex said.

Jamie scowled and rubbed his shaved head, flinging a cigarette on the floor.

'Thanks,' he said, grinding it beneath his boot.

They got Jamie's errands done, lugging stuff in and out of Chances, putting things in the van, taking things out of the van, cups of tea, more cigarettes. As evening approached, so did the gig, right there in Chances. It was a popular venue for music that endured the decades, music that was too weird or too aggressive for the current fashions that found their inspiration in arch irony and depressed hedonism. Alex loved it here, and he wondered how long the place could last. There must be an offer just over the horizon.

Job finally done, they headed over the road to The Beehive for a few pints, met the usual faces. There were Hank and

Roberta, and Sally came and Alex kissed her on the cheek. They became more animated and the world swirled and became a bit more colourful and the dark dreams that plagued Alex faded out of view and he could see better visions of the city for the time being at least. In the gents, at the urinal he noticed stickered images of golems and djinn and Clapton FC on the hand-dryer.

Heading back to Chances they walked half-cut and myopic into commotion all around them. Police on the street and a crowd of fifty, maybe a hundred, of the local teens all in their weekend glittering finery stood there. Some of the girls were crying and then some of the boys, masked up and hostile, chucked a few bottles at the coppers and things got hairy for a bit. Bouncers from Chances tried to defuse the situation and Alex thought some of the local gang kids were here, but it was weird seeing them next to the crusties and the old guys with the tatty mohawks and the shaved-headed girls in their vegan boots. But this was London and this was Tottenham and this was, in some strange way, what Alex enjoyed. He dragged on his cigarette and asked what was going on and the hulk of the bouncer, a Cuban guy called Tony, told him it's an end of term party that was happening in the hire-room upstairs, advertised on Facebook only for half of Tottenham to get wind of it, like in those stories you read in outraged and titillated papers. They all turned up. Turf rivalries, too many drunk and excited teenagers spilling out on the street, and a police force that dealt with black kids in a bad and violent way added up to an incident on a sweltering London night. It shouldn't be like this, and this is what it was like.

The girl who had – Alex guessed – planned the party, wept on a wall and a policeman was trying to gently tell her that it's probably time to go home and disperse. Her friends made concerned faces in a circle around her. The punks watched, talking in groups, not sure what to do. They didn't like the police but this wasn't their fight, they reasoned. Above them, in the sky over Chances, Alex saw more of the swirling ifrits who now seemed less mischievous and more curious. Even they knew this was a place, for better or worse, where things happened.

Slowly the crowd dispersed, with minimal violence,

'What the fuck was that all about?' wondered Jamie.

'I'm just glad no-one pulled a blade,' said Sally.

Or let the nightmare loose, thought Alex.

That's what counted as result in the city that summer.

*

Why would you choose to live in a city of dreams and nightmares?

Alex had followed Sally to London a good decade ago, her lucky landing of a decent job in the city prompting them both to make the decision to leave the towns of the Hollow Shore where they'd grown up. A common enough choice, but it had felt big to them, as it does when you're young.

They'd both been attracted by a place that was, as any sane person agreed, more of a fiction, a dream, a myth, a nightmare, than any physical reality. This is what cities were, Alex and Sally agreed. This is what made living in a metropolis worth it. Choose to live only in its physical reality and you were doomed before you'd even started. Alex almost admired those people who had spent decades not realising they were living in a fiction.

He considered the physical spaces they had lived in, fucked in, danced in: The Balustrade squat, Chances, The Beehive, RampArt, The Railroad Café, The Stockwell Arms, dodgy flats above chicken shops in N16 and small terraces in Tottenham. Alex often wondered if Tottenham would be the full stop on his London story; that was fine, all a person could ever do was contribute. When all of those who said London was dead had themselves died, the city would still be living, pulsing vigorously with polluted health.

All these places he and Sally remembered, where their lives had formed and crystallised, had changed or been demolished, been done up or run down. They had photos of the two of them, young and in love, then older and still in love, posing in places that no longer existed.

Yet somehow London itself just kept going, a monster without clear boundaries that couldn't be stopped. Punch a hole through it or slash a rent in its side, the wound would simply seal up seamlessly and the juggernaut would keep going, barely noticing. Alex wondered when his and Sally's experiences became memories, when those memories became myths, and when those myths would be forgotten.

They both knew that this was a city of the mind, and they knew it was an example of city-as-beast, and as such it was thrilling and terrifying. It was where life, and correspondingly death, happened. If you wanted the dreams you had to accept the nightmares. People made the place and the places made the people, and every Londoner, wherever they were from, brought their own stories and myths and monsters to add to the giant tapestry of stories that comprised the city. A city of immigrants and a mongrel culture in every way you could imagine, and many more you could not. This is what gave the city strength and what made its brutal imaginings so vivid and potent.

It was hard for Alex to watch the nightmares rise, because he and Sally had made this place their home and though he loved the mythologies and haunted spaces of the coastlines of their childhood, this city, London, offered up so much to those attuned to the right frequencies. Languages spoken by the hundred, revenants sitting and staring on steamed up winter buses, ghosts on every street, deep history and a constant amnesia. You could lose yourself here and find yourself again in an altered form. Sally particularly loved the melting-pot myths, the city that was home for all the folklore and weird fictions you could ever want.

Sally was, of the two, the most enthusiastic consumer of the novels and films of London until she was convinced it existed more in print and celluloid than in concrete and glass.

'We navigate this city, and we navigate it together, yeah?' asked Sally, more and more worried as the summer progressed.

But Alex was tired of navigating. He was ashamed, but he didn't want the fiction anymore.

*

He was pleasantly buzzed, not smashed and not totally out of it, but feeling good finally about the world after the summer months of horror. It had been a good gig, uplifting, cathartic, energetic and positively aggressive. There was comfort in being surrounded by those like yourself, in sweaty, dimly lit rooms with bad ventilation. They were nights that could fight off the creeping fear, the bleak visions and the redeveloped memories.

There was a party going on at Jamie's, where he was going to meet Sally in a bit; she was still dancing with Hank and Roberta back at Chances. Alex had forgotten his stash and was heading home for it. He walked back from Chances, under the railway bridge at Bruce Grove where a drunk gibbered and spat in front of San Marco, the Italian restaurant, up past Bruce Burgers with its painted art of the Incredible Hulk that always made him laugh, the KLM ministry, and the alms houses that look imported from another England that Alex suspected no longer existed.

He approached Bruce Castle Park; he opted to not cut through, deciding to go up the road flanking the breaker's yard, the beginning of the cemetery and All Hallows Church, and the Haringey Mortuary. All those places where the dead lived. How strange, he thought, to find the dead more of a comfort than the living. They offered a kind of safety. Alex suddenly felt ghoulish, mischievous, thought it right to take a walk through the cemetery. He loved the Celtic crosses colonised by lichen and moss, faded and broken faces peering blindly out from the walls of the church. He took solace in the table mushrooms that grew out of tree bark, of the monuments to those who died in Tottenham during the bombings of a war now approaching myth itself. The man whose death sparked a riot that sent the city down in flames for days was buried here. The dead here were multicultural and mixed and that always cheered Alex up.

*

In the All Hallows cemetery where no shadows fell, in summer moonlight were arranged the strange dreams of London. Two djinn with parchment skin stood atop a green and weathered headstone, their ears thick with piercings, telling each other stories of blind men left for dead in the deserts of long ago. A clay man, like a Hebrew bouncer, slowly nodded its frozen features as Alex approached. The crackheads were there shouting in their ancient language of the city, and the barking woman too, her face a mess of smeared lipstick. Further in the undergrowth, arranged amongst the trees were the leaf-faced people, like trees themselves. They watched him with eyes the colour of rosehips. Sad eyes that knew even shadows would fall here, in time. Scarred harlequins and pierrots and pulcinellas sat playing cards and drinking using a tomb as their improvised table. They paid him no attention. Acid-burned boys stood and grinned, fiddling with mobile phones as their remaining flesh smoked and bubbled. Charred skeletons who had forgotten their own names stared mutely at the ground, not knowing what to do.

Alex cracked open the can he'd brought with him for the journey. He sat down in the cemetery with the crowd, and gave into the bad dreams of London.

The party could wait.

A Constellation of Wondrous Places

After many years of mapping the city's interior I became tired and my enthusiasm that had powered me like strong amphetamine through the metropolis for a decade and a half began to wane. My own interests began to embarrass me; they felt like clichés, painful and obvious and trite. History had caught up with me; I'd gotten to the point where I was no longer the fresh-faced newcomer, an urban explorer forging new paths and scribbling down raw fieldnotes. Now I was a resident of London, firmly weaved into the warp and weft of the things I had once merely observed. I was no longer an outsider; instead I was part of a club I never wished to be a member of.

But slowly it dawned on me that I did not know the city at all. I was being self-pitying, melodramatic, ridiculous. I had only cherry-picked the parts I once considered interesting, fashionably liminal or artfully decrepit. I talked a lot about London writing, and wrote it badly myself, but much of London seemed to be missing from those works.

After Alex died that night in Tottenham Cemetery, after a long period of mourning and self-destructive behaviour, I became increasingly drawn to an obscure and esoteric strain of the metropolitan artistic movement known as 'London Incognita'. London Incognita was a method and genre that searched for the stories hiding in the suburbs, the mystical revelations contained in backstreets, slip roads, underpasses and shopping centres. Many of the short stories and novels that formed the loose canon of London Incognita writing were now out of print, published by defunct houses such as the Malachite Press and sold for large amounts on the internet. Publications like *Magnesium Burns* carried on this tradition into the present day.

Like a satellite drifting out of Earth's orbit, I began to frequent the ends of the underground lines, those places where things stopped; or at least where you had to jump on a bus or national rail to continue your journey. Places that had, in my myopic life in the inner areas of north-east London, almost seemed mythical and now possibly transcendental places.

In the fiction and travel guides of London Incognita, a constellation of wondrous places presented themselves. Edgware, High Barnet, Cockfosters, Upminster, Amersham, West Ruislip, Uxbridge, Ealing Broadway and, most mysterious of all to me, Morden.

One day I ended up further south than I had ever been – within London, of course; I had holidayed below the equator and enjoyed the Mediterranean, Latin America, a girls' trip to Barcelona. Morden, end of the Northern Line, a place when mentioned to colleagues they wrinkled their noses and feigned ignorance of its existence. I felt they were hiding something from me. Protecting me, or wanting to hide the place for other, more selfish and sinister, reasons.

'But you can see it is there,' I said, pointing at Morden tube station on the ripped page of a battered A-Z.

'Why do you still have that A-Z?' they asked angrily, batting the book from my hands before dismissing me and my outlandish suggestions. I clicked frantically at my laptop, swiftly trying to summon up Google Maps, but they had already left the room before I could show them the truth.

It didn't matter. I went there myself and I travelled alone, on foot. I tracked the old Roman road, read up on the Garth family, and admired the size and scope of Baitul Futuh Mosque. Not a religious woman myself, I still marvelled at the diversity and complexity of religious architecture. I could barely believe I had stumbled upon the largest mosque in the United Kingdom; I fondly recalled my trips to the Hindu temple in the grey pollution of Neasden. My enthusiasm was flowing back, and I began percolating with love for the city, a feeling I had not had since my time with Alex.

Every day I ate sandwiches and crisps bought from the local high street supermarket and sat by the River Wandle as it flowed through Morden Hall Park. It was the first heated flush of summer and it was a pleasure to be there. I wrestled with profound questions, such as whether I was in Surrey or in London, and what did London mean in the first place, and what were my true motivations?

I texted my friends pictures of the Wandle, of Baital Futuh, of the park's National Trust signs and footbridges. I photographed herons and tried to record the sound of a green woodpecker I heard hammering in the trees.

'This is fake news, an obvious hoax,' they said. 'A clever use of Photoshop.' But by now I suspected the truth, that my so-called friends were already privy to the secrets of London Incognita and were trying to deny me access. But I was ahead of them; I had seen through their cheap deceits.

*

'What do the people in south London think of it being called the Northern Line,' a friend of mine asked me in Irish chain pub near Wimbledon. We had taken to meeting in arbitrary drinking holes in areas we felt we knew little about but wished to explore further. I had no answer.

Many months went by uneventfully, until one day in early Autumn. I was walking back from my daily circuit of Morden and South Merton, along London Road and towards the underground. The sun was beating down without remorse, but this I enjoyed. I was a Londoner and appreciated being scorched, reddened like lobster, dried out and cracked. The street was dusty, with an Oxfam, a Greggs next to a newsagent, a Sainsbury's and an optician's. Approaching Morden underground, however, I realised the station had moved, or disappeared. In its place stood a group of teenagers smoking, a sick-looking tree hosting a resting flock of green parakeets and an elderly man sat on a bench reading yesterday's newspaper.

'Am I in Morden?' I asked the old man. He laughed hysterically before breaking into a hacking cough, spittle flying from his mouth. I left it at that.

And then I imagined myself falling into water and drifting down through the layers of London, as if it were an ocean, which in a way it was. Did this make Morden the abyssopelagic zone, and I was now stuck there?

Sky City

by Melissa Eider

His nights fill with the vision of a shimmering city high above this one, a better reflection of the metropolis projected into the skies above. Its streets are clean, neat, almost deserted, only populated with the quiet shades of denizens long past who pay him no mind.

Each night he walks this city in the sky, alone and disoriented, the streets illuminated by an inflamed moon and shredded with sharp-angled shadows. Some nights, the shadows seem to twitch and writhe as if a lithe-limbed and cruel man were moving under their cover. He senses a flash of a grin, narrowed eyes observing him, a delight in his unease.

Other nights, he encounters a woman standing below a sputtering streetlamp in a near-deserted square fringed with wooden benches and plane trees. The woman below the streetlamp reminds him of every woman he's ever known, he just can't say how exactly, but he knows he has met her before. She is the homeless girl near his flat, Auburn; she is Linda and Lucy; and she is his mum and his Irish grannie. She is his first girlfriend whose smile still burns brightly in memory. She is skeletal and voluptuous, shy and brash, and as she begins to walk, he knows he is supposed to follow.

She walks ahead of him for many miles through the streets. He hopes she will lead him to the city's edge so he can stare down at the city in which he sleeps. But he always loses her as she turns around a sharp corner, and he is left with only the shadows for company.

*

Mick's phone buzzes, gyrating under a pile of worn clothing that lays crumpled on his bedroom floor. He stretches out an arm and roots around for it and opens up the text. It's from his ex, Linda, texting him as if she were their four-year-old daughter, Lucy, aping the way she speaks. Confirmation of Saturday's day out – the next day he has access. It gives Mick the creeps, an adult's parody of cutesy childhood language, but he knows not to do anything to rock the boat and so he keeps his opinion to himself. Duvet still draped over him, he lights a fag and sends an enthusiastically-worded text in reply; after all, he's looking forward to it. Their last trip, London Zoo, was a joy.

Time to get up soon – a job in Wood Green today. Mick works as a bailiff in the boroughs of Haringey, Hackney and Waltham Forest. But for a while he just lies in bed and watches the smoke coil into the funk of the poorly ventilated room. It is 2006.

Mick likes his work. It's not that he enjoys turfing people out of their gaffs, not as such – though, with the junkies and the vermin and the other fucking spongers, there is a certain satisfaction in that – but he does like being out and about in the city. He is spurred on by the energy of the place and what he does for a living. Even if that energy is negative, it can power him, for a while at least. If there is a comedown, he can drink through it. In that way, it's like a drug.

It's a warped sense of how most would think of it, but he likes working with people. Or at least encountering them, exerting some power. Being in the world. Escaping a life spent within four walls. He enjoys coming up against all kinds of situations and meeting the full spectrum of London's desperate and indigent, and Christ aren't there a lot of them. This endless drip of dregs. Diseased insects running out from under their rocks, sewer rats with their tails entangled with filth forced from stinking nests. Being a bailiff gives him a range of experiences that a desk job in an office in Holborn or Angel would never provide. If Mick feels contempt for those he evicts, then he also felt it towards the corporate nine-to-sixers and the city boys and middle-classes out in the suburbs, places like Mill Hill, Bromley, Barnet. Comfortably well-off but dull-as-shit places that are nothing but endless hushed rows of suburban streets. Residential spatial warps in which a man can get lost forever. A form of dying, a willing sort of purgatory, Mick thinks. But he's done evictions there too.

Some were grim, others comedic and good fuel for pub banter with the lads. But there were the other times, experiences that would get to him if he let them; they'd burrow in like a hungry worm through any chink left undefended in his armour, lodge themselves deep in his being like a virulent tick. So, no tears, Mick, you've got to be tough in this line of work. These animals will have you otherwise. Spend enough time in the scum of the city and you'll become scum yourself. If you let it.

So, Mick has become adroit at ignoring the pleas of single mothers, the shrieks and bubbling tears of their toddlers who don't know what is going on, only that it's bad. He is immune to the wailing and tears when he clears out an illegal sublet in Woodberry Down, a tiny two-bed with half of fucking China in it; they could all go jump in the reservoir for all he cared. Even when it's the turn of the oldies, he feels nothing for them. His grandparents had worked for what they have; these shambling things could only deserve what was happening to them. They made the wrong choices.

Mick doesn't flip coins to the young ginger dreadlocked girl near his flat as she sits by the Halifax cash machines on a tatty cloth. She holds a bit of cardboard Sharpied with 'Hungry and Homeless'. He doesn't know her name but mentally christens her Auburn, in honour of her filthy hair. He pictures her nooks and crannies crawling with lice. You can't encourage them, can you? It'll only go in her veins or up her nose or down her throat.

'Spare some change please mate?' Every morning the same, as if Auburn's never seen him before.

'Sorry, love, I haven't got anything on me,' he replies each time, almost angry.

Mick has a job to do and everyone has to earn a living. The vermin he evicts should have paid their rent. Simple as. Anyone can work if they really want to, it's 2006 for fuck's sake. Just get up off your flabby arses. Crybabies and spongers and immigrants expecting to just be handed everything without lifting a fucking finger. It's not on. His grandparents, when they came over from Ireland, they dealt with a ton of shit, didn't they? Paddy jokes on the evening telly: *next time tell your man to lay the turf green-side up*. Alf Garnett calling for the navy to sink the island; worse than the Pakistanis. And so on. People now don't know they're born.

His grandad worked digging out tunnels for the trains that now shuttle mollycoddled ingrates to and from their desk jobs. Nan and Grandad never complained. Not like this generation.

Some might say, if asked, that he was a bit numb to it all now – his ex Linda certainly would, she just couldn't deal with the emotional blank anymore – but they have a little girl together, little Lucy, aged four, and he loves her with a fierceness that surprises him. Everything else he can block out; he tells himself there are no compromised areas. But there are chinks he won't admit. Tiny cracks. Everyone has them. He's never told anyone about his dreams of the city in the sky above London – they'd think he was a fruit, going soft on them or losing the plot like so many others do. A man keeps it together. For the kid, if nothing else.

He sees Lucy once a week. Their last trip was a Saturday outing to London Zoo. Mick doesn't know why he knows this, but he does – the world's oldest scientific zoo. Maybe his old man told him once; he loved facts about London like that. It gave him a sense of pride. It was like the underground, thought Mick. Oldest in the world and showing it: creaky, splitting at the seams, but still there. The city must be senile now, losing the plot, right? Mick knew it was. Despite all the building work, the endless demolition and reconstruction, Mick had seen the rot in the foundations. Black mould creeping up the walls of the bedsits, the track marks on junkies' arms; the way some people live.

'Look at the animals,' he whispered into his daughter's ear, pointing at a pair of African hunting dogs trapped in their cages, yelping sadly in the light spring drizzle. Lucy seemed excited and shouted 'Doggy' a few times, pointing in their direction and trembling with excitement. She was hankering after a pet, but Linda had to go out to work didn't she. It wouldn't work.

Mick thought of the couple of crackheads he'd cleared out of a stinking basement flat in Bounds Green a few weeks ago. The dark red sores on their pale and clammy skin, the woman's skeletal frame, the man's weirdly shrill shouts and incoherent abuse. Something scrawled on the wall opposite their tatty and lice-crawling sofa, above the TV that got smashed during the scuffle. 'We pass under,' it said, in spidery, jittery handwriting – whatever the fuck that meant. The couple had had a doggy too, a sickly yappy thing that Mick had to boot hard with his right foot when it came for him. They'd left it whimpering and wheezing in the corner of the front room, its ribs snapped, pink foam forming at the corners of its mouth.

The man had taken a swing at Mick but was so out of it he'd failed to even graze him; slapstick out of an old children's cartoon. Mick and his mates had laughed about that in the pub, come up with names for the junkie double-act, weakly flailing against these giant bailiff men. Pinky and Perky, Tweedledee and Tweedledum, Ant and Dec, Bodger and Badger. As he had sipped his pint, Mick thought of the city above this one, how we all passed under it and lived in its invisible shadow.

A lot of the time Mick wasn't sure if the scum he evicted knew who he and his colleagues were – they could be social, the old bill, private enforcement, anything. To his clients – ha – Mick was simply one of *them*. The system. Whatever you want to call it. How many times has he been called a fascist by young ones who had no idea what they were talking about? But perhaps a bit of that old discipline could help the city. The thought had a sense of scandal, titillating. Exciting. People were so soft now.

Mick did some freelance gigs too. Private work. Squatters causing problems, parasites who had to be gotten rid. They had some sort of legal right, Mick understood, but fuck that, they were in the way and if certain people were prepared to pay, then he was going to clear them out. And so he did. The extra money was always handy.

The bailiffs know stories of dark things. Stories half-alluded to. Narratives imported from the paramedics and the coppers and the social workers, then told to a friend of a friend and diluted with booze then repackaged and spilled out again over a pint of London Pride. Mick tries not to think too hard about them, the tales of people and other things that stayed incognito and operated outside of the light, deep down in London's tunnels and disused underground stations. Women like rats, men like shadows. But he has heard no one, ever, discuss the city above this one.

*

Mick is in Wood Green, sat in a van with the other bailiffs parked on a side street not far from the shopping centre. He hears the laughs and screams of young children passing by, on their way home after school. He thinks of Lucy, doing the same thing right now, most likely hand-in-hand with her mum.

Him and the boys are going in for a routine job to a flat in Sky City, the housing complex three-storeys up that sits on top of The Mall, Wood Green's shopping centre. A firefighter Mick met once told him that, due to the design of the stairs, it's incredibly difficult for emergency services to reach anyone in the housing estate. Well, he and his bailiffs will get up there. They don't even think anyone is still living in the place. The neighbours haven't seen anyone in years, think the flat is empty, but there's a funny smell coming from somewhere. They can't look directly in through the windows, but it's clear no one's home. Probably the smell is coming from the waste bins – you should see how some people live. Animals not fit for the zoo.

Empty flats with years of arrears are nothing unusual. So many people just disappear or dive willingly into the cracks and leave their shitty little lives behind. Mick can't blame them.

They make their way up the stairs and to the flat.

Bang bang bang.

No answer.

'Okay lads, time to go in,' says Mick, grinning.

With a crash and a crack, they're through the door. A few of the neighbours and their dirty children have appeared to watch them at work but Mick pays them no mind.

Four grown men, big lads, hard, break into the flat and are hit with a stench none of them have encountered before.

Decay and refuse and spoiled meat and old stains.

Something is wrong.

It is rotten.

Sour.

When they enter the living room, they find her lying on her back next to a shopping bag and surrounded by Christmas presents she has wrapped but, for obvious reasons, never delivered. Mick finds himself unable to read who the packages are intended for – knows it might be the thing that snaps him in two. The television is on, playing a mid-morning gameshow. A buzzer sounds as a cheerful contestant answers a question incorrectly. She lies on the sofa, grinning and sightless. Hot liquid rises up Mick's throat, and he runs to the woman's bathroom.

Her remains would later be described in the papers and documentaries as 'mostly skeletal'. Three years spent on the sofa, they say. Poor girl.

*

In the weeks after the Sky City skeleton, Mick finds himself in his car alone in a Sainsbury's car park in Holloway on a Tuesday afternoon, taking hits from a bottle of economy vodka. All he can see is a grin without lips and when he puts his hand to his face, finds that he is crying. For her, or for himself, or for all the endless futile waste in this joke called life he cannot say.

He drives for hours along the North Circular late at night, with two a.m. thoughts of his daughter and his ex-wife and how he fucked it all up, how he could still have a chance with the little girl but knows that he'll ruin that too. He's ruining it right now. He's missed two access days and Linda is not happy, no, not at all. Slings accusations his way: he doesn't care, he must have a new woman, all the usual. But he can't bear to look into Lucy's face because all he sees there is her in the decades to come, desiccated on an Ikea sofa, unloved and rotting for years without anyone even to notice. How can he bounce her on his knee now he has seen the fate that awaits us? Look into any crowd on any street in London, any packed tube carriage, at any football match or gig or gym and see the future bodies, the beings of blood and bone soon to be the forgotten remains of unfulfilled lives.

The Sky City skeleton evicts him from his own life. He has stopped going into work and presumes he is now unemployed. Linda has given up on him. Maybe, Mick thinks, this is what I deserve. I couldn't hold it together, I let it all get to me, and this is what a man gets for going soft. Spend enough time deep down in the dirt and you're going to get stained.

And finally, he is in a world of eternal night in the city above. Sky City. He finds the woman standing in her square beneath the streetlamp. The leaves of the plane trees ripple and whisper. The benches seat one or two shades of a London long past, who watch Mick without malice as he steps into the light of the lamp.

As the woman begins to walk, he follows her once more through dark and winding alleyways and this time she does not disappear from his view; he manages to keep pace, dark energy powering him one last time.

They reach the very edge of the city's limits. They look into each other's faces. All of London stretches below them, beautiful with a million pinpricks of electric light, the Thames writhing like a worm between the north and south.

The woman's face. She is Auburn, she is Lucy, she is Linda, she is all of them, and she grins a lipless and toothed grin as she gently takes Mick by the elbow and aids him as he steps off the edge of the city and into the void below.

Staples Corner, and How We Can Know It

One – On why you are at Staples Corner

Weak and watery November light. A Monday afternoon. You sit with your nose pressed against the cold glass of the 266 bus, breath fogging the surface and revealing the finger-traced declarations of a thousand other travellers. GAZ 4 LUCY, John B is a dickhead, a misshapen anarchic A.

You think on what awful chain of events led you here, to the end of your known world, over your horizon. Dimly, you are aware you have lost something and that you must replace it. As the 266 chugs and rumbles, Nina checks emails on her phone and you try to remember. That's it. A robbery. You were drunk, Highbury Corner, the Hen & Chickens pub, meeting two old schoolmates. A few lagers turned into many. You never normally keep your laptop in your bag, but that day you'd come straight from the office in Tottenham. Then the bag was gone, and you were panicking in a toilet cubicle.

Being informed by the bar staff that this kind of thing 'happened all the time.' That's it. That's why you are here.

As penance, you travel to Staples Corner.

Cricklewood fades as you escape the Broadway, and concrete begins to colonise the landscape. You know you are headed to a divine meeting of arteries. Repeat their names. M1. A406. North Circular.

Aeons pass. Then Nina's elbow is nudging you to let you know it's time. We are at Staples Corner, she says. We are here.

You exit the 266, listening to the doors hiss like malicious laughter.

Look around you. This web of underpasses and roundabouts, of concrete walkways and steps to nowhere, how can it function? You are trapped in the fevered dying dream of a brutalist architect. You stand where logic has given up, and perhaps hope too. Perhaps this is what you see when you peer behind the veil.

You are here. Your destination stands temple-like over there. As the lorries force fumes into your lungs you panic and wonder how to cross. Slowly the scene assumes logic. A zebra crossing, an underpass. All is well. You cross, breathing in exhaust, clutching Nina's hand.

Two – On how Staples Corner got its name

Not from the Staples stationery store that sits there now. There are no easy solutions here. You think how you could do with a new ruler, better pens, a notepad more befitting a proper writer.

Staples Corner, against all odds, has history. For sixty years Staples was a mattress factory, dealers in sleep and nightmares. Then an upstart, B&Q, took over. It couldn't last. Come 1992, the Provisional IRA detonated a device below the A406 flyover. B&Q, damaged, was demolished, and replaced by another Staples; pens and pencils, not mattresses and their illusions of comfort, where fevered town planners laid and dreamed of Staples Corner.

Three – Currys car park, Staples Corner

You stand insignificant in front of the hangar-size stores. Here, you thought it would be simple. But your eyes dart nervously from PC World to Currys, Currys to PC World, heart racing. You are blinded by choice.

You notice that here, in the car park outside Currys, Staples Corner, no people come in or out of the doors, no customers return to their parked cars. You and Nina stand in the car park, the only couple in existence, alone. A flock of diseased pigeons pepper the sky over the North Circular with an awful flutter of wings. It is cold, and you shiver. Panicking, you head into Currys, drops of sweat beading your brow, whispering to yourself: M1. A406. North Circular.

Four – Inside Currys, Staples Corner

Inside are many shoppers. Assistants lean on white counters and follow buggy-pushing families, imparting wisdom. They wear dark blue fleeces and smile without pause. Customers enter the store straight after you, but you know there were only the two of you in that car park. These other customers form on entry, visitors from a world you are not privy to. The carpet is womb-red. The air is artificial and warm. The atmosphere flickers.

After half an hour of talking, misunderstandings, boredom and a final decision, your elderly male sales assistant informs you that the model is not in stock. A leering, spiteful face grins at you from the screen of every tablet and laptop. You hear a hissing and malevolent laugh leaking from a boombox speaker. All others seem oblivious.

You fight the bile that rises, try to ignore the spirit of this place, Staples Corner. You never considered a genius loci could be fucked-up, malicious, out to get you.

The sales assistant continues: Go next door to PC World. We are the same company. They have five.

Five – PC World, Staples Corner

You find your model quickly. You recognise it, even obscured amongst the other screens with the grinning and juddering face.

You didn't see her arrive or remember instigating conversation, but the short woman who is now your sales assistant is in full flow. She has watery blue eyes, or perhaps they are contacts or perhaps something else entirely. This will be over soon, at least, you think.

Twenty minutes pass. You are still fending off add-ons and extras that she flings at you with the remorseless energy of an algorithm. A stone-tape recording of a PC World, Staples Corner, sales assistant, stuck on loop. Nina, driven hysterical, starts to laugh and laugh and will not stop. You sadly realise the only way you can break this endless cycle, give this fretful ghost-assistant some peace, is through gritted teeth and complaint. It works, but you feel no satisfaction.

At Staples Corner there is no comfort in being right.

Sir, I regret to inform you we have no bags.

The watery blue eyes betray no emotion and the leering juddering man in the screens sneers. The checkout beeps and a man speaks into a walkie-talkie somewhere in the distance. Nina is holding her stomach, bent double by the iPads, spasms of hysterical mirth ripping through her.

Six – Staples Corner and how we can know it

Your replacement model, boxed up but not bagged, is tucked uncomfortably under your right arm. You stand shivering, waiting for the 266 and look at the monolithic mass of Staples rising high over the other side. You think of stationery and mattresses, bombs and watery blue eyes. Repeat your mantra. M1. A406. North Circular.

You think on what you have learned at Staples Corner as you head home, re-entering the world. You have been handed a question mark formed in concrete, and you know you must return.

What Never Was

As a child on the wintry coast of Bexhill, the sight of frayed photographs depicting moments corroded by time moved me to a degree considered unusual amongst my peers. I was odd, a slight embarrassment, deemed overly sensitive by teachers and family. But perhaps this was to be expected: I had lost my mother at the age of seven, and had no siblings.

My mother was a modest-sized woman with shocking blonde hair and a small smile who enjoyed taking me on short walks along England's southern coastline. One day in the spring of 1990, when the swells were aggressive and unpredictable, the sea took her. I imagined it as a reclamation, as if she had been on loan.

It is unanimously agreed amongst my family that my mother and father loved each other greatly, though he is understandably quiet when the subject ever arises at infrequent social gatherings. I wonder how he resists the thoughts of what was denied to him, the life he anticipated that never came to pass. I am a symbol of that lost future. I am a piece of bold post-war British architecture; a piece of

Soviet cosmonaut metal rusting in a quiet meadow; a promise of progress rescinded.

I lived through dark nights as freezing rain from the continent battered the windows of our house, my father drinking from bottles as he looked out to the black sea. By then, my mother existed only in frozen staged moments framed on our mantelpiece. In my adulthood, lost images of forgotten families wreck me like a ship striking sharp, submerged rock.

*

On a drizzly September night in 2016, as I approached my thirty-third birthday, I came across a box filled with sepia images of a family of six, speckled with abstract patterns of mould. There was Mummy, Daddy, Brother, Sister, Baby, and a scruffy Irish terrier. The box, its cardboard damp and flaky, had been dumped by a green recycling bin outside a large house in the throes of refurbishment common to the area. I was walking in a quiet and relatively affluent suburb of north-east London, near Bush Hill Park overground station, on one of my many solitary explorations through the outer reaches of the metropolis I had undertaken since Stefan's death. Rain speckled the grey pavement as I crouched by the recycling bins like one of the scavenging urban foxes I saw so regularly. Despite my expensive winter coat, had anyone passed at that moment I would have looked feral, indigent, a woman to be avoided. But the streets were empty of human life.

The orange lights in the windows of the suburban homes were warm and possessed a comfort denied to me, and at that moment I heard the strained bark of a fox further along the road. I took the box of photographs, glancing at the house to see if anyone would care about my theft, and poured the images into my grey rucksack.

Nightly now I look through the rescued pictures, drinking glasses of rosé wine on the balcony of my flat on the northern edge of the city, near the stinking roar of the Great Cambridge Road. The photos date back to a lost London of the nineteen-forties and fifties; blue ink inscriptions in the script of a forgotten hand date and annotate the backs of the pictures. Stefan, I think, would have enjoyed these.

*

In the office, at lunchtime, my colleague Julia asks me, 'Whatever happened to that fella you were seeing?' She crunches through a tasteless supermarket meal-deal lunch as she interrogates me. I study her face, the make-up applied exquisitely and with practised precision. Julia learned, she tells me often, from online tutorials in the dead hours while her partner Baz was away on one of his many business trips to the continent. Her and Baz have been married for nine years, together for fourteen. No children, and I wonder why that is; she seems the type and she lacks the imagination for anything else. There is a small piece of iceberg lettuce stuck in a gap in Julia's teeth that I decline to point out.

'It wasn't working,' I say. 'We weren't compatible. You know how it is.'

'Not really,' she laughs. 'Baz was my first and only. You met on one of those online things, right? Where you swipe?' And she laughs again, miming the action with her small hands. It makes it look ridiculous, like the actions of a defective or a simpleton or a carnival freak, a child in adult's clothes. Grotesque.

Julia thinks herself lucky to have been spared my sad life by an accident of timing. We are the same age.

'That's right,' I say, nodding. 'One of those online things. They're pretty popular these days.'

Julia doesn't know what happened to Stefan, so she chuckles some more, in a tone that suggests she could never understand, or lower herself to such things.

'I'm just *so* glad me and Baz dodged that bullet. Things used to be so much *simpler*, didn't they?' she says, assuming the role of wise grande dame who remembers better times, a person I could learn from.

In the days before dating apps, my mother was taken by an angry black sea on the south coast of England. Things were never simple.

Julia grins, lettuce still stuck in her teeth.

*

There are days in London that stop my heart. Autumn days with damp hanging in the air and a sharp bite to the temperature. White breath-clouds shrouding people's red faces like spirits or essence unleashed. Slicks of brown leaves carpeting the paths that weave through the city's parks I love. Stefan loved them too. On these days of russets and yellows and deep reds I drift through London like a spectre of myself, heading to parts of the urban sprawl I have yet to discover, watching couples walk arm-in-arm and encouraging their children as they pedal on miniature bicycles with the training wheels attached.

I wrap thick coats and knitted scarves around me, imagining I am the heroine of a popular and melancholy BBC drama about a resilient woman's loss. My reality is nothing so glamorous. You cannot miss what never was.

I have drifted from the centre to the outer reaches of London. Something draws me to these spaces, ever since Stefan. So many sights I have seen, with no one now to share them with. But the city's endless mystery keeps me going, giving me a reason to leave the flat and not get tangled in the dreams of a lost future.

Only last week, I walked for miles from my home to reach the Dollis Brook Viaduct and its magnificent brick arches. I ate my lunch in Hendon cemetery and caught the train home from Finchley Central. These activities keep my body busy, my mind occupied.

I love the clank of the overground trains as they shuffle across the arches above the city. The ripple of yellow and orange leaves in the plane trees. The whistle of an owner summoning his loyal pet. Surly young men who sit on wet benches smoking pungent weed.

The night before he died, Stefan said, 'I think I could be falling for you.'

Last night, as I drank my wine and flicked through my rescued photographs, I texted him, 'I miss you and wonder what could have happened.' His mobile had by that point, of course, been disconnected.

*

Julia was correct, it was one of those online apps where you swipe left or right depending on your preference. A bit of silly fun, my friends and I all agreed, but it was worth a shot. That was how I reasoned it. It had been six months since my last romantic interaction, and eight since my last sexual encounter – a grimy bunk-up in the toilet of a Camden pub that played out-of-date punk and garage-rock songs. I wanted to scrub the event clean as soon as it had happened. I said to myself never again. I thought of myself as the kind of person who didn't need a relationship, was content on my own, didn't enter relationships purely due to the pressures of society.

But I wanted one, and the old ways had not worked, so it was time to try something different.

After signing up to the app and uploading a photo that I hoped suggested just enough of myself and who I might be, I began to swipe. I ignored the messages I knew were coming from my positive matches: quick to the point and full of sexual aggression and threat and unearned confidence. I wondered what these men's success rate was – likely higher than I would have liked. There were fat men and thin men, short men and tall men, men with tattoos and men with disfigurements and disabilities. There were men who worked as bankers and as bicycle couriers and bar managers and editors and builders and estate agents and film-makers and even men from the London Metropolitan Police force. There were paramedics and lecturers and chefs and sous-chefs and guitarists too full of themselves. There were unemployed men, and men who spent too much time at the gym and men who still lived with their mothers. There were English men and Irish men, Polish and Nigerian men, men from France and Israel and Canada. There were black men, Asian men, Mediterranean men and pasty white men. As I swiped, I wondered what my mother would have made of these men; if any of these men would stand next to my father in Bexhill sharing bottled beers as they looked over the dark waters towards France.

Eventually I swiped on Stefan and an alert buzzed announcing we were a match.

*

Stefan and I met for a drink in the French House in Soho on a Thursday night and we clicked. Sometimes it really is that simple.

For our second date, he suggested we visit the Horniman Museum, in Forest Hill in the south-east of the city. Stefan lived nearby in Bell Green. I jokingly said I mistrusted the places he frequented, as a north London girl of many years. Though, in truth, I was barely joking at all. The south of the city below the great river was unknown territory, a bandit country, as my friends and I joked. The vanity of small differences is very real, I realised. Stefan took it all with good humour.

I loved north London, despite my precarious and solitary existence in the Canonbury flat my ex, Terry, evacuated the year previous. On my own I was barely making the rent, regularly having to lease the place out on Airbnb while I stayed with friends in Hackney, or my ageing father in Bexhill. I had grown accustomed to a lifestyle I could not in truth afford but didn't want to let go of. It meant jettisoning how I saw my future self: a warm and self-satisfied life as a Stoke Newington mother pushing a plush buggy to the organic vegetable stores and meeting my friends in an upmarket Italian café on Newington Green. I had dreamed this dream of myself, an inevitable spectre of the life I was going to live, for so long that it felt that this woman had died an obscure and painful death. Murdered by a tide of rising house prices and unaffordable living, drowned without ceremony by the city. Ruined by Terry and his hollow promises, his endless solipsism.

I met Stefan at Forest Hill overground station. Minor details linger: a small polystyrene cup of white coffee he carried, a small greasy smudge on the left lens of his glasses, the crackling and broken speech of the tannoy, the pair of small children who scrabbled and scuffled as their mother shouted from her metal bench.

We walked from the station up the hill and into a realm of curated flower patches and vibrant green grass that held the museum amongst its grounds. Friends picnicked on the hill. I took in the view, stretching from the twisted metal sculpture of the Olympic Park in the east of the city to the new developments parasitising Battersea Power Station.

'Great, isn't it?' said Stefan.

'I've never seen London like this, from this perspective,' I said. My vision had been inverted.

At the desk, Stefan paid for both of our tickets despite my weak protestations that we should split the cost. We descended the stairs into the rippling light and shadows of an aquarium. I photographed poisonous, psychedelic tree frogs from South America and squeezed Stefan's hand with joy. I watched a ray lie flush against the glass of its tank, the pulsing mouth and gills sexual, fleshy.

Different coastal and tidal environments were recreated in large tanks, and for a long time Stefan and I observed a recreated environment of the cold English coast, a wave machine imitating the swells that had reclaimed my mother, stubborn starfish clinging to rock alongside limpets and barnacles. Bladderwrack waved in the brine. As I stood and observed, I felt a kinship with my father, this water a reminder of all the futures denied to him and my mother.

'I'd love for you to visit Bexhill,' I said eventually to Stefan, still staring into the water.

He squeezed my hand. 'That would be lovely,' he said and, as I turned to look at him, I saw a coastal swell reflected in his glasses.

We moved on. In an ambient room, small jellyfish hung in an endless blue. I felt a rare moment of peace and could have stayed suspended in that empty cosmic space, my tendrils dangling and intertwining with Stefan's, for all time.

And finally, in one small tank that seemed almost like a throwaway thought, a pair of flamboyant cuttlefish. Rippling, polychromatic things that often settled on dark purple and frills of burnt yellow but just as often buzzed and flowed with a dizzying array of palettes. They were the size of floating slugs or fat sticklebacks, tentacled, bobbing in their tank far from their native seas of the Indo-Pacific.

Alien beings and memories of the sea. All a part of what Stefan is to me.

*

After Stefan died, I moved out of my Canonbury flat, seeking cheaper rents and isolation from my peers, and found my balcony apartment near Turkey Street, in what was once the county of Middlesex. I enjoy it here, as it gives me easy access to the canals and reservoirs I like to haunt.

I often walk through Brimsdown to the King George's Reservoir, standing over the still water and imagining Julia's struggling form as I hold her under, her movements getting weaker and more pathetic with every minute until she goes limp.

On a recent walk along the Turkey Brook to the Forty Hall estate, I saw a mandarin duck perched high in the branches that arched above the water. Its colours were lurid and obscene in the grey of a wet London day. I lay in bed that night and thought about the cuttlefish dreaming on Forest Hill, in the dark of their tank after the visitors had left for the day.

*

Stefan and I had six dates, one night of sex, and the feeling that something was germinating and sprouting into life. And then the future, for the third time, was stolen from me.

Stefan died an everyday, dumb, pointless death. He didn't look as he was crossing a backstreet and a reckless seventeen-year-old kid on a scooter hit him full on at high speed. Stefan was killed outright, the kid left with a broken clavicle and four smashed ribs. I wondered if Stefan had been on his phone, distracted due to texting me perhaps. Or maybe he was still swiping left and right, which would have stung but I would have understood; I was doing the same but was ready to stop if he asked. I wanted him to ask me to stop.

It was too soon for anyone in his life to know I existed. I only found out about his death through an online post, thinking for a week that he was ghosting me. I have no idea what his funeral was like.

*

One of the photographs rescued from the bins shows a young man and woman, dressed in the clothing appropriate for their period. They are on London's south bank, amongst post-war splendour in front of a giant sculpture titled *The Islanders*. 1951 is inked in neat handwriting on the back.

I hold it up to the light, as dark mould has greatly corrupted the image, and drink deep from my wine glass. In a certain light, the couple resemble Stefan and me. Angled again, it becomes my mother and father.

There is something corrupting the images. Maybe when I found the box it was already too far gone. The dark mould and a pale lichen-like substance is over all of the images. Powdery to the touch, with the smell of age.

*

On the morning after our sixth date, Stefan and I woke early in my Canonbury flat. We were not tired, as if sleep for once had the power to refresh us rather than fill us with panic at the thought of another day in the hostile city alone. We decided to do something spontaneous. I had the car. It was raining persistently and it was early. We knew few people would be about, so we drove beyond Chingford and parked up at Connaught Water on the fringes of Epping Forest. In the car park we sat for a while listening to the soft tattoo of rain on metal and sipped Italian coffee as steam enshrouded us. A dog walker in a red cagoule wandered past with his cocker spaniel straining at its lead.

We walked the circumference of the water, and as the drizzle speckled our faces, we watched mandarin ducks float silently over the water. I looked at Stefan, the charming crease of his mouth as he smiled.

Enfield Town in the mist
as the Asphodel Meadows

Look from the balcony, where we have arranged empty plastic pots ready for compost from the garden centre. The blinking skyline of lights and cranes and skyscrapers – a skyline many people think of as London, but I don't, no not at all – is obscured today in thick mist that swaddles the city, mutes the noise, dampens everything down. It has been like this for days and it makes me want to write down in my notebooks such trite phrase as fugue state, or dream state, or waking dream, or collective dream, or, worst of all, phantasmagoric.

We are in outer London, or maybe Greater London, or possibly Middlesex the county that both does and does not exist; or are we now living in the suburbs? The debatability of the geography I find appealing. Friends tell me it suits me. I am predictable, and happy with that.

But we look down from the balcony at the overground station that connects us to Spurs country where that girl got shot the other night, to friends in Bruce Grove, to parts of

Hackney and the beginnings of the East End and on to that skyline we observe from our balcony. Most days, of course, because like I said, the mists are everywhere and obscure everything, there's no visibility and we cannot see. It is so thick it may even be fog, and I really hate to draw anything from Classical myth, from the Greeks and Romans – it's such a cliché – but all I can think of is the Greek afterlife for those not good enough to get to heaven but average enough to not deserve hell. A meadow of endless asphodel flowers, a plant ghostly and pale itself. And if that sounds harsh, I don't mean it to be, because it's more about atmosphere and the mood and the vibe that this weather creates than anything else, and anyway, I would be destined for the Asphodel Meadows myself. A strange nowhere land – I never say liminal – between one thing and the other is a kind of heaven itself.

So today I picture Enfield Town, and Southgate, Enfield Chase, and Winchmore Hill as the Asphodel Meadows, where people wander forever in a misty pale world, shades or reflections or shadows of their old lives of flesh and blood. Nothing feels real to us today as we listen to a downstairs neighbour coughing constantly – is it bronchitic, cancerous, we don't know for sure, but it doesn't sound good. It is hacking and horrible and wet and a cause for concern. We nickname him 'coughdrop'.

Time pauses. The inhabitants of the city withdraw into themselves, insulated by the mist, insulated against each other. These are days for thoughts not conversations.

The mist is spectral up here on the balcony, like a gathering of melancholy wraiths, like cotton wool suspended in polluted air.

My Queen

Jim 'Tosher' King, watching the light of London ripple on the dark surface of the river Thames, the wide water that splits the city. It's gone midnight in this part of town, but it's never dead, never silent or pitch black. Nothing above can compare to the darkness below. But it's okay: there are few people around on this Tuesday night, and he's far from the big stations. St Pancras, Paddington, Victoria: those places crawl with life at all hours. Tosher avoids them if he can.

He recalls what the guy asking for change said to him, as Tosher and The Priest sank pints of craft ale in a pub on the Caledonian Road.

'After dark. That's when the creepy crawlies come out.'

And after he'd placed a few ten pence pieces in the guy's hand, Tosher sipped his pint and imagined himself and The Priest as arachnid beings, agile as spider monkeys traversing the brick and piping of London's depth. As leggy as crane flies, bodies writhing like worms.

He supposes he's one of them: these bug people, rodents in the ship, beings that hide in daylight and only reveal their true form when the sun dips beneath the cluttered skyline. Tosher is an urbexer, pushing himself now to be bolder and better in his explorations. In the light of day, he's one of the rats running the rat race, but at night he's one of those urban creatures intent on standing in the ruins of the man-made, dedicated to seeing the structures most don't see, don't care to see and will never see. This is what draws Tosher to the tunnels and sewers of London; what gave him his nickname, bestowed by The Priest and Grubber. His sporadic draining companions, at home in blackness, who know the good spots where to descend, how to avoid getting nicked, how to come back up again and into the light. The Priest, an expert on the lost stations of the city. Grubber, a mucky bastard.

Tonight, though, Tosher's going solo.

So, here's the spot; where he knows he can force entry and descend into the city's bowels. It's been researched, checked out weeks in advance and planned and thought about endlessly. It was recommended, given a nod of approval as they discussed the plan in The Priest's sparse flat in Bounds Green, the walls covered with old maps and blueprints, one solitary photograph of The Priest and an unknown woman on a shelf. Grubber silently nodding and sipping cheap black coffee, The Priest animated and sermonising. They were happy to initiate one they recognised as their own into this closed circle: this drain cult, dank sewer tribe, thinks Tosher. With their help, he's noted the locations of the CCTV near the entry point and the ways to avoid it, discussed the site in depth on the online forums with other drainers across the globe.

This spot, within sight of the mighty river, is deemed a safe place to descend into danger. Standing there he feels watched, observed. He looks again: there's no one around, and all the windows of the nearby flats are dark. Much of the city sleeps; or lays in bed staring at the ceiling next to a softly snoring partner, pricked with anxiety about what the next day will bring. That was me, for so long, thinks Tosher. He's happier single, he tells himself, but is yearning for a connection that may be love and companionship or may be animal lust and debased fornication. He can't summon the energy to work himself out, to discover what he wants. For now, he is a drainer. An urbexer, dropping out of sight of humdrum reality.

The spot is safe, but it's time to get moving.

*

Tosher takes his name from the sewer hunters of the nineteenth century, men who'd force entry to the stinking underworld via the Thames at low tide. Men who risked getting lost in the maze of foetid tunnels beneath the city; drowning in effluent when the sluices were lifted; breathing in noxious fumes and braving pockets of sulphurated hydrogen. Imagine that, thinks Tosher: being trapped by the rising tide as it pours in. Knowing you could not get out in time, that the water was going to fill the tunnel to the roof. That you would soon be one with the city.

Down in the tunnels the toshers sought out scrap metal, dropped coins, bones both animal and human, sections of rope, lost jewellery and trinkets. They carried hoes with which to haul themselves from the muck if they found themselves sinking; implements that would double up as weapons to fend off the packs of rats they inevitably encountered. Tosher has read the accounts and the hearsay and the myth and legend: large creatures unafraid of humans, in groups of over a hundred, that would attack when cornered. This is why the toshers rarely went alone into the sewers of London.

Tosher recalls briefly, absurdly, a set of books loved in childhood. Mice down south in Deptford, a demon feline in the sewers.

For the toshers, it was their living; and he just does this for fun, it's a hobby, to fulfil a need other than survival, and this fact gnaws at him like a rodent chewing through electric cable. He is a fake even when he's down there alone and surrounded by the soft darkness and sniffing the stink of the city.

To Tosher, everything these days is a simulacrum; all human actions are now parts being played, based roughly on ideas and archetypes badly researched and lifted from the past. Even his high-wire antics and chthonic urges feel like they're done for the benefit of the audience in his head. For the guys on the forums like himself, for other losers incapable of love like Grubber and The Priest. At times, he feels he's nothing better than a high-risk Instagrammer; what's the difference between his photos of a sluice gate beneath the streets of Bruce Grove and some idiot's selfie in front of a popular London tourist attraction? Nothing. All there is is the burning and futile desire to prove we exist.

So, tonight's mission is a corrective. He's going alone, and yes, he'll take photos and record what he finds, but that information will be for him and him alone. No sharing. In this way, Tosher believes he can regain something he has lost, cultivate a sense of purity. He is, he admits, looking to regain a lost authenticity. He pictures it as a personal heirloom, dropped in the buddleia bushes that flourish along the tracks of the Thameslink trains that run through Finsbury Park, hidden in the dirt and the gravel but still there if only he could reach it.

*

The problem is, despite everything, Tosher is still in love with the city. He imagines the river larks of the nineteenth century river singing their salvage songs, the chatter of the bone grubbers and pure finders and Hindoo tract sellers. On the wall of his rented flat in Mile End hangs a cherished framed print: Gustave Doré's rendering of Old Father Thames looking out, Britannic lion by his side, at a Thames stygian and fogged. To Tosher, it's a world more brutal and dangerous, with a mystery to it, and of course that's attractive to a man like him. Somewhere deep inside he's aware of the contradictions. The time he is harking back to is a time when the river was dead, a poisoned thing; surely that cannot be better than a place where you can now see grey seals and a beluga whale can exist upriver in the estuary at Gravesend?

This fantasy of the old city, it's a Dickensian thing as treacherous as the mud out on the estuary at low tide. He knows this, but he can't let go; and why should he, anyway? Shit and mud and the physicality of fatbergs counteract the glass edifice in which he works, the thrusting cocks that stab the sky. He spends time among the hidden and the forgotten to combat the amnesia of this place. He hides in darkness to prove he exists.

Tosher loves the lore of the city he chooses to explore, the place he and his fellow drainers call London Incognita. He knows the stories of the tunnel tribes, and despite the impossibility of their existence, he yearns to encounter a group of fish-pale troglodytes down in the depths in which he and Grubber and The Priest explore.

He's heard of the thing the women of London call the commare and what has been seen in the underpasses around Brent Cross shopping centre, and he knows the tales of the judderman and what happened to the Eider boys in the nineteen seventies. It's all online, in the more speculative and conspiracy-minded sections of the internet. And he knows the story of Jerry Sweetly, the bears of the Hackney Marshes, the aggressive black swine in the tunnels beneath Hampstead. The flood barrier at Barking Creek is a temple to him. He has spent hours reading about and debating who committed the Hammersmith nude murders – Jack the Stripper, a sixties knock-off of the guy who set the bar for all the murderers of the city.

It is this love that has ruined his relationships with women. Initially they found it charming, were attracted to his passion. Then the slow dawning realisation that this was obsession, morbid and misanthropic when it got out of control. They all left him; yet still he has the craving. Part of him still believes in romance, in a happy ending.

And Tosher is keenly aware, too, of the popular contemporary narrative, that the city is now dead, drained of vitality by the vampires of capitalism, written about too much or written about in a way that has hastened its demise. The sense that by making your presence known, you invite the dark energies you are trying to ward off. And maybe that's all true, but fuck that, says Tosher. I'm still here and there are still things that I have not seen. If being seen is the problem, hide then in the shadows and crawl through the unlit underworlds with the rats and pigs.

*

He's about to descend. He looks again at the river, at the glimmering skyline and its buildings. Does anyone live in those? He pictures spoiled Saudi princes beating their Filipino servants, grim city-boys fucking Latin prostitutes pressed up against the glass, a thick line of coke neatly chopped on a bespoke coffee table offered to a pricy escort.

He shakes his head, shrugging off the visions; to his lasting shame, they're tinged with jealousy.

If the energies of the city are all pointing up, Tosher's

drive is then to go down, to descend, to explore the miles – some say hundreds, other thousands – of tunnels and sewers that coil beneath the metropolis. He imagines the tunnels interconnected, twisted and tied together like the tails of a rat king, that near-mythic mess of rodents with their tails bound together. Entangled and trapped together with plughole hair, flushed gum, the cloggy mess of a fatberg fragment.

He's never seen one but knows a guy who has.

His cousin's boyfriend, Teddy, works for Thames Water. The guy has seen things, tells funny, truly disgusting stories. Like: unblocking a pipe and getting hit full in the face with a used tampon. Ha ha. The things people flush; you wouldn't believe it. Well, Tosher would, he's seen some of it himself. He reads all the drainer reports on the urbex forums. Some of his own trips, ones he took with Grubber and The Priest, are documented there. The pornography of brickwork to be found at Counters Creek beneath Hammersmith, the sensuous terracotta curves. The ladders to nowhere and gorgeous sandstone-yellow patterns of the Ranelagh Sewer.

He's watched the footage of the fatberg too, over and over again, a colossal lump that ran the length of football pitches found beneath Whitechapel – night-vision recording, a skittering rat slathered in fat and grease, running at the camera over the colossal berg. He'd love to see it with his own eyes, in its natural state; something real and a product of the modern world. Something the toshers never saw.

Instead, he's had to make do with a trip to the Museum of London to see a dried out and preserved chunk of the thing encased in glass, now looking like powdered and moulded cheese. It's strange, he concedes, that if the museum sold small chunks of the berg, preserved inside acrylic glass, he would buy one for his home. This is why he can't hold on to a girlfriend.

He knows that the bergs are formed with all manner of things: piss and shit of course, non-degradable wet wipes, used cotton buds, flushed condoms, all glued together with congealed fats and oils. Leftover grease from a million frying pans poured down the plughole, sure, but also from the shampoos and gels the people of the city use to wash the filth from themselves. Tosher thought soap eliminated grease and fat, broke it down, but he's willing to believe the science. The fatbergs are there, after all; they exist.

Teddy found the king rat. Most of the creatures were dead, a few still wriggling on and feeding on the decaying flesh of their partners, all entwined in their awful death spiral, fur foul with the grease of the sewers. Teddy had the nearest thing these days to proof – photos on his Android, a minute of footage too of the wriggling mess that was uploaded to YouTube. It's vile, fascinating, unmissable. Hundreds of thousands of views.

Crowbar out, Tosher jimmies the manhole open and is down the metal ladder, closing the manhole back behind him like he's climbing into a World War Two submarine; like he's a man with a mission and purpose rather than a hobby. The darkness envelops him like a warm shroud, and down here he knows he is nothing and nobody and the feeling is glorious. Something skitters away as he approaches, and perhaps he feels curious eyes on him, but he believes himself to be a rational guy and knows when his imagination is playing up.

He spends a minute, maybe ninety seconds, engulfed in the blackness, luxuriating in it.

Click. Light floods the sewer.

Headtorch on, he makes his way into the tunnels.

*

He meets Kate one night in a pub just off Brick Lane. The Pride of Spitalfields. It feels cockneyish, almost authentic, though it's full and popular with the bright young things of London seeking something the gastros can't give them.

The way they meet is refreshing, almost old-fashioned in its simplicity. They get chatting outside the pub; Tosher is sparking up a rollie and this woman, Kate, approaches him and asks for a light. An old, classic tactic. And if he's unsure why she seems to be at the pub alone then the thoughts are pushed aside because she gorgeous and funny, and listens to him when he speaks of his love of London and exploring the city (he keeps the urbexing to himself of course, for now at least, you never know how people may react), and what surprises him is that he's interested in her when she speaks, not just her body and what he wants to do to it.

She nods when he mentions parts of the city he believed to be obscure; he'd admit he was showing off, enjoying the opportunity to verbalise his interests. She adds streets and brooks and parks to the places he names and suggests parts of the city that she could show him. Dollis Brook Viaduct, the Crouch End Spriggan, Mark Lane station. They could go together. Tosher wants that, badly, realises he would follow this woman through a deserted suburb at five a.m. in pouring rain on a Bank Holiday morning; go with her hand-in-hand down deep into the tunnels searching for the lost tribes; run with her into a rioting estate in high summer, threading through lines of armoured police, with the temperature at fever pitch.

He notes her eyes, beautiful and shining like an animal's. One is blue as a blackbird's egg, the other grey as the Thames Estuary in October. He is merry on London Pride and realises he would worship her as a goddess, a commare, a queen. Pictures her pedestalised astride a chariot like Boudicca at Westminster. He desires to genuflect and beg her for forgiveness, for her to release his pent-up and straining lusts that have surprised him in their severity, for her to end all this, for her to show him something authentic.

Please, he thinks, *let me show you my city, take the metal ladder down into the depths where the brickwork curves and the fatbergs float. You'd like it there. We would be at home.*

And, a few drinks later, she is saying wants to come back with him, to his flat, whispered obscenities in his ear urging him to ruin her. She's forward; but he supposes young women are now, and Tosher is not going to turn down an opportunity like this. There's something giddy in this evening, these rare moments when the animal attraction between two people crackles and sparks, the sheer rarity of such encounters itself something to celebrate. Life can be so crushing and dull. For Tosher, Kate is a rush akin to that first descent into darkness as the manhole closes; she is like the first time he sat atop a crane watching eight million people below him; as mysterious as the sights he and Grubber saw in the Williamson Tunnels running beneath Liverpool.

For Kate, the feeling is pleasant, something like a hunger sated. She's done this many times before and it doesn't have the shock of the new; but she's taken a shine to Tosher and wishes him well.

One thing they can both agree on is that this doesn't feel like chance. These things never do. Tosher doesn't believe in such nonsense – the universe is a cruel and indifferent place, he knows that – but this meeting with Kate, now this fumbling and hungry pulling of clothes with Kate in an alleyway off Brick Lane, his hands between the legs of Kate, it feels like it could only have ever gone one way. They stumble and giggle into an Uber, a short ride back to his, stop at the offy for some more booze, and then home. He fucks her imagining she's pushed up against glass in one of the high towers of London, like she is a voiceless servant, like they are embraced by the pulsing warm darkness of the city's tunnels. She bites his neck to test him out, and he passes the test. Then they lie entwined, coiled together, king and queen.

Both Kate and Tosher would agree, it is quite a night.

Unexpected, inevitable.

In the morning, Kate is gone. She leaves a yellow Post-it Note scrawled with a number. Tosher stares at it for a long while as he emerges from under his duvet with a pulsing head and a sense he has crossed over to a new place. Kate is gone, for now. He rubs his neck, nipped by this woman he met in The Pride of Spitalfields. A tiny smear of dried blood yet to be washed away.

Two days later, he sends an exploratory text to the number. It sends, but there is no reply. Maybe it was too soon. Maybe he's too keen. Maybe he has scared her off; did she seem a bit skittish on the night? Yes, maybe.

In the weeks that follow Tosher is consumed with images of her, and dreams of her naked as she stands ankle-deep in the sewers of London, the accumulated filth of the city splashing at her shins. Her pubis is greasy with the muck of fatbergs and the thought is so arousing it enrages him; he takes numerous trips to the bathroom at work. In his fantasy, wet wipes and used cotton buds float past, brushing her moon-white legs. She drapes herself over the lurid and salacious brickwork that winds like rodent tails under Hammersmith. She swims through the flooded tunnels at high tide, a pale and sensuous wraith suspended in grey-green water.

Yet during this time, for reasons he cannot explain, the world shines for him. He's promoted at work and receives a pay rise. That tax rebate he's been waiting on for the best part of a year comes through. His sister gives birth to a healthy and happy child and he is pleased for her. A new draining lead comes through from Grubber. His conversations with his parents seem warmer, less strained.

But at night his dreams go further, to truly shameful places, warped images of Kate and muroids and wormlike things with segmented bodies, and he wakes nightly now panting in a puddle of his own creation. He is grateful he has no flatmate, thankful for his isolation. He's sick, he thinks, a fucking pervert, a corrupted version of his teenage self, full of rage and surrounded by crusted used tissue.

Is this love? Tosher thinks. *Is this what infatuation is?*

Sod her. She never texted back.

I don't know what to do.

I need to get back out there.

And so he does. Another mission, with The Priest as his company and guide; the strain and adrenaline of going back into the tunnels beneath London a necessary distraction, this time somewhere far to the east of the city. That's what he likes about these missions, they take the mind off the rest of life's shit. It allows him to forget briefly the cluttered skyline and what the lights reflected on the river mean; to indulge in the dreams and fantasies of a city long gone. To take his mind away from Kate.

The toshers were, in fact, a healthy and robust bunch of men. Perhaps due to their immune-systems having to work flat out, perhaps just due to the fact that it was a profession that only attracted the toughest and most determined. Tosher read about Queen Victoria's rat catcher, the descriptions of rat bites that festered with a hard core the size of a fish's eye, how the bites had to be cut clean out with a lancet and squeezed to prevent infection. How the vermin were a constant peril to the men of the tunnels.

He rubs his neck where Kate had bitten him, a small yellow bruise now the only trace. As much as he fetishises the past, he knows he is too weak for it.

'A love bite, like a fucking teenager,' laughs The Priest.

'Piss off.'

'She was a right sort though,' The Priest continues, grinning. 'You did well there.'

Tosher shakes his head slightly. Despite his sick imagination, he's never been much good at male banter.

It's two in the morning and they are far from anywhere but still very much in the city. Where they have chosen to descend is in an area of waste ground primed for redevelopment, dimly lit by the glow of streetlamps from the road nearby. Concrete and rubble sprout with plant life. They're ready, but before they go down into the darkness, Tosher sits on the remains of a brick wall and rolls cigarettes for himself and The Priest. He pictures Kate asking him for a light outside The Pride of Spitalfields.

The Priest ignites and drags on his cigarette, looking out towards the road, checking for traffic. Tosher listens to the rustle of cow parsley and buddleia and nettles in the breeze.

Imagines things lost in this rubble and never regained. Somewhere far off in the distance he can hear a group of teens laughing and jeering and smashing bottles. Sirens and an ambient traffic hum.

Lighting the cigarette, he inhales and exhales slowly, blue smoke coiling like a tail, and sees an animal, a brown rodent, snuffling through the weeds. It notices him, disappearing into the shadows.

His phone buzzes discreetly.

Hey, sorry for the late reply things have been mad busy. Hope you're not too mad at me. I really enjoyed our night together. K x

Kate. She hasn't forgotten him. Parts of him spring violently into life.

His phone buzzes again.

I knew you would make it. See you soon. K xx

Tosher flicks his cigarette into the darkness impatiently.

Yes, my queen.

'Come on,' he says to The Priest. 'Time to go.'

They descend into the darkness, headlamps on, and they walk for miles through the tunnels, talking softly of what they are seeing and what they think they are seeing and what they might hope to see. The Priest claims to know a guy who knows a guy who has seen the tunnel tribes. 'Bullshit,' says Tosher, even as he wishes it to be true. Occasionally they hear a splash, a screech, a strangled moan from what must be ancient piping. The skitter of rodent paws echoing far away.

'Remember, in London,' says The Priest grinning back at Tosher, 'you're never more than ten feet from an estate agent.'

Tosher grins. The obsessions of the world above seem absurd down here. As The Priest walks ahead, Tosher observes scrawls of old graffiti that cover patches of the tunnel walls. Tags of older drainers, hard to tell how old, scrawls from people whose purpose down here it is hard to imagine. But there's something fresher – new paint – too.

'Wait up,' he shouts to The Priest. The air around them is warm, ripe, sweet and sour with rot nibbling at the edges. It's a stink they have come to enjoy.

The Priest is ahead of him; he likes to take the lead and is the more experienced drainer, Tosher has always been happy to allow that. The Priest stops and looks back at his younger friend. 'What is it?'

'This bit of graf. It looks new.'

'What does it say?'

'"We Pass Under",' says Tosher. 'Can only be a few weeks old.'

The Priest chuckles. 'There are no new ideas, eh? No virgin territory.' And he resumes walking.

Tosher snaps a picture before following.

They keep walking, occasionally stumbling in the darkness, inhaling the stink of London. The two men arrive at a strange intersection of brick, many tunnels of many sizes converging on one point, the architecture of a madman who designed this underground city drunk and blindfolded. There is more of the graffiti, spelling out 'We Pass Under' in fresh paint on the brickwork. It is beautiful in its construction, a wonder that the majority of this teeming antheap of a city will never see. Leave them to their anxieties, thinks Tosher. We have this.

'Look at that,' says The Priest, exhaling with satisfaction. He removes his camera and prepares to take a photograph. Tosher watches his friend, The Priest already picturing how this photograph will be received on the online forums and what the admiring comments will say. Really, they are no better than the world they reject. He has a moment of intense yearning, wishing the pair of them were genuine, the hardy men of the real, physical Victorian city, toshers with lanterns strapped to their chests, wearing huge coats with deep pockets, old slops for shoes, rugged constitutions staying one step ahead of the law. What did the toshers themselves yearn for? He cannot imagine.

The Priest stops for a second, delaying the photograph, and he chews his lip in thought as if there are words wriggling inside of him waiting to get out. Tosher waits for one of The Priest's sermons.

'Before I was a drainer,' The Priest begins finally, 'I was what, I suppose, you'd call an average guy. I was nothing really. Poke a hole in my skin and you'd find me paper thin, hollow, a construct of other people's ideas and hopes and aspirations. If I think back to those days – this is the mid to late noughties I'm talking about, just before the crash, you know – I can't recall much of anything. I know that I got up each day and I went to my work in an office near Clerkenwell and I travelled on the underground and I bought chicken-salad sandwiches from the local Sainsbury's for my lunch, had a few pints on a Friday night with my colleagues. I had a partner; Gemma. A great woman and I fancied the fuck out of her, for a long time. You never knew her, Tosher, but she got fucking sick of me in the end and who can blame her. But that was all after the switch in me was flicked.' The Priest laughs. 'All those years, and I can barely remember anything. Time passed and things happened, but we could have been anyone. Well, anyone like us, from our backgrounds. We met through mutual friends and we dated and then we moved in together in a little two-bed flat off the Green Lanes, the Newington Green end if you know it. I worked and she worked, and we put a bit of money aside and we took nice daytrips on sunny days to the coastal towns of Kent and Sussex and Essex and holidays to the places where you're supposed to holiday. Paris, Berlin, Barcelona, Rome, not taking much of it in, and on and on it all went. We had our tick sheet of things that average middle-class white Londoners do. We ticked the boxes, performed our duty. I bought books from Waterstones and filled our shelves. We cooked healthy dinners based on BBC recipes. Gemma joined a yoga class.

'But there were times when I'd look at Gemma and wonder who she was, and considered that she couldn't possibly know me, because I was nothing and nobody.

'I can remember the day it all switched. I was on the underground going to work and the train shuddered to a halt, and just sat there, immobile, not moving, no announcement from the driver, nothing. You know how it is, Tosh, we've all been there. And while everyone around me was tutting to themselves and doing these big exasperated sighs, as if Transport For London would somehow hear them and leap into action, I just looked out through the glass I was pressed up against and I realised in the gloom that we were at a station. One of the dead stations of London. I'd read a brief mention of these stations in the few books about London I felt I should own, that we kept on our shelves at home. I'd never really considered them as real places in the physical world. I'd never really considered a time other than *now* or a reality different to the one I was blindly leading. We were at Snow Hill, near the Holborn Viaduct. I could see the remains of this dead station, just about, and there was a bit of graffiti down there and I realised people must have *been* there, and there was a way to access this underworld.'

Tosher nods, smiling through the corner of his mouth. He recognises the feeling that even his articulate companion, The Priest, struggles to put into the words. The lure of the darkness. The sense of the world opening up into this giant, complex, infinitely strange and dangerous place.

'And that was it. Well, that was the point things changed. Suddenly the thought of a little maisonette with Gemma in Chingford, then a bigger house out in Hertfordshire and commuting in and out of the city and maybe a kid or two and the dog and barbecues on a sunny Saturday seemed laughable ambitions. For *me*, do you get me Tosher? It's okay for people to want those things, of course it is, but I didn't, and I never had, but I'd never even considered that before. I was comfortable, safe, secure, and I was nothing. So, I resolved to find Snow Hill. I found it.' He pauses, wrinkles his brow.

'You know what I mean?'

'Of course I do, mate.'

A silence, not awkward, follows The Priest's sermon. Tosher wants a cigarette but deems it too dangerous down here. There's a sound from a trickling pipe nearby that sounds like a gentle flowing stream, despite the stink and darkness around them.

Tosher thinks of his failed relationships and he understands The Priest; thinks of Kate and twitches with hope and hopes he will never be like his friend.

Now Tosher thinks he can hear something, a scratchy sound, creatures moving quickly and quietly. A flicker of shadows in the small tunnels that lead to where they stand.

Who was the last tosher, and what was his name? All these histories lost.

We're all used cooking fat poured down a drain, he thinks, just as The Priest's flash goes off and the first rat hits his body with a meaty thud. The thing is big, the size of one of those awful dogs walked by the posh girls in Chelsea, dark brown fur and nicotine-yellow teeth that sink deep into The Priest's arm, and the camera is dropped, cracking on the curved brickwork. A second rat appears from the shadows and rips at the tendon of his left foot. He seems surprised, not making a noise until a third creature has landed on him and bitten deep into the fleshy muscle between his thumb and forefinger. Thick crimson flows and the screaming begins. Then they get to his throat and the screaming – shrill like a whiny posh girl's, thinks Tosher – becomes a wet gurgling screech. Bubbling sounds, pipes blocked with accumulated gunk.

The camera is lost, kicked into murky water with a splash as The Priest thrashes about and more of the creatures pile on top of him, biting legs, feet, genitals, ears.

Tosher watches as the torrent of rodents swarm over his friend, biting through flesh, gnawing at exposed bone. He doesn't understand what he's seeing and his heart is pumping like the piston on a steam locomotive. He's frozen to the spot, terrified or excited, either way paralysed and he knows he can't help his friend. And anyway, Christ, this is really something *happening* isn't it? What a way to go. The Priest would appreciate that.

We should have brought a hoe, he thinks uselessly, as he waits for his turn to be ripped and torn and gnawed upon.

But the rats ignore Tosher completely.

As The Priest's vile noises filling the tunnels weaken, and his burbles and chokes get slowly softer, Tosher sees a figure, unclothed, striding from the darkness towards him.

Kate, as she was in his shameful dreams.

'You made it,' she says, and she's smiling, and my God doesn't she look fine.

He wants to fling her into the sewer water right there and then, to repeat the actions of their first night together in full view of this legion of rats as they devour his friend. His lusts are unbearable. But he controls himself, knowing it won't be long.

Jim 'Tosher' King steps off the walkway and is now in the grey-green water, genuflecting before his queen, the watery filth of London flowing around his ankles and shins. The Priest is gone, swept away, or sunk to merge with the greasy bergs, to be stripped clean by the rats and the other things that live down here.

Kate squeals and shrieks as Tosher bends the knee, a gorgeous noise that sends his arousal to impossible heights.

He kisses Kate's outstretched paw, thinking he may finally have found the one.

Red

2007

Auburn's her nickname. It's the hair: rust-red, chestnut, auburn. A few mates call her Boudica. She's the indigent Celtic queen from High Barnet.

The nickname is so all-consuming it has gotten to the point where her own rarely-used Christian name of Aoife is a thing alien to her. It sits oddly on the tongue, like a piece of indigestible food. When teachers, social workers, police, bailiffs, magistrates have used it throughout her life, it's as if they are talking about another person. Which they are, really. They know the details as recorded in the paperwork, but they don't know anything of her life: knocked around by her old man as her mother watched mutely in a pink dressing gown, waiting for her turn. What a cliché to have an abusive, boozy dad who was busy with his fists. Something that appals Auburn is how common the story is. These little humdrum atrocities are taking place all over the city, behind closed doors in Totteridge, East Finchley, Ladywell, Bruce Grove, wherever. Well, fuck him and all like him.

After that she was fostered in a few places across London after the social services got properly involved. Eventually she thought sod all that and ran away. It's better to go it alone. I was escaping from their world and into a parallel one, this invisible reality rubbing up next to the fake one people think of as normal life. I escaped to a London in plain view but out of sight. So she likes to think.

She spends her time in the squats, on the streets, in the homeless shelters. Sofa-surfing, sometimes, with mates and acquaintances. She has an auntie in Burnt Oak who lets her stay every now and then, a warm sofa and a plate of hot food. Mum's younger sister. But she doesn't stay there long – it's a dirty and boring part of town, and anyway, her welcome only lasts a night and a morning.

Often when she's out begging – maybe by Angel underground station under the arcades that flank the banks, by the Sainsbury's cash machine in Holborn, or watching the tourists flood in and out of Victoria – she's approached by God-botherers, street pastors they're called, who squat down on their haunches in an attempt to be on her level. They tell her they can help. That there's a better way, a way out of this. The crosses around their necks glint. So she calls the men nonces, kiddy-fiddlers, laughing in their faces as she tells them to jog on and leave her alone. She tries to make a scene, embarrass them, make them feel bad, because if there was a god, he departed this city long ago.

Auburn may have had a rough start in life, but she isn't stupid. She got taken to church, clutched rosary beads and said her Hail Marys and looked at the stained-glass windows whilst zoning out as the priest said what he had to say. Stories about Mary, the saints, suffering that was supposed to be celebrated. Pain as a virtue was something Auburn could never get behind.

As she watched her father rearrange her mother's features and then kick her while she was down, curled into a ball on the carpet, Auburn decided that if some being higher than us had created all of this – *allowed* all of this – then it was sick and with a degenerate sense of humour. What if the creator itself was flawed? You couldn't ask that question at Catholic school, but it was clear that the architect was a drunken madman, a strung out junkie who had once been a successful artist. It was the only explanation; other than, simply, there was nothing.

The street pastors always leave with fixed smiles on their faces as they retreat and melt back into the crowds of human life that wind and writhe in the streets.

Auburn is twenty years old and has been on the streets for a few months. She has a good begging spot by a Halifax cash machine, and once or twice has been gifted a few notes, fivers and tenners mainly, from the friendlier types who pass her. Women, most of the time. A couple of creepy geezers who are best avoided if possible. She may be young, but she is not stupid.

She remembers that big bloke – Mick, he was called – who passed her most days. Never gave her any change but she asked anyway on the off chance. He'd answer no with a grunt. He topped himself, threw himself off one of the roofs in Sky City, Wood Green. He'd travelled there especially to do it. The place, they say, had a special significance to him. He left behind a young daughter; maybe she's better without him, thinks Auburn.

She remembers reading about it in the *Metro* last year. So it goes. He'd probably turfed a lot of her mates out of their squats, or when they'd fallen behind on the rent, kicked out the needy and most at risk to face greater dangers. This surplus, nuisance population that she strangely enjoys being a part of, he was their enemy. Mick made people homeless when he knew there was more than enough space in this city to keep everyone warm and out of the rain. Let him rot.

The winters in London, whilst not as brutal as other parts of the world or even the rest of the United Kingdom, are harsh if you're on the streets. Winter is a time of four p.m. darkness, stinging rain, puddles and splashes, and it's cold, always cold. Wet shoes half the time. It's miserable. This is the time she aims to be in the squats or with her auntie in Burnt Oak as much as possible. It's no time to be outside. She weathers the Christmas of 2007 and heads into a freezing January. She's doing fine by herself, feels like she has the run of London, enjoys the time she spends wandering and how she is imprinting a map of the streets, her brain rewiring to match the city. Auburn thinks of a map in terms of arteries, veins, capillaries, the nervous system.

Skin me and spread me out like something at the Body Worlds exhibition in Piccadilly. It would form a map of all the streets in the city I have wandered down, begged on, the alleys I ducked into and made my escape through.

After Christmas, she parties with a few people she knows – PK and the rest of that crew at their ropey place in Deptford with the fag burns in the carpet, piles of moulding plates sitting in the kitchen and a stereo always on full blast in an empty room. They're a good craic, this lot. They've got the stamina to carry the party on until its bitter end.

But she leaves to find somewhere else to sleep – she has a promise of a bed elsewhere, somewhere warm and perhaps a friendly warm body to share it with. But she's fucked, ruined, decimated – they've all been drinking since midday, smoking a few fat spliffs and on the bags of jittery amphetamine and ket that these lads seem to have around them at all times. She wants to clear her head a bit and decides to walk – it's not too far and anyway, she can't afford a cab can she? And she loves walking through the city when she's smashed. Auburn knows people say it's dangerous, but then isn't life itself?

For whatever reason – the alcohol, the ketamine, the mandy – she decides it's a good idea to have a little sit down in an alleyway near New Cross Gate station and smoke a cigarette, by the recycling bins, on her way to her promised bed. It's freezing out in London that night, but she doesn't really notice it. She is buzzing, happy, enveloped in a warm chemical blanket.

When she wakes up, she notices a body splayed out on the ground, with auburn hair fanned out like fronds of pondweed.

The body's face is frozen to the pavement.

Damn, she says.

2017

Auburn spends her days wandering the city at a steady pace. She has all the time in the world.

She has had time to think about it properly, and if one of the other shades of this other London she lives in were to ask – they never do of course – what her favourite haunts were she would answer with the following:

The Barking Creek flood barrier standing mighty and iconic, a London temple, the mud of the river glistening in summer light as wading birds tread through shallow water.

The Dollis Brook viaduct, hushed and muted with snowfall, the gorgeous white contrasting against its red brick work. Trains shuttling overhead.

Under the Westway near White City, hanging out with the memories of a thousand forgotten BBC productions. The traffic roaring, as she passes under en route to the crowds of Portobello Road.

Sitting silently in the bombed-out ruins of St Dunstan in the east. Perhaps her favourite spot – a place that elegantly turned the scars of the city into something beautiful. Memories of the great fire and German bombs are here; it is so peaceful.

But today she has appeared at Hyde Park Corner, to take in the sight of *Boadicea and Her Daughters*. She likes the statue, despite its Imperial flavour. It reminds her of her other life, when friends would call her a Celtic queen and she would laugh and stick her tongue out at them. Diseased pigeons perch on the statue; tourists take photos and wave selfie sticks. They pay no attention to her.

She shoos away a pack of Blackguards, little dead boys and girls talking in an antiquated slang who infest this other city – the place she slipped into that night in New Cross Gate. She is wary of these children, feral underfed shades who never had anything and never will. She has learned how the city swelled in those years of Empire and how many of its own London devoured to power itself and to get to the point where it is today.

As Auburn watches a snivelling spoiled rich kid, screaming in a tantrum at the bottom of Boudica's statue, throw its ice-cream cone at its mother – one of those women with pumped-up lips, botoxed cheeks, orange skin – she wonders what all that sacrifice was for.

She has spent this last decade learning about the city. She has listened to the stories from the slums of Whitechapel, women who died in the 1880s of starvation and disease and neglect and exposure. The black street kids she never knew existed, over a hundred years before Windrush. The jakeys and boozebags and every hobo and derelict and drunk who died on these unforgiving streets. She even saw Mick once, as she drifted through Wood Green on a sunny spring afternoon. But he didn't notice her.

Auburn now knows that the only gods are the ones we create. We get what we deserve. The shadow-man, the woman who does nothing to help the women of the city, flipsides of each other. Useless, redundant things. Our gods.

They can't see her, but she observes the people who fall through the cracks swelling and growing in number as the years go by. A decade ago, it was bad enough, but this decade of encouraged selfishness and enforced austerity – a mean, pinched existence that has sapped even the most hopeful – has taken its toll. Rough sleepers are everywhere, they die every day, and no one cares. She often sees a girl who reminds her of her cousin Wendy, sat on a pile of blankets and a handsome Alsatian with a black-and-red bandana around its neck, by the bank near Angel underground. Maybe seventeen, at the most. Predated on by some of the men around her, Auburn is sure. Angels – what a funny thought.

She tries to help the new ones as they enter this new reality. The women with collapsed faces, the ones slurring and not right in the head. The ones that can't stop crying.

It won't seem like it now, she tells them, but you really are in a better place.

Later that evening, having left Hyde Park Corner and Boudica, Auburn is wandering unseen through the crowds at Borough. The crowds are thick and vibrant, the bars are full, the stalls packed with enticing and pricy produce.

She likes to absorb the happier side of London sometimes, to see people enjoying a bit of life. She was only just starting hers, really, and this is her way of getting a taste of what she missed out on. Auburn spots a woman she thinks she recognises from back in the day – that's it, it's PK's sister. She saw her once at his place in Deptford. They were having an argument. Auburn recalls how she tried to ignore the shouts from upstairs, concentrating on a small dog on the sofa that she played with until they both grew tired.

Cerise, another shade of red. I wonder how the decade has treated you, she thinks. Cerise is drinking with friends, puffing on an electronic cigarette, talking, happy the week is over. Normal boring things.

And then Auburn hears a bang, of a vehicle colliding with something or someone. Screams and shrieks and the sound of mass panic surrounds her.

People are running.

Shouting.

Dying.

The police arrive at some point. Gunshots.

Auburn drinks it all in; now for her it's just another small chapter in the history of the city.

Borough is quiet now, empty almost. Someone is sobbing in the distance.

She sees that Cerise is lying on the ground. Her clothes are red.

You're Already Dead

WALK I: THE CROUCH END SPRIGGAN

My whole life I have navigated this city, tried to understand all there was to understand. I swim through its arteries clogged with fat and oil and accumulated filth.

I dive deep into its bowels, explore its wounds and trace its scars.

I rummage through piles of rubbish and rubble at the city's periphery, sift for secrets in the bins out the back of restaurants in Soho's Chinatown. This, perhaps, is a family trait.

As I approach something like an understanding, over the fence I go, into the land of the dead boys. A place where no shadows will ever fall. There are some things you cannot unlearn.

Time is short; I have to understand the dead brothers, the Eider boys, my relatives, before we all sink. We're all sinking.

And the show is coming up. I have to get this done.

I have to find the flickering woman who lies to us, the women of London, promising an escape, a way to pass under the city to somewhere better.

You're already dead, Gary, but I am still here.

*

I am heading back out in the field again for the first time in an age. I decided to start with a short walk to get my rhythm back, with my camera, notebook, a flask of black coffee and a spliff, up from Finsbury Park – where Gary disappeared all those years ago – to Highgate. A walk along the abandoned train line, dodging the cyclists, to see the Crouch End spriggan. It seems like a logical place to start, and it's a route that means something to me, and to the city.

Twenty years have gone by since the first issue of *Magnesium Burns*, and it's now my time to take stock of things, but also to create something new. If all you have is nostalgia then you're already dead, right?

So, I am writing the anniversary issue. The retrospective at the TeXt gallery is coming up, so now is the perfect time to do something I've wanted to do for a long time. I want to solve a family mystery. I need to find out what happened to my uncle Gary. To my uncle Danny. Were they just entertaining nutjobs, or was there more to it? Their concept of London Incognita is one I feel myself, bone deep, true. It's an innate understanding that I share with my own brother.

Why do we put off the things we most want to do? Answering my deepest desires feels like a painful extraction, giving birth to something necessary but disliked. It's a great expense of energy, and it's almost an embarrassment. I picture myself ripping wisdom teeth from my jaw without anaesthesia.

I understand why so many people do nothing, why they never know themselves, how years slide by in a blur of neither happiness nor sadness. It's easy to swipe a phone, buds in ear, as the underground speeds you to work, day after day. I get it.

I step off the tube at Finsbury Park, ignoring the pleas for change from a handful of homeless guys loitering around the station. I must look unacceptably serious and thoughtful as a dickhead in one of those tracksuits that make a grown man look like he's wearing pyjamas, a body warmer pulled over it, shouts, 'Cheer up gorgeous,' at me. I shoot daggers at him and he wanders off laughing to himself. This shit never ends – or maybe when I get old, it will stop. From harassed to invisible. Where is the in-between time?

I turn left out the station, over the lights and through the side entrance into Finsbury Park itself, heading in the direction of the overgrown entrance that leads onto Parkland Walk. The park is full of kids and picnicking hipsters and over-serious joggers. It has other, darker, associations. This is where Gary Eider disappeared. He'd been in a bad way beforehand, apparently, according to the scant information I've managed to dig up. The stuff I inherited from my great aunt Sarah.

There are suggestions that Gary was homosexual, a cottager, a fucking queer – that's why he was in the toilets here and why those skinheads had battered him. The park is notorious for it, or so people say.

Maybe he was – who gives a shit one way or the other – but I always felt like that story was used to discredit him.

Especially in my family, in an age when homosexuality was in-and-of-itself, *funny*. Ha ha ha. Or to suggest he deserved what happened to him, in some way. It makes it all easier to understand; people don't want the complexity.

There are many other stories living hidden in the park, resting dormant in the polluted soil. Stabbings and shootings and beatings, of course. A few loners and bagheads who'd seen a giant green man moving around in the undergrowth – clearly fragile imaginations who'd seen the spriggan and let their minds get away from them. When I'm here, I always think of the tiny tattooed Greek girl, a barmaid in Camden, found dumped in a burned-out hut, dead of course, with the Superman logo carved into her chest with a broken bottle. She died on a Christmas Eve. I remember her pulling pints of cider for me as Andy and I drank before a Sick of it All show at The Underworld. I remember the dirty rain that day, lashing the windows of the pub, the traffic snarled on Camden Road, cabbies beeping at herds of cagouled tourists.

I've gone dark again. Cheer up, love. Happy memories, Melissa, come on now, force them out of hiding, this misery is so fucking easy – the punx picnics here in the park, pissing in the plants by the railway sidings, a few cheeky tabs of mandy from Cerise's stash before heading to a show at The Dev or The Gunners. Laying angel-posed on the green grass in the sunlight of the early noughties with PK, Andy and Cerise. Cold bottles of cider, cheap bread and hummus from the nearest Turkish shop, Golden Virginia tobacco, crumpled Rizla tossed on the green grass.

Gary and Danny lived, and possibly died, during a time of the city's great sickness. That's what they imagined as a thing called the judderman, the illness of the urban environment manifest. A grim metaphor, maybe something more. Obviously influenced by the old Michael Ashman novels, but what was he influenced by, other than the city itself?

Perhaps they spent too long in the darkness and the sickness, the stories of humdrum brutalities and disappeared children and IRA bombs shredding the bodies of civilians. And if you do that, maybe you attract that darkness to you. Spend too long in the muck and you'll be stained forever.

I feel that impulse myself, to wallow in the murk and rummage in the void, to the point where it distorts and infects all life, and then life itself becomes a bleak farce. I loop back to certain events with grim fascination: the 1973 Old Bailey bombing, the riots of 2011, the rat queen that keeps popping up in the online lore of the urbexers, the 2005 tube attacks, the Nazi scumbag who nail bombed the Admiral Duncan in '99, the judderman, that grim Yewtree stuff, and of course, the attack at London Bridge.

I know what has fed this fascination. Cerise.

Down in the void, the world becomes a freezing dark day in January, still and dead and silent, frosted over with my breath fogging the polluted air. These are the times when it is most important to remember the sun will return and swallows will once more fill the skies. Then the sun arrives and scorches all life in its path.

Jesus.

Cheer up love.

Did Gary and Danny live through the tragedy, and I live through the farce? It's true that the skies over the city are darker again and the shadows cast last longer. It's so hot this summer, all of the time, none of us can think straight. My brain is cooking in my skull, my thoughts are burnt scraps. Everything seems like a bleak joke badly made, or misremembered and recounted drunk. An unidentifiable burnt body was found in Tottenham cemetery surrounded by a ring of cheap cider cans. My friend's Tinder date died in a stupid absurd accident and she lost the plot and moved to fucking Turkey Street. A pair of urbexers were ripped apart by rats that must've been the size of Irish Terriers, according to the sewer workers who found them. Their bodies could not be identified. Cerise went under in the attacks at London Bridge. I lost her. Something as dumb and banal as a cheap ceramic knife can end everything.

Grenfell blazed and sub-letters burned to death. I took a walk out there recently with PK, to the memorial and the gutted tower nobody knows what to do with. We hadn't managed to summon the energy to do it before, just thinking about it all shredded me. The logo of the London underground styled into a heart, with GRENFELL the station's name, attached to a white wooden wall. Messages of love and solidarity were scrawled over every available surface and I'm not ashamed to say it choked me up. I couldn't breathe.

Young men died in police cells across the city. The venues where I had danced and made my life all closed one by one. Train lines designed to shuttle in tourists and commuters ever faster destroyed all in their path; franchise coffee stores sprouted in small spaces that were left. I sat in steamy cafés watching people take photographs of their cupcakes, listening to them talk about new hot yoga classes. These people all seemed to work as freelance SEO optimisers. They holidayed in France, dragged little pet dogs with degenerate genes and breathing problems around with them, loved combinations of egg and avocado arranged on toasted sourdough bread. A new London, perhaps, or maybe I just focused on these people to confirm my worst fears. Worst of all, I had to travel to south London with increasing frequency for gigs. Even my retrospective at the TeXt gallery is being held down there.

And the homeless were everywhere. I couldn't spend more than thirty seconds outside a pub having a smoke without being asked for a bit of change to get the bus, a begged rollie, a bit of food. I looked into the eyes of women with collapsed faces, scraggle-beard men with wild eyes and skin a mess of psoriasis. Saw a group of aftershaved lads out on the town, trained in from some cesspit in Essex, spit on a beggar in Old Street and piss themselves laughing. 'Get a fucking job, mate, you stink.' I waited for a bus as a gang from near the Woodberry Down estate battered an old homeless man who didn't know what was going on. I wanted to intervene, but all I could think of were knives being drawn. We call this austerity and the way, simply, things are. But each day I see the small homeless village growing under the arcades near the Angel, and the girl who must be no more than seventeen on her mattress. I think about what happens to girls like that. The goddess of this city does nothing to protect us. The commare will let her die, fall into the hands of people who will destroy her.

But I need to stop this. The city is my home and it can be beautiful.

It is beautiful, in its endless labyrinths and infinite stories.

We carry on.

What else is there to do.

*

I find the entrance to Parkland Walk. The city will spark me back into life; the city has always fired me, and always stokes my imagination. I feel those hot coals glowing a hellish red. This city made me who I am, and I owe it something. It created me, and I create it.

In preparation for the new issue of *Magnesium Burns*, I've been feeding on as many books of London lore as I can find, like I used to, back then. Everything from *Neverwhere* to *London Orbital*, *King Rat*, *A Journey Through Ruins*, *Savage Messiah*, *The Great God Pan* and *The London Adventure*. I reread *The Good Terrorist*, *The Lowlife*, *Duffy is Dead*, *NW*. I dug out my copies of *Yardie*, *He Died With His Eyes Open*, and *Robinson. London Bone, King of the City, Mother London.* I can picture the fight in *King Dido.* Some of us have always known. I'm back with the children of the Jago, I am bouncing over fences with Springheel Jack, I am Dora Suarez, I am a tosher grubbing through the sewer muck, I am red London, I am Staples Corner and how we can know it.

These words map a place I sense is there, just out of sight. I know it is there. I always have done.

Onto the path now and I am walking Parkland Walk. It's hot and the mud of the path is baked hard and powdery dry. Crickets are chirping, a few small brown birds hopping amongst bramble and bracken. It feels wrong somehow; my image, my memory of this walk is always autumnal, everything overlaid with grey drizzle, mud slippery beneath my feet.

I have a natural pull to the useless, to the broken down, the arcane. In London before the Olympics there was a lot of that. I looked at strange graffiti on the walls of friends' squats, smoke leaking from the roofs of houseboats and I saw, like so many before me, the city as strata, layers of packed story, myth and heartache. It was in those years I found the stories of giant beasts in the marshes, skinned and headless bears, reptiles pulling down geese in the river Lea. They seem quaint now.

I filled my head with shibboleths, knowledge at odds with the pace, the dirt, the press of crowds. I love all that too – the life of the city, the sheer human chaos of it: but this feeling, this pull towards something deeper, perhaps ageless, is real also.

So, I walked amongst Victorian ruins on the Middlesex Filter Beds, broke onto reservoirs with friends, marvelled at the lost rivers buried by time and development. On Horsenden Hill, where they say an Anglo-Saxon king fell long ago, I disturbed cottaging men and watched a crow pluck the eyes from a mouse on top of a windswept mound.

I read the stories of Nematoda and wriggling things on the message boards and fan sites full of sad lonely men.

I followed stories of a golem on the streets of Stamford Hill; ifrits brightening the skies over Edgware Road. Tokoloshes in Tottenham cemetery. Good stories.

And today I walk along the abandoned train lines through Crouch End, to see the green man who slides out from brick, the thing that solidifies all this for me, gives it physicality. A carved thing that tells me it's not just me and my imagination: this is something legitimate, something I can touch. Here I can renew my sense of history, urban narrative, of stories trapped in soil, encased in the mortar and concrete. Some deeper or parallel reality right there to see, if you are willing. London Incognita. The Crouch End Spriggan.

It lives on Parkland Walk. Always pictured in the rain, a greasy city drizzle, but today is scorched, uncomfortable, dying in the blaze. I see bracken threaded with spiny thorn branches, diurnal foxes, Lycra-clad cyclists taking a route both scenic and convenient from Finsbury Park to Highgate. The old Edgware, Highgate and London Railway line, through a platform mossed and overgrown.

It's popular with dog walkers, couples arm in arm on a Sunday stroll.

In the disused railway arches near Crouch End, that's where I find it; not that it could have moved. The spriggan. It slides out of the brickwork as if caught between dimensions, perhaps seven feet tall if it could stand. Much like how the brothers – my uncles – saw the judderman slipping out of the shadows, peeling itself from architectural interstices and coming for them.

It's a marvel, amongst the overgrowth and the lurid graffiti. It reminds me of the old Arthur Machen stories, relics of older mythologies making themselves felt in the city.

I take photos, jot some ideas down for the new issue, a sketch of the spriggan's leering face in biro. I light my spliff and sit down, inhaling deeply. I observe the green man for a while, willing it to move. A few people pass me on foot, more cyclists, a homeless man with a trolley full of crumpled plastic bottles and shredded scraps of cardboard. The day is still, rendered near-motionless by the heat.

The funny thing is, the spriggan is not even part of London mythology. It's a Cornish thing, a monstrously ugly protector of treasure, a kind of heavy, a bouncer for the fair folk. It took me years to find who made it, but I was never sure exactly why it was there. I'm sure I could find out if I really tried, but the mystery of the thing and the shocked joy upon discovering it is a feeling I want to preserve as long as I can. I can spin fictions from it.

It's a place I take friends, partners, family members to. I walked here with Cerise, with PK, with Andy. With a few boyfriends. I've promised to take Debbie, the girl from TeXt who is helping me set up the exhibition. She's texted me, *Good luck with the walk! X.* Though why I need luck I don't know.

Away from the high streets and the chugging traffic, London still conceals marvels.

The spriggan on Parkland Walk reminds me my burning interest in the stories of the city is a valid thing. It's all still real and I am still alive. London Incognita is still here, away from the coffee shops and the Instagram posts. I'm glad I have made the time to come back.

Walking here reignites an obsession, a desire to track and know as many stories and myths as I can, here in the city that is my home.

Unlearning

I dug out one of my unpublished flash fictions this morning, and I'm thinking of using it as part of the *Magnesium Burns* retrospective. It's kind of a B-side/rarities cut, if you like to think in the language of London's music scenes, which I do. The story is kind of naïve in its anti-hipster posturing but I like the city it depicts, my London Incognita from about fifteen years ago. It's based on a period of my life when I was seeing a feller who just wasn't right for me, which should become clear. It's funny reading it back; that venue I allude to on the Holloway Road is a now a Costa Coffee with all the memories and experiences there wiped clean. A flat white sipped in the exact spot where a crowdsurfer's boot smashed into the left side of my face. I have a crystal clear memory of seeing Scarp play there, and a little scuffle breaking outside with PK getting his nose busted by a Motörhead-biker type guy. PK was off his nut in those days and he deserved it, the gobby twat.

Anyway, this is the story:

Unlearning

[Collected in *Magnesium Burns: Two Decades in the Underground Capital 1999-2019*, Melissa Eider, Positive Press, 2019]

I was unlearning.

I should have been feeling my insides burn and sweet cider running through my veins, standing on the edge of Holloway Road surrounded by black hoodies and Harringtons and combat boots, an endless roll-up blazing in my mouth, discarded fliers pushing up against my feet.

I should have been standing under canvas on Blackheath, whipped by cold rain and wind but glowing with human heat and energy.

I should have found that squat out in Bermondsey, a party to continue the feeling that something, somewhere, mattered.

I should have been anywhere but here.

Instead I drifted through phantom bars, pricy alcohol nights where I tried to convince myself I belonged. No luck; just hundreds of human beings with nothing to say dislocated from time and place. A line of coke on glass and a sad handjob in an alleyway. Maybe, as many told me, it didn't matter.

My doppelgänger: she had tried to change herself into someone who neither deserved nor desired this life. The other lives, the heat and flesh around her, swam in and out of focus. They were multi-national but rootless, transitory, paper thin. She could push her finger through their skins. She had to run, regretting her failure. Leave your brain at the door.

I thought about cockney prostitutes ripped apart and the morbid tourist industry. Plague bodies sleeping forever under the market. The Jewish Anarchists. Banglatown. If you asked me, I could never fully articulate why it all bothered me. A sadness that the new residents didn't care, I suppose.

But I unlearnt, escaped.

'Still Burning'
Andrew Eider

[From the introduction to *Magnesium Burns: Two Decades in the Underground Capital 1999-2019*, Melissa Eider, Positive Press, 2019]

I have this burning bright memory of my sister – Melissa Eider, author of the book you're holding in your hands right now. It was the early days of Scarp and we were touring our debut album, *Songs of the River Larks,* doing the usual run of grotty beer-soaked venues and DIY spaces that stank of stale cigarettes and spilled cider, playing anywhere that would have us and having a few adventures along the way.

We were doing a date at the 1 in 12 Club in Bradford. Melissa was with us on tour helping us do the merch stall and along for the ride – and using the tour as a chance to get the zine she'd been working on for the last year or so into the hands of scene kids and interested folk all across the country. I remember an older punter sniffily looking at a copy of *Magnesium Burns,* flicking through the pages to find it was nearly all *words.* It was issue number six that features the now lauded story 'A Monument to Nothing'; one of Mel's first forays into the fictional London narratives that the zine would become known and justly celebrated for. My sister and I always *loved* the weird stories of our home city, London, and drew on it for constant inspiration. They are an endless resource.

'What's the point in this then?' the old scenester asked with a sneer, flapping the pages in her face like a wad of counterfeit notes. 'We're here for the music, aren't we?'

Her reply took him off guard, being a long and impassioned speech from a nineteen-year-old woman about the importance of telling stories and why we all needed to document and record the underground cultural and creative scenes we were involved in. No one was going to do it for us – and even if they were, it was extremely dangerous to hand your narrative to someone else and expect them to tell it truthfully for you.

'Because you'll forget,' was how she signed it all off. She could have taken a bow at that moment, and I would have applauded. I remember the intense pride surging through me.

At the end of the gig, the guy bought a copy and even got Melissa to sign it with a thick black sharpie. If he still has it, it's worth a lot of money; the issue is a sought-after collector's item. Everything becomes history, or else it is forgotten and lost – a dominant theme in one of Mel's most powerful later stories, 'We are the Resurrection Men'.

What Melissa and I, I think, shared, was a get-up-and-go attitude, a willingness to put our work out into the world before anyone told us we were allowed to. The sense that if we didn't make the work we wanted to see in the world, nobody was going to do it for us.

I still see a young woman of nineteen, answering back and educating a man twenty years her senior with a poetic skill that still makes me smile. It's one of those memories that only becomes more real as the years roll by.

After that tour, *Magnesium Burns* started to go from strength to strength and it just kept going; while Scarp and the scene that birthed the zine folded, Melissa kept writing and gaining more readers. It helped that she was a brilliant writer, naturally gifted, able to open up the world in ways I never thought possible. I am more than happy to admit that Melissa was a crucial inspiration to some of Scarp's best work – I even dedicated our song 'Burn Forever' to her, my sister.

Magnesium Burns is still going strong; Melissa is still writing and editing and publishing and flying the flag for independent culture.

This book covers the first twenty years of *Magnesium Burns*. Here's to twenty more.

– Andrew Eider, North London, 2019

The Beehive

'Mel— Melissa, you know what I'm saying. Everything is a saleable commodity, you know, even these experiences that are designed to fucking—' PK sighs theatrically, wanting me to know how heavily the burden of late neo-liberal capitalism is bearing down on him '—liberate us from the pressures of consumerism. From all of this shit.' He waves his hands vaguely to indicate the wider world beyond this pub, all of London, the entire stinking country. He's getting worked up as usual, battling straw men in his head while I nod along. I indulge him because he's had a shitty few years and that gives a person a bit of leeway.

We're sat in the beer garden of The Beehive in Bruce Grove, a pub just off the main road, not far from Tottenham police station. We're near where the riots kicked off in 2011. I remember those nights: a city on fire, broken glass confetti tossed on concrete and tarmac.

That summer the tarmac of London oozed in the heat. Hotter than Spain, screamed the headlines. Flesh on display. The city was burning. Five nights of riots, triggered by something so common we'd almost all forgotten it was a travesty. The police killed a black lad, as they do.

PK and I had taken our fair share of batterings out on the demos, and Andy once took a kicking in the cells of Stoke Newington for having too much of a mouth on him.

What were we going to do, go to the police? Ha ha. But we considered ourselves lucky – we put ourselves in those situations. I see that now. The police didn't come looking for us, didn't persecute us simply for who we were, other than the squatters maybe – however much the London punks wanted to believe they were the oppressed, we had it lucky. Sure, the London Met hate crusties, but who doesn't?

For whatever reason, people weren't having it that summer. Who can blame them? Push people too far, then punish them for having the gall to react – that takes some nerve. So, the put-upon of London reacted with torched squad cars, bricks through the windows of Currys, looting all those things they were told they needed to be a proper person but could not afford.

A petrol bomb bursting on a riot shield is a truly gorgeous sight. The memories I have of London streets lit at night by an oily flame – so fucking beautiful. Rip it up, tear it down, smash, start again.

If only it had been that way.

Even back then I knew the violence, the unhappiness and unrest, was nothing new to London. This ancient city, a place I knew like one of its rats, eking life out in the cracks and gaps.

I could see the ghosts of the all the cities London had been. I'd catch glimpses of men and women in outdated clothing and wonder whether I was just seeing hipsters or something deeper. It was so hard to tell who was living and who was dead – with retro fashion booming, second-hand chic a thing, even skinhead fashion suffering a fashionable re-appreciation, how could I tell *when* anyone was from? And who was I, anyway, to pass judgment on this? Whether I was decked out, like I was back then, in the black and white T-shirts of bands from the early nineties, or smartened up in polo shirts, when the hell was I from? I burned with nostalgia for times that never really happened. This older London we fetishised, even as we knew it never quite existed. A different place to London Incognita; that was a place half-seen, misunderstood, but very real. The imagined London was overexposed, a fake city crushing the life out of the real one. Sometimes I fancied I could see a distorted reflection of the city up over the clouds, floating above me.

The weight of the city I lived in almost flattened me. I couldn't verbalise it. It was a drug. I'd sit and watch old Pogues videos on YouTube, flick through my shelves of London fiction, stare out high as a red kite over the view from London Bridge at five a.m. as the sun came up, and the knowledge of where I was, what this city was and the fact that I lived in became unbearable. The feeling was like a pill you'd taken that you knew was too strong, the rush of emotions enough to buckle me at the spine. I never knew what to call those feelings. Some kind of extra, unnecessary sensitivity.

I saw the spriggan on Parkland Walk struggling to get free of the brickwork when no one else could; I knew the golem in Stamford Hill was real. I studied the tarot, I loved weird fiction, and took an interest in things like the collective unconscious. I had taken mushrooms, acid, even DMT in a plush flat in Muswell Hill, an experience which almost made me believe in an afterlife.

That night as the city burned, we thought we'd sniff out what was going on, try and live up to some of the creeds we claimed to adhere to. I can still see my ex-boyfriend, Jim King, long disappeared now into his own obsessions. I still sort of miss him.

We were running down a side road off the Green Lanes, fleeing it as a whole unit of riot police done up like RoboCop marched down the street. Turks and Kurds were leaning out of their windows above the kebab shops and grocery stores. I have a memory of a tipped-over box of Turkish peppers, those pale green ones you cook up with eggs in a metal pan, arranged like an absurd, crushed corona on the tarmac.

The Turks were out on the street ready to deal with any potential looters, tooled up with cleavers and bats that should have been hitting softballs in London's parks. They were a community prepared to look after themselves. I always respected them for that. They were defending their property from people we presumed they knew as neighbours.

We ran down the alley as the Green Lanes went up in flames and came down in smashed glass and scorched brick. Jim and I had lost the others, and it felt like we were in *Sid & Nancy*, excited and adrenalised by the fact that things were happening and for once the status quo was wobbling. We kissed in the shadow behind a green industrial recycling bin, a piece of smouldering cardboard wafting above us like a burning angel.

I have seen great spotted woodpeckers and table fungus and the graves of tiny children festooned with toys in Tottenham cemetery; felt my eyes prick with tears, on a comedown after a night at Chances, as I floated through the graves in September mists with Jim's hand clutched in mine. Inviting trouble, I suppose, but there's a pleasure in that sadness.

PK is sucking hard on his vape and is taking little sips from a Becks Blue bottle with a label sloughing off like the skin of a dead thing. The garden is busy with drinkers, the air thick with vapours and voices, blue smoke, the clink of glasses. It's Saturday afternoon and the weather is fucking roasting and the place is swollen with people; I love all this human life, but I could give the heat a miss.

We're wedged onto an uneven and splintery wooden table, trying to hold onto some space for the others who should be with us soon; five minutes, their messages say. A few afternoon beers and a bit of chat and a catch up before we jump in an Uber and head up to Tufnell Park; we're adults and we pay for cabs. So that's the plan. Scarp's big London reunion show.

I try and think what to say to PK; he is essentially correct, of course, but what are we to do – just sit here in the pub agreeing with each other like we have for the last twenty years? The sun is pulsing above us like an inflamed gland; it's too fucking hot, I can barely think when it's like this, the city melting in heat we know is not right. The wrong thing no one speaks about. It's like the sun itself – we can't look directly at it. Like in the Jawbreaker song: the man who saw everything and went blind.

Finally, I say, 'I know, PK. We all know this, don't we?' I try not to let my voice betray my boredom. I'm stifling a sigh. I swig my drink instead.

He looks at me curiously, like I'm letting him down. '*We* do, Mel, we always have. I'm not sure about anyone else.'

PK has an arrogance he never really earned. I think of all the times he was so fucked up he couldn't string a sentence together; or the time he pissed himself during a Capdown show at The Underworld and didn't notice.

I'd never say this to him – he's an old mate and we're all supposed to stick together –but Jesus fucking Christ. Though he bought my book, which was nice of him. I'd have given him a freebie, the idiot, but a sale is a sale and I'd like to make at least a bit of money out of *Magnesium Burns*. Credibility and respect *is* nice, but I can't eat a write-up in *The Quietus*.

I take another gulp of sharp fizzing cider and I am about to reply, maybe start an argument or vigorous debate just to stop all the excruciating mutual head-nodding; this is exactly what they mean by an echo chamber.

Then I feel a slap on my back, and hear a male voice directed at PK: 'Oi oi dickhead, still decoding the great swindle for us all? Opening the eyes of the sheeple.' PK laughs nervously as the voice continues, 'You're becoming like one of those truthers mate. I give it six months before you become a Flat Earther or start getting into some Nazi occult shit that you pass off as "art". Those guys were all smackheads too.' This is followed by deep laughter with the texture of sandpaper and gravel.

My brother, Andy. We're all heading up to Tufnell Park together for the show. His reunion show, really.

PK's face contorts into a combination of wince and smile, like he's happy receiving low-level abuse from one of his cultural heroes who he thinks he's lucky to also call a mate. We call this stuff banter and that makes it all okay as long as we don't examine it too closely. PK, at this moment, reminds me a dog desperate for love despite the beating it's just received, and I hate myself for thinking this. Where do these uncharitable thoughts, about even the people I love, come from?

Andy has a point, though. PK thinks he's more enlightened than he is, but at least he's coherent these days. Never try and talk to someone after they've been smoking heroin, or drinking for a week, is my advice.

'Hello sis,' Andy says crouching down for a hug and a peck on the cheek. 'Need anything from the bar?'

I shake my head, gesture to my nearly-full pint of cider.

'And you're still off the sauce, PK, is that right?'

PK nods, leaking vapour. He gestures at his blue-labelled bottle to suggest he'll have another. Andy fights his way back inside, card already out and ready to tap on one of those machines. I watch my brother and think about the days when we must have come to the pub with wallets bulging with enough cash for a night. But I can't remember when that ended and the world went plastic, and who cares anyway.

PK starts up again. The McMindfulness conspiracy, app-sedation, the psychotic narcissism taking over all our brains like a creeping fungus as the world outside of London burns and drowns and rips itself apart. As toddlers' bloated bodies are washed up on Mediterranean shores, as piles of dead Vietnamese are found in the backs of lorries in Essex, and so on.

I zone out thinking about the passing of time, how Andy has reached the stage of his life where he can reunite and resurrect parts of his past, and the exhibition I am preparing for where I'll edit my work and myself into a narrative fit for public consumption. It was nice what he said about me in the intro to the book – I'd forgotten that night in Bradford, but it all came flooding back. Now it's part of the official story, though he embellished a little bit, of course.

I wanted to create something new for the twentieth anniversary, a new issue of *Magnesium Burns*. Maybe a limited run only available at the gallery and online, something like that. This one will be about trying to solve the mystery of what happened to Gary and Daniel, my great-uncles. To try and crack the mystery of what they called London Incognita. *In Search of Family Ghosts,* or the title I'm really leaning to, *You're Already Dead,* from the Crass song. Keep in line, stay in line. It's one of my favourites, after that one about Myra

Hindley. It always makes me think of the commare.

The anti-mother.

Mother, is that you?

I snap back into the conversation.

'PK. Can you shut up for a second, I'd like to enjoy today, let's try and cheer up a bit.'

He sucks his vape and rolls his eyes.

*

Eider. I'm not clear where the surname comes from. I'm aware that there are hints of Huguenot deep in the family history, according to my mother who has gone down the *Who Do You Think You Are?* route. But an eider is a type of sea duck. I used one as the cover image for an issue of *Magnesium Burns*: a solitary bird alone on an empty ocean.

The eider has always captured my imagination, the pale minty greens, sharp blacks and whites of its plumage, the thick banana-mustard-yellow of the beak. Pillows and quilts were once stuffed with its feathers; eiderdown to keep the cold at bay. I have never seen one, can't be arsed with birdwatching outside of the M25 to be honest, but I like the thought of them bobbing on the waves far off of a cold British coast, sleety rain sliding from their oiled feathers. They are pretty things.

At night, when I cannot sleep during the intense heatwaves that are searing the city with unchecked brutality, I imagine myself in freezing waters off the north Kent coast where the Thames becomes the North Sea, a pod of narwhal spearing and breaching around me, a creche of young eider ducks forming an enclosing circle as I float, then sink gratefully into the chilly brine; woman down, eider down, Melissa down.

I set up the fanzine *Magnesium Burns* in 1999; two decades documenting the world I inhabit, or perhaps the fish tank I swim in. Twenty years of writing interviews, short stories, fantasies of a city life lived in London Incognita, record reviews, book reviews, guest spots from other writers I liked and admired and invited to contribute, even the occasional and regrettable poem. Twenty years of work that now has to be organised and put into a select order with the help of the curator of the small gallery in Peckham, TeXt, where we're doing the retrospective. Not my ideal location; it's in bandit country for a start, and Peckham – south London in general, really – was never a focus of *Magnesium Burns*. I'm a north London girl when is all said and done; give me the ecstatic joys of Wood Green and Bruce Grove and Ally Pally, the outer reaches of Enfield at Forty Hall, pints and powder at a punx picnic in Finsbury Park. Fugazi recorded *Margin Walker* at Southern Studios in Wood Green. The Battle of Wood Green in '77, beating back the National Front. My north London has got history.

To be fair to the south, it has some decent areas. I've been to belting gigs at the New Cross Inn and The Bird's Nest in Deptford, done some great bookfairs at Goldsmiths, attended some of the most insane and memorable squat parties in Bermondsey and Camberwell. Happy nights at The Balustrade. But it isn't home.

Debbie works at TeXt, a little slip of a hipster who'd like to be ethereal but is only ever earnest. She's lovely but I do wonder where her mind is sometimes. Face buried in her Instagram feed a lot of the time. I'd have preferred someone with more of a grounding in the scene, but then I'm not sure what I expected. I'm a relic of that world, I realise. Andy too, and PK. I am the resurrection woman – ha ha. Picture me as a discreetly tattooed coelacanth, swimming against the tide up the Thames.

Debbie gently pressured me into a photo of the two of us that she uploaded to her Instagram feed – as a good way to tease out details of the upcoming show, she said. 'Making battle plans with this gorgeous trailblazer,' she wrote below the photo. Ooff. But I looked pretty good in it, luckily, in a denim skirt, black Lifetime T-shirt from the *Hello Bastards* era, green vegan Docs. Debbie was wearing dungarees over a Ramones shirt – I believe, bless her, she thinks that's punk – and glasses too big for her face. She was making the peace sign with her fingers.

Lots of likes for the post, and some creepy comments from a couple of men. One of them is from a guy I know, who feels the need to declare himself a feminist despite no one asking him. He takes an avid interest in female wrestling, claiming them to be iconic role models for young women.

I try not to think about Cerise too much, but every day I

fail. How could I not think of her? This exhibition is, I suppose, time to take stock and make sense of everything. I am not sure why twenty years has any greater significance than an eighteenth or twenty-third anniversary, but it does. It is something to do with how we measure and understand time, to trick ourselves into believing the world is not formless and without meaning.

This is something that has always interested me: the fact that I cannot really control my own mind. Be it the memory of a murdered friend who was like a sister to me, or a graphic sexual image as I look at an unattractive and acne-cratered guy on the bus, or images of eider ducks and breaching narwhal and writhing worms in the tunnels of the underground, or simple scraps of memories from the old days before PK got into the junk and when Scarp were first touring all over the country. No amount of mindfulness techniques or meditation can stop that, and I don't want them to anyway. This is me. My uncontrollable mind is where I get some of my best ideas, and life is about responding to stimuli, right? I can't become one of those people who have given up, no matter how tempting it may be. Life has to be about embracing the unexpected, relinquishing the control that you never really had. And sometimes it's natural to be anxious, depressed, melancholic, fucking angry, just as it's natural to have moments of euphoria, ecstasy, peace, raging lust, gentle love.

I hate the question, *Where do you get your ideas from?* As if ideas were a brand of desirable groceries available to pick up at select stores. The ideas come from my own mind, obviously. I generate them from the raw material of what I see and experience. Duh.

Of course, I don't control the ideas I have; in my more pretentious moments I imagine myself as a conduit for the stories of the DIY scene, of the people I knew and the things I cared about, for London Incognita itself. But I try and reign those thoughts in when I speak publicly about my work and try and remain a little more enigmatic and elusive. People give far too much of themselves away these days. And I'm aware how stupid and up-my-own-arse the idea of being a conduit for something greater than yourself sounds, but I feel it regardless. Like an idiot savant but not as stupid – that's me.

I presented a heavily edited version of my own life in the zine, a fictionalised and perhaps an idealised one, one I was careful only to reveal certain aspects of. The Melissa portrayed in those pages has a life of her own; we get on well, but she has her life and I have mine.

Magnesium Burns started as a perzine – a personal fanzine – with a lot of biographical detail and day-to-day stuff, the idea being that the mundane could be beautiful and the everyday was infinite and strange and ultimately as unknowable as the far reaches of the cosmos. To see a world in a grain of sand, or in my case, to see the universe in a flyer for a DIY arts space, glimpse reality in the tomato relish smeared on a tofu burger.

The problem I encountered was that, often, the mundane really is just crushingly boring.

The title itself doesn't mean much, I just felt that the

words had a nice ring to them, a dim memory surfacing of chemistry lessons at school in a comp in north London. And then the idea developed in my head, a free association that led to picturing things like a harlequin with a face scarred with bad burns from igniting magnesium, though I don't even know if that is possible. I always liked harlequins, clowns, Pierrots, fools. Pulchinella, all that Italian stuff, Mr Punch battering his wife on English seasides, chain-smoking alcoholic misanthrope Mr Jelly from *Psychoville*. There's a gorgeous little sea bird, much better looking than the eider, called a harlequin duck, that lives in the cold and frozen north. Also known as the painted duck, totem pole duck, and the white-eyed diver. The drakes are beautiful.

So, this idea of the everyday being magical was pretentious, yeah, but it's a concept I still fundamentally adhere to. Reality amazes me, the fact that anything exists or ever existed: I visited the Natural History Museum in Kensington for the first time in many years recently and stared at the fossilised ichthyosaur held behind glass for a long time, considering that, fuck me, this thing really existed. Bizarre reality. Like the tiny flamboyant cuttlefish in the aquarium below the Horniman Museum in south London and the jellyfish that seemed to hang in an eternal blue void from a far future. Like what happened to Daniel and Gary in the nineteen seventies.

After those first few issues of *Magnesium Burns*, I began to read and delve heavily into the odd fictions of my home city. I can't remember who it was who turned me on to the works of

Arthur Machen, but they came as a revelation to me. I loved the idea that a fragment of paradise – frightening and awe-inspiring rather than comforting – could be found in a back garden of Stoke Newington. Stoke Newington in a different incarnation, of course, before it turned into a cupcake yummy-mummy hotbed – though there is mystery and horror even in that. I loved novels from the nineties like *The Course of the Heart* and *Signs of Life*, the sense that unknown knowledge, Gnostic mysteries, were just around the next street corner, to be found by the Grand Union Canal or in the swaying grasses on Horsenden Hill where cottagers congregate and crows rip the eyes from rodents. I had my own Jumble Woods to explore, and so I did.

In my early twenties, I found the work of Michael Ashman. I was nosing in the Fantasy Centre bookshop – sadly closed down now – on Holloway Road, and came across a couple of old, fairly pricey editions of his work. But I had to have them. Ashman's *The Salvage Song of the Larks, and Other Stories* was hugely influential on my writing and my brother's music too. 'A Life Constricted, or, These Serpentine Coils Will Crush Us Both' remains a personal favourite of mine, that I placed at number one in my top ten short stories. The list was for a piece that I was invited to contribute to and in the end was never published due to a change in editors; in the end I just stuck it on my website. I know Debbie, at least, has read it.

I adored the Vincent Harrier novels too, the brutal and gritty depictions of a city I had never known. I considered the work to be up there on a par with Derek Raymond's *I*

Was Dora Suarez – a book I loved and hated so much I wrote my own conflicted tribute to it. 'I Was Melissa Eider' was my clumsy attempt to grapple with the fact I admired a work of art depicting extreme brutality against women. Eider down.

I'm putting together the new exhibition at TeXt. I slide rare early copies of *Magnesium Burns* into plastic protective bags, first pressings of Scarp's debut album on grey vinyl, signed and dedicated to me by Andy, sketches Cerise made for some of the later books I put out in 2012. I listen to *South London VS the World* as I work, a decent album despite being from bandit country.

I marvel at the physicality of the things I'm handling. How did *we* make this? We are nothing and nobody; yet here we are. Human beings remain a question mark to those around them and to themselves. These walking talking mysteries create words, pictures, music, all trying to decode the great mystery. But we only ever add to it.

This isn't entirely an exercise in self-congratulation, however. Looking at the early stuff now, something becomes very clear: I liked to examine the contents of my own navel. I had a lot of *feelings* as I made my way bumbling and cocksure into the adult world. It makes me alternately smile and cringe to look at those early issues now and the young woman depicted there. Romantic tribulations where I mooned over a tattooed dickhead with a drinking problem, no prospects, and even fewer ideas; fretful essays dissembling the patriarchy whilst pointing out the bleeding obvious; handwringing over my dietary decisions. But also, and this is what interests me more: depictions of London, *my* city, in a time period that feels intimately familiar and shockingly alien. I'm glad to see the kernels of this interest in my younger self; good on you, girl. Well done Mel.

Magnesium Burns #5 is simply a documentation of travelling to Highbury Corner with PK and Cerise to see Leatherface play at the Highbury Garage in 2000, supported by Nomadic Tribe. There's something in the depiction of London that pleases me still, the little sketched drawings I did to accompany the text, of Chapel Market near the Angel where we gorged at the all-you-can-eat vegetarian Indian buffet, the tins of strong Polish lager we sank on the walk up Upper Street – PK necking his beer like children's lemonade – and a pen and ink drawing of Highbury & Islington station in its Silverlink days with the punters and beggars fanned out around it; I like how I captured the worming coil of smoke rising from a *Big Issue* seller's cigarette, a crumpled empty pack of Bensons on the pavement.

I have a photograph I've managed to keep hold of, that was xeroxed into the design of the zine, of the three of us standing in front of the venue. I must have asked a passer-by to take the picture. My hair is short, bottle blonde. I'm wearing a white T-shirt emblazoned with the logo of a lame Californian pop punk band under a light denim jacket, short skirt, leather Docs. Oh well. PK's wearing shorts, Vans, a black Scarp T-shirt, the outfit he largely adheres to even now. Cerise is in a Harrington, black jeans, her shoulder length hair a dark green, though the image in the zine renders it merely dark and murky grey.

I miss you Cerise. I think of you every day, mate.

Issue five, looking back through it now as I select material for the exhibition, was my first attempt at creating a sustained narrative, albeit one that only ran to ten pages of photocopied A5. I even gave the issue its own title – *In the Real World* – but I wouldn't say the meaning behind that choice bears up to much scrutiny, it was just one of my favourite songs and I liked the scraps of meaning song titles and lyrics could impart. What's important is the time and place it captures. What might have been just a floating scrap of memory eroding as the years went by given some permanence, a permanence through the filter of me and my writing, sure, but I make no claim to any objective truth and I never did.

Always this urge to document things, terrified that I would forget, or that none of it meant anything unless I pinned it to paper. At times I feel grateful I live in a time where I am able to do that.

Putting together this exhibition, delving into my archive here in my home in Tottenham, I indulge my thoughts that revolve and spin around accidents of birth, the insanity of history. What kind of person would I have been had I been born in the seventeenth century in rural Norfolk? Burnt as a witch no doubt. What if I had been birthed into a South African township during Apartheid, or a hut in ancient Sumeria, or in an empty city in a former Soviet republic, or perhaps in Herculaneum before the volcano? What an impossibility it is to exist now, right now, and certainly in 1999.

What did I feel was so important to document? I loved the Riot Grrrl stuff from North America, the zine culture that exploded out of Washington, Olympia. Of course, being here in London, I couldn't really read much of it but the very idea of zines like *Jigsaw* and *Girl Germs* and *Bikini Kill* were enough of an inspiration to me. I have always been a disciple of Heavens to Betsy, Bratmobile and L7.

But I am a Londoner, and I was trying to explore and write about the trials and tribulations of a young feminist woman in the London underground scenes, not merely aping my American influences or pretending I lived in the same world as them. And I am proud of my city.

I harboured artistic pretensions, little scraps of creative writing decorating my bedroom floor, pencil sketches tacked to walls, and I liked the idea that not only could I document things but that also I could tell a story. What I liked about zine culture was that I could chuck it all into the mix and try and make it work. A big inspiration of mine was Cometbus #47, *Lanky* , that I'd picked up from a distro at one of Andy's gigs, a shithole toilet venue in Manchester. This was a zine as mini-novel, and I loved what the author had done, these little accumulated vignettes of a life lived around San Franscisco and a first love inevitably lost, nights at punk rock shows, days spent working at a photocopy shop, the aimlessness and infinite potential of life lived at age nineteen. I loved Screeching Weasel and Crimpshrine, too, which certainly helped.

The format and the way I encountered the work seemed highly significant to me. The audience almost seemed irrelevant. It wasn't anything like contempt or disdain towards them but getting the work down on paper and out into the world seemed to be the most important thing. How it found readers seemed incidental – a terribly naïve attitude, I now realise – but there also felt like there was an implicit trust that it would find appreciative readers. And it did.

I loved the stark black-and-white photocopy cover, that long-standing aesthetic of the DIY scene that still gets me right now in 2019. Could I do something similar about London, about me as a woman in the late nineties?

Of course I fucking could.

I love the whole history of zines, from their roots in the sci-fi and fantasy scene in the 1930s, then into the first punk era, *Slash* and *Sniffin' Glue* and all that stuff. And as I've said, zines were a huge part of the Riot Grrrl movement. These days there are zines about pretty much anything, most of them twee and pretty dreadful in my opinion – cutesy comics about how to make vegan cupcakes, oh fuck my life – but, like with anything, the good stuff survives and persists whilst the chaff falls away. This is what distorts our view of the past, I realise.

Early *Magnesium Burns* was too earnest, I can see that. I hope it was never twee, but it was *heartfelt*. Emocore was a big thing back then, remember. Those early issues and their achingly sincere vignettes of a life lived in vegan cafés, DIY social centres and failed relationships. I think it does accurately capture the pretentiousness and certainty and self-centred seriousness of young adults who think they have found an answer to the world. It's painful when you realise the solution is not a solution at all; and I wrote about that too.

As I sort through my material, I can now see the cliqueness of it all. At times a self-conscious and smug showing-off, like, look at me I've found this underground scene and now I'm going to bang on about how great my friends and I are.

Fucking great for me, eh? Luckily, at that time it was only my friends and I reading it. I'm glad I started *Magnesium Burns* before the real onset of social media. This is something Debbie at TeXt treats with a weird reverence – being a digital native, as she is, but artistically inclined, she fetishises this kind of work made before the Internet made everything easier.

Occasionally, if my senses are all still working, I get the sense Debbie is attracted to me. I catch her looking at me and notice how her pale cheeks bloom crimson. It's a little ego boost, making little Debbie in her dungarees and Ramones T-shirt flush with blood. You've still got it, Mel.

Emerging in that pre social media era allowed the zine to grow, to try and fail and succeed at a few things before settling into a comfortable shape. Write all those naïve and cringe stories out of me before I found what I was really trying to do. I grew in public, if anyone had cared to look.

That can be the benefit of no one caring or paying attention to what you are doing; you can develop with no one really watching. Mistakes could be forgiven.

I loved zine culture and more importantly the idea of zine culture, as part of a DIY underground community of self-expression and artistic freedom. God – it sounds so innocent, and yet I still believe it. It's not that I wanted to publish any old shit, and I believe that people almost always need an editor, but I wanted to create a platform for the things I found interesting and to get on and do it without someone telling me I was allowed to do so before I proceeded. I always pictured this someone as a surly and patrician gatekeeper with a fuligin-black uniform and a heavy brow, the gate made of thick Victorian iron with rusted and squealing hinges as it opened the barest inch before being slammed shut in my face.

The London obsession came a bit later. I started to write longer bits of fiction, or fictionalised biography, after the sense of satisfaction I felt doing *In the Real World*, but thought I could broaden the scope beyond 'Mel attends a gig by band she likes with some friends of hers.' Think big, girl.

I had always had a fascination with the weird stories of my home city, the scraps of folklore and urban myth and stuff that gets spouted in the pub after a few pints but rarely written down. Why not work that stuff into the stories? After all, I was rapidly coming to realise that my life wasn't interesting enough to fuel this zine through the coming years, and I could just start a dreadful blog if all I wanted to do was document my trips away and the bands I went to see. Fiction got me out of that bind.

So, I started by writing a little short story, about a female protagonist I named Melanie. I was very subtle. It was about having to change trains at Bank-Monument underground station on her way to a Nomadic Tribe show in east London. A simple, vapour-thin plot, right? That was my speciality. Bank-Monument station is routinely voted the most hated in London, and it's not hard to understand why, but more interesting to me are the stories that have always surrounded it, the fact that it operates as a London-commuter version of the Bermuda Triangle. Did you hear the story of the Belgian tourist changing platforms who never came out again, lost among the worming maze of tunnels connecting the two stations, who now wanders for all eternity with a A-Z in his hands and looking around confused? Or the yummy mummy who disappeared into what is described as a 'wormhole' trying to get to the District Line, her outraged protestations of 'Can you move up the carriage please?!' and 'This is bloody well not on' heard distantly in the tunnels at night? On it goes, deeper and darker: there's the ghost of a murdered nun that haunts the Bank of England and is sometimes sighted in the tunnels, Blitz victims who died in fiery torment, the many suicides, the giant segmented worm spotted by track workers in the tunnels about two hundred metres from the platform at Bank, dismissed later after it was discovered they'd been smoking weed before starting the job. A dodgy, trippy strain, apparently.

Three times the capacity of Wembley Stadium pass through that station each day. How could there not be stories to be mined from the place?

My story, for issue six of *Magnesium Burns,* was inspired by the stories of the station, and I titled it *A Monument to Nothing.* It was the first time I had the inkling of this thing I would later call the commare, this sick goddess of London. I sensed her more as a presence in those days, a useful embodiment of the female-focused ideas I was groping blindly towards, and I didn't have a name for her back then.

A Monument to Nothing

Melissa Eider

[first self-published in 2001 in *Magnesium Burns #6*; reprinted 2019 in *Magnesium Burns: Two Decades in the Underground Capital 1999-2019*, Positive Press, 2019]

The interchange between Bank and Monument underground stations is interminable; what was noted on the 1985 tube map as an escalator is, in fact, one endless connecting tunnel, dimly lit, often packed with unhappy commuters and bemused tourists and the lonely ghosts of the city. The occasional beggar, a few pickpockets. Today is the first day of the weekend and the tunnels that worm beneath the streets are quieter, gloomy, filled with strange echoes and the shuffles of unwilling feet, whispers of things that once occurred in the darkness. This is where Melanie, twenty-one years old and a native of the northern suburbs of the city, finds herself. This is where she will find herself.

It is Saturday, early evening, and Melanie travels alone, en route to meet friends in a dirty but charming pub in Mile End to see the live music they all thrill to. The pub has fabricated associations with East End gangsters, like all those pubs do; maybe the Krays did drink there once, and Melanie and her friends wish to believe so. They are young, after all. Death still seems glamorous.

She is heading to see the Nomadic Tribe, to catch up with friends and acquaintances and perhaps further things with a young man who has been circling her these past few weeks. The mutual attraction is tacitly understood, acknowledged by all of the group. Melanie is the one with the decision making in this situation, not him, and she wonders why this may be. She feels powerless in so many other ways.

Why does she travel alone? Come on, it's the dawn of the twenty-first century, it's nothing special, there's no reason at all really. Melanie just had a few errands to run in the centre of the city, a bit of shopping and a new plastic case for her Nokia, a cheap cigarette smoked beneath Centrepoint, then a nosy in the shops on Denmark Street, noting what shows are coming up at the 12 Bar. Then it's onto the Central Line at Tottenham Court Road, change at Bank to Monument, then get the shitty shuddering District into the east. Melanie likes traversing the city alone; she's a woman who hates waiting for her friends and having to adjust to the pace of others. It's self-centred, she knows that, but better to be honest about it right? As she boards her carriage, she hears a woman, a city derelict probably on the game, muttering, 'You're selfish you sell fish you are selfish.' An everyday nutter who looks sixty but is probably half that age. Crack or skag, most likely.

The woman's face looks like half of it has caved in. The gear, a pimp's fists, too long weathering on the winter streets, a battering from a punter. Melanie gives an internal shrug. It's sad, but what is she going to do about it?

For a young woman in London in the year 2001, when you'd hope life had progressed a little, she still has to be alert. Careful. Melanie takes the leers and suggestive glances from the men of the city as a price she pays for the freedom she understands herself to have – by the standards of generations that went before her, it's not saying much, and this angers her – and today she knows she gets many looks but also generates a little bit of fear and misunderstanding and this suits her just fine. Her right arm is black and blue with fresh needle ink, her black boots are on and firmly laced, her hair is dyed an inappropriately bright colour. She thinks, bless her naïvete, that this is a form of rebellion. But Melanie knows her look will put some off, invite attraction from others, and hostility from others still. She was spat at once, near Mornington Crescent station. Whatever; she looks fucking great and they all know it. People hate what they desire, right?

And she needn't have worried. The tunnels, as she navigates her way in the gloom towards Monument, are deserted. She thinks she can hear the skittering of rats, or those tiny black London mice, or some other monstrous rodents adapted to a life in the pollution and stink of the city. She ponders whether larger rodents have larger fleas, the parasite scaling up with the host. Like in the Michael Rosen story; Mel liked that one as a kid. Chitinous, blood-hungry things clogging up the Bakerloo Line. She allows herself a flight of fancy, giving these giant rats a leader, a queen.

Where is everyone? Ah, of course: there are no bankers or suits out and about today, that must be it. They're all at home in the home counties, spending the day with the wives they cheat on, the children they rarely see. She pictures these men tending a barbecue in a clipped green garden in an exclusive hamlet outside of Guildford. Not that she's ever been to Guildford. A jug of cold Pimms with condensation beading on the outside of the glass, clear and crisp white wine bought from Waitrose, high-end nibbles. On some level, she knows she's being unfair.

Melanie looks around again. Seriously, where is everyone? This can't be right. There is no one in the tunnel but herself, a tunnel that reminds her of the segments of a worm, as if she were inside the hollowed-out body of a nematode. The tunnel is plastered with adverts for recent pop albums, new Hollymood movies and skinny models hanging ash-grey jeans from bony waists. Keep going, of course you're going to come to the platform, she says to herself, and anyway she has loads of time. The band won't be on until about eight, she just wants to hit the pub early and shoot the shit with her mates and get a few drinks down her.

But hours pass and she wanders the tunnels feeling a distant sort of panic; this can't be happening and yet, well, clearly it is. Her boots are now starting to hurt her feet –

they're new and they cut rather than cushion the flesh – and she is thirsty, parched. She can feel her skin cracking as it dries, her throat is sandpaper and sand and ash and dust. She considers the possibility that has she has stumbled into a kind of limbo, a between place, and she tries to trick her own sense of direction, take a different side-exit this time even though it feels like the one she just used.

It works, to a degree. She finds herself on an abandoned platform. She has heard about the lost stations of London, the derelict and the disused and the redundant. Along the platform, standing in front of adverts from the 1960s for a women's perfume, stands a flickering female form who beckons to her. This woman is lithe and voluptuous, vampish and impish and buxom and Rubenesque, she is waif-like, a hag, a witch, a scrubber, slag, skank, a slut. She is gorgeous and repellent. What attentions does she endure on the night bus, thinks Melanie. What have men murmured to her? Has she been spat at near Mornington Crescent?

There is a man also on the platform, further away from the flickering woman. Melanie hears him muttering in Flemish, his sweaty face buried deep in a London A-Z. He doesn't notice her.

The flickering woman stretches her left arm vertically above and points her finger, indicating the streets and life and city above. Melanie considers the Monument somewhere far above her, on the intersection of Fish Hill Street and Monument Street, and she is filled with a knowledge of the tragedies that surround her; she is flooded like Canning Town in the year of the North Sea Flood. The suicides from the gallery: bakers, Jewish diamond merchants, a fifteen-year-old boy all had to die before the Londoners of the Victorian age installed an iron cage. The fifty-six people burnt, destroyed, killed by the bomb that fell on Bank station, January eleventh, 1941. The fire of London, that failed in its job to rid the earth of this festering city, breaking out on Pudding Lane. Didn't they hang a Frenchman for that?

Melanie smiles thinking of the phallic commemoration to flame, sticking into the sky as commuters rush past like mice, ants, worms, rats. It is a monument to nothing, because the suicides, the Blitz victims, the crisped and charcoaled bodies are not dead, nothing ever dies and everything is *right now* and always has been. She hears in the distance rough cacophonous music, abrasive and scorched, dissonant.

Melanie will never reach Mile End, but she will not be without company. The flickering woman who stands on the dead platform will lead her out of here, in time, will help her pass under the monument and on to somewhere better.

The Commare

I read *A Monument to Nothing* now and see how unfair, how harsh I was about certain things. My obvious and cliched hatred of the city workers and the 'suits'. How radical and punk rock of me. Bleugh. The slapdash infodump of little bits of London lore without any proper explanation. I think I'd just got into Machen at the time. Does the title even make sense? Well, it sounded snappy and like it could mean something, and that gets you a long way in the creative industries. People often don't have the courage to say they don't understand something; nonsense goes unchallenged.

My depiction of the woman I would come to know as the commare stands up when I read back through the story; I am happy with that. I could have expanded on the concept, I'll admit. But I would do that later. I think I'll read the story at the opening night at TeXt as it highlights a few key themes that run through my work. I like live reading, and I think I'm pretty good at it.

Recently I have been reading a British Library edition of old ghost stories; I picked up a few in the shop after a morning of working on *You're Already Dead*. That's the title I went with in the end.

The edition that most caught my eye was one called *The Platform Edge: Uncanny Tales of the Railways*. Not all London stories sadly, but it made me think fondly of Melanie and what happened to her. Is she still down there, trapped between Bank and Monument? The odd sense that I'd condemned an image of myself to wander eternal in the twilight of the London tunnels. There's an intriguing idea posited in one of the stories in the anthology: the subway system in New York as a Mobius strip. Fuck, I wish I'd had that idea back then. It's perfect.

It was strange, reading back over the story, how accurate my imagined version of the commare had been. When I saw her for the first time, I was approaching my twenty-fifth birthday. I was with Cerise. The writer in me, the lover of the lore of London Incognita, would have hoped for the commare's entry to be grand and dramatic, appearing at the perfect moment, but no. That is not really her, or London's, style.

Cerise and I had taken a trip to Wood Green shopping centre; I had to buy a new bra. It's as exciting as that. Around this time, a desiccated and skeletal body that once was a woman had been found in her flat in Sky City, above the shopping centre. It is a famous story of the city, of loneliness and how we can disappear in plain sight: the television on for three years, Christmas presents she'd wrapped but had never delivered scattered around her, the heating still running, half the rent still being paid by housing benefit and druggies hanging around the flats all the time so no one questioned the noise. Don't get involved, it's not worth it. It took years for the bailiffs to finally bother to batter down the door. I still wonder what the reaction of those men was, what they felt and how they processed it; I had tinkered with the idea for a story for a number of years, a narrative of a bullish and alpha London bailiff, hench from the gym and with failed aspirations to join the Metropolitan Police force, being confronted with grim mortality like this. Did the image of the skeleton on the sofa come back to him at night, as he drove his car to Sainsbury's and sat briefly alone in the desolate carpark, staring into the blackness; as he bounced his young daughter on his knee and imagined her future; as he waited for the traffic lights to change on the North Circular at two in the morning on a wet Wednesday in November? Did he think she was pathetic, that she'd brought it on herself somehow?

Really, I should write the story. The story of the Sky City skeleton should have let me know that the commare was not the salvation of the women of London. There was a documentary about the whole sad story made later, in 2011, with that Hackney girl playing the role. Sad times, yeah, but the film made me perversely nostalgic for a late-eighties and nineties London I never really experienced as an adult. The seeming impossibility of anyone ever existing in a historical moment was drilled into me. We're all history and you're already dead.

Wood Green is a place I enjoy for its rough and dirty life, with very little green and no woods unless you walk up the hill into Alexandra Park. The packed pavements and the honks of cars and vans and lorries. Shouts and curses. Laughter and high-pitched screams. Skeletal bagheads asking for change.

The roadmen gathering outside the Nag's Head for a fight after closing time. Irish karaoke nights at Monaghans.

The shopping centre that day was heaving, teens hanging around in groups and chattering shrilly, mums pushing their buggies laden with bags and shrieking infants, serious men in cheap shiny suits bellowing into mobile phones.

'Why the hell are we here?' Cerise asked with a sigh, and I laughed, as I browsed the underwear in M&S. It was then, standing among the racked clothes, that I saw the commare, as she was in my story, a flickering form that changed from idealised feminine beauty, a boring dyed-blonde bimbo, an Aphrodite emerging from a shell, then to a slattern, a hook-nosed Baba Yaga, a lank Jenny Greenteeth with tendrilled locks, a nervous young punk girl with shaved and dyed hair, a pierced scrap-metal face and heavy boots. Her skin changed tones at high speed, like a flamboyant cuttlefish fluttering in a tank beneath Forest Hill. She, or it, watched Cerise and I with a passionless interest, and I held her eye for a while. The commare remained motionless.

Cerise, it turned out, had seen her too. Or some version of her, at least.

'See that weird old bat looking at us? Bag lady, stinking of piss.'

'Yeah,' I said and sort of shrugged with my eyes as I looked at my friend, as if to say *What are you gonna do?*

'Do you ever get sick of the psychos in this city?' Cerise seemed weary.

Everyday nutters. Flotsam of the streets. The beggars and junkies and crack-thin women probably on the game. Broken teeth and bruises blooming purple.

I shrugged. What *are* you going to do?

When I looked back, the commare had vanished.

I really do regret what I wrote in *A Monument to Nothing* about the city boys. I'm sure some of them love their wives, you know. They can't all be philandering cokeheads. Sorry about that, lads; forgive the posturing of a young punk rock girl.

Where We Reunite Briefly As One, and Live the Past as if It Were the Present

The Dome in Tufnell Park is heaving tonight. A sold-out show. I've bumped into so many old faces and people from way back when and it's fucking great to see them all. I am alive with the blood flowing hot through my veins; there's a sense of occasion in the air. Hugs and smiles and many a *hello mate, bloody hell it's been a while!* followed by slaps on the shoulder and back. Hands gripped together. People from the old days, here, right here in the here and now. Where have we all been? Tonight, we're resurfacing.

There's PK and Roberta and Hank, Jess, Adrianna and Simon. Canadian Dave is wearing an atrocious and offensive grindcore T-shirt in a near-indecipherable font. *Exhumed Abortion*, this time. John Whitefield, a mate of Simon's, is here too, a nice bloke judging from the few times I've met him. And the lad who's name I never seem to catch, with the cropped skull with a haunted look and melancholy air that always seems to land him a younger girlfriend. He told me this story once about this monster thing in the Black Forest in Germany and his dad one time, at about six in the morning, when we were all smashed on amphetamines. This was years back, after a Hard Skin show at The Stockwell Arms down south. The story stuck with me. It was probably bullshit drug talk, of course, but he could adroitly spin a tale and I liked that. Sometimes that's all that matters.

It's unspoken for now, but we all feel Cerise's absence. It's like someone has taken a pair of cheap children's scissors and cut her out of the picture, the ragged cuts and tears still visible for all of us to see. She is a page ripped from an ancient and irreplaceable book. She is a wound I never want to heal. I will never stop picking at it.

I look at PK, chatting with Jess and Adrianna, sipping from a bottle of Becks Blue, and despite his unbearable proclamations about the world, he's staying sober and that must be hard.

Staying clear-headed in this mess of a world. I couldn't do it myself. But I never went to that dark place, down deep into that lightless hole, that PK went to. But this is the important bit: I understand why he did, and I understand how it happens. I don't judge him, much.

Here at The Dome, celebrating Scarp's reunion, PK's in a place and an environment that facilitates and encourages the drink, be it bought from the overpriced bar or smuggled in in a hipflask, or sucked greedily from a tin from the offy over the road, sat on a chipped brick wall. No doubt there's someone selling grams of cheap speed here too, those irresistible ten pound bags, usually from one of those rat-haired little crusties with a silly nickname. There is always someone. In London a dealer is only a text away, they come to you like fucking Deliveroo. So fair play to PK. And despite his sour attitude to a lot of modern life, he's right, that *Keep Going* album *is* utter dogshit. I gave it a spin on Spotify out of morbid curiosity and it didn't go well.

This, here, where we are in Tufnell Park, is music. This is what it's all about. This is the stuff that helps us keep going, keeps us afloat on this dark ocean.

Unhappy recollections hit me now, of Cerise trying to help PK out again and again. I take a swig of cider and try and ward off the memories as I take a look at the merch. New ethical Scarp shirts, being sold on the No Sweat stall, looking pretty tasty. The image is a line drawing of a tosher sifting through the muck of London in the Victorian sewers, one of my brother's big interests. Mine too, actually. I'll pick one up after the show, I could cadge a freebie of course but it's for a good cause. There are badges and pins and limited seven inches at the distro that take my eye; this is something I'll never grow out of.

But the images still come to me like a moth driven mad by light, banging repeatedly into the window of a north London newbuild. The puke and the piss and the sketchy Italian crusties PK squatted with in that massive house in Stamford Hill. His dark days. The old Jewish lady who owned the place seemed to let them get on with it, which always baffled me. I never found out what the full deal was there. I can still smell the stench of that place, the unwashed sheets and the dog piss and piles of shite, a physical force that hit Cerise and I in the face when we stepped over the threshold. Like you could chew the air.

We were checking if her brother was alright, when we knew he wasn't. Of course he wasn't, but the human capacity to try to believe things are okay in the face of evidence is a strong and burning one. PK was living in the basement of the house, in a pit that smelled of black mould and pungent weed and old cigarettes. Tatty cushions and an ochre throw tossed over a sofa that was bleeding foam.

I remember passing the kitchen on our way down there, that I imagined as descent into the bleak underworld of London peopled by rat queens and toshers and emperor worms, and seeing this horseshoe of young men, all of them smacked out of their heads, spread around the kitchen table. Ratty dreads, filthy jackets, patched green shorts with unidentifiable stains – could be blood or spunk or encrusted vegan stew. Mud spattered combat boots. The smell of dogshit, from the ratty little thing that was whining and shivering in the corner unattended. Not one of them was moving or registering each other.

What a way to fight the system, lads. It was so fucking sad.

In PK's room, we had a chat with him and listened to a bit of music – Etiäinen, one of PK's favourites – and tried to pretend things were normal and okay when they so obviously were not.

I remember Cerise getting teary in the Royal Sovereign afterwards. Maybe drinking wasn't the best way through it, but we needed a pint and a few vodka and oranges after that experience. I can still smell the place. The sweat and the cheap drugs and the unwashed plates.

Bad memories. Memories of the city, my city, the city we chose to live in when we could have become standard nine-to-fivers hating the commute to the hated job we were grateful to have and terrified of losing. I see them now as memories of London Incognita too, all this stuff going on below, or behind, the official story. It's a dark city, and always has been.

I need a smoke, so I dip outside. My phone buzzes, it's a message from Debbie, bless her, saying she's on her way. This is not really her scene, but I couldn't really tell her not to come, could I? Maybe she'll enjoy it, and I hope she does, I'm just desperate to dodge the inevitable Instagram picture. She'll probably be a hit with some of the young, and not-so-young, men here, the dirty bastards.

My brother is outside too, here with Jed, Scarps' bass player, and a few hangers on. I recognise the young lad who wrote a recent *Quietus* piece about the band, comically hovering around them not quite knowing what to say and gripping his beer bottle too hard. He's wearing a Shellac T-shirt.

I go over to them.

'Easy sis,' says Andy. I light my cigarette with his lighter that he hands to me and absent-mindedly put it in my pocket.

'When I get to heaven, I'll get all my lighters back,' he says, and I pass it back to him, sticking my tongue out. But it's all good vibes. His hangers on laugh on cue.

Happier memories now. Exploring London with my brother, trying to spot the peregrine falcons perched at the very top of the Tate Modern on the South Bank; posed photos at the Hardy Tree in the cemetery near St Pancras that ended up in an issue of *Magnesium Burns*; a supermarket sandwich eaten in the Blitzed ruins of St. Dunstan-in-the-East as a light drizzle came in off the river. Exploring the polluted, less walked reaches of the Lee Navigation where it passes under the North Circular, and on towards Ponders End to find the flat where the Enfield poltergeist took residence.

The back-and-forthing of ideas, going through all the books and old songs we could find for inspiration. We took our patchwork inspiration equally from late seventies London Oi! anthems, the *Doctor Who* shop near Upton Park, the novels of Derek Raymond, Maureen Duffy, Doris Lessing, Alexander Baron and Henry Green, our rummaged stories of the toshers and grubbers in the sewers, Machen's London adventure, the DIY scene we grew up with and helped define. For a while they called it the landscape punk scene, and yeah, it's a crucial part of London Incognita.

All of this never gave us a living, but it gave us a life.

I smoke my cigarette and chat out there on the pavement and even have a cheeky tin of Tyskie that Jed sneaks to me, in timeless DIY scene style. Support your local scene – after you've necked a few drinks outside first – have you seen the prices at the bar? I'm feeling that mild thrill of being in the inner circle for a little bit. How smug; but I'm going to enjoy it. Like, I know that people milling around us *know* who my brother is, and they know who I am. Amongst a group of about a thousand people worldwide, we're famous. Ridiculous, isn't it?

Debbie arrives – I see her hopping off the number 4 bus like an excited wallaby, spotting me and waving – and gives me an awkward hug. She's tried to make herself look a little bit more sceney tonight, going in hard on that look that was popular in the early noughties. Charcoal jeans rolled up, a pair of black DMs. All she's missing is the little black flesh tubes. But, oh God, she's wearing a Scarp T-shirt under her black jacket. She's wearing the T-shirt of the band who are playing tonight. Fuck me. She really is clueless.

'Andy, this is Debbie. She's helping me set up the exhibition.'

'Ah, Debbie my darling, great to meet you finally. Mel sings your praises.' Andy is accentuating his north London accent here; I'm surprised he didn't call her 'treacle', and what's worse, she would have loved it.

'It's *great* to meet you too. I feel like I already know you from being with Mel and reading *Magnesium Burns* and putting the exhibition together.'

'Don't believe a word she says; it's not worth the paper it's written on.' He winks and Debbie blushes. 'Nice T-shirt,' he adds.

'Oh this? Well I've been listening to your stuff and I just thought I had to get one.' Debbie has gone beetroot.

I roll my eyes.

My brother's band are definitely one of those whose fanbase picked up and grew and multiplied in the years after their dissolution, like it was super-cool to know about them and even cooler to have seen them play, a sense that by knowing about them you were tapping into the patchily documented and true lifeblood of Britain's cultural underground. There is an undeniable appeal to that. I think his association with *Magnesium Burns* helped, and my association with Scarp helped me in reciprocal fashion. It helped, too, that they are simply a good fucking band.

An interview on the Noisey website last year only helped this, one of those 'rank your records' pieces, then a gushing commemorative anniversary piece in *The Quietus* written by the eager young man in the Shellac shirt hovering around Andy, who seems like he only discovered post-hardcore last year. I wonder if he knows about Fugazi in Wood Green. That piece was about the reissue of Scarp's second album *Your Degenerate Architect*. The article was accompanied by a photo of Andy looking moody in front of Balfron Tower, hands dug deep into the pockets of his Harrington.

You pretentious prick ;) I texted him, with a screenshot of the picture.

Whatever m8. Says the artist and the writer with the upcoming exhibit, she thinks she's Kathy Acker? Winky face and an emoji of an aubergine and some water droplets. I think my brother was calling me a dick. Or a wanker?

He can piss off. I love Kathy Acker.

Obviously, because of this exposure, some of the more zealous DIY elements of the UK scene sneeringly called him a sell-out sucking up to the hipster press, and told odd anecdotes about him secretly eating meat in 2002 when he claimed he was vegan. I now can't get out of my head this image of my brother secretly scoffing down a pork pie in the toilets of the Cowley Club in Brighton before a Scarp show.

I often think about whether Gary would have been into all of this stuff. I suspect, I hope, he would. For me it's all part of the myth and the lore of London Incognita and I'm still trying to explain why, though I've been attempting that for twenty years now. I loved the idea that a city was this living breathing entity, a gestalt or many gestalts and the number of stories you could dig out of a city like London was mind-boggling.

'Shall we go in?' No one seems to hear me.

Debbie seems a little starstruck being around Andy and Jed and me. I introduce her to PK, and we smoke another cigarette. She asks if she can have a rollie, and I hand her the packet but it becomes clear she can't roll, so I do it for her feeling like a particularly irresponsible mother. Andy leans in and lights it for her, and she blushes. He'd better not be trying it on, the cheeky bastard.

Debbie holds her cigarette at an odd angle, sucks too hard, coughs.

'Debbie, do you smoke?' I ask.

'Not really,' she sputters. 'Only socially like this.'

My brother and I share a look, as if to say: young people.

A few pints later and the opening support acts have finished. They were decent, but tonight is not about them, and the crowd has swollen and buzzes with anticipation. I've secured a good position near the front of the crowd, but to the right of the stage as I don't fancy getting a boot in the face from a moronic crowdsurfer.

Scarp come on stage, to ragged cheers.

Andy introduces them simply with, 'Hi, we're Scarp from north London,' before they launch straight into 'Bilocation'.

The crowd erupts and Debbie, jittery and excited and unused to punk shows, upends half a pint of cider over me as the crowd spasms around her.

In many ways, it's exactly like the old days.

WALK 2: TOTTENHAM HALE TO MILLFIELDS

I am meeting Debbie at Tottenham Hale station. She's wanted to accompany me on a walk for a while now, to get a feel for the work and the exhibition. She says she wants to explore more of London, there's so much of it she doesn't know. You have to really make the time to get out on foot, don't you? I was at the Body Works exhibition in Piccadilly – it was explaining the importance of motion and movement and the beneficial effects to circulation and emotional wellbeing. It's hard to start but once you get moving it's easy to keep drifting for hours. These are the things she says. I hope today can meet her expectations.

I wait for her near the entrance of the station, listening to the new Petrol Girls album, scrolling through my social media on my phone. The usual bullshit, but also some nice feedback and excitement for the upcoming exhibition; there are some positives to engaging.

I wave away a woman in a headscarf, a Romany I think, asking me for change. I watch two junkies with pockmarked faces squabble by the bins. Holiday makers dragging heavy suitcases trundle past me, heading to the Stansted Express; I never understood why people left London while it was hot, but people must have their reasons.

I see a billboard poster for *Keep Going*, a mindfulness app, and an orangutan listening to an audiobook. Modern life. The sun is remorseless, pulsing like a boil fit to erupt.

I consider the point of the TeXt exhibition, as I wait for Debbie's face to appear out of the steady stream of people emerging into the light from the depths below. I'm trapped in an endless discourse, held in London beer gardens, on the Suffolk coast, among ruined churches in Kent, in a friend's house in Hastings. A conversation trying to tackle the question of London Incognita. It's an impossibility, and I have no answers, but I hope I can pose new questions.

I hate the people writing opinion pieces on why they're leaving the capital – they're so unbearably smug, like an ex-smoker or a new convert to veganism. I'm jealous of everyone who does manage to leave. I'm terrified by the thought of leaving, and sick at the thought of staying. When will I be done with all of this? uPVC nightmares and Lego-block newbuilds climbing into the skyline and I feel the urge to just hit the canal towpath and keep running and running until I escape the city, only to be crippled by questions of would I be bored? And what would I do? Even my worries are prosaic and clichéd and shared by hundreds of thousands of other Londoners.

The problem is, I love the city. Always have done. My London Incognita. The city I love is inefficient, weird, overgrown, ripe for development, a place whose creases are being ironed out. This is a common argument, a point made many times before. What else is there to say? I've thought of leaving and I've thought of staying and so far, I am still here. And today Debbie and I are going for a walk. That is all that matters.

It takes time to dig into an area, even a small patch, to get to know it in any meaningful way. The best parts of London are the ones I never went looking for, the ones that just slowly made their presences felt. In the city, I still believe in the opportunity for the unexpected. There is still an element of chance, if you allow it. The route Debbie and I will take today is familiar to me, but new to her, and perhaps I can see the place anew through her eyes.

Finally, I spot her exiting the station and I wave. She sees me and smiles.

'Hi Mel, sorry I'm late,' she says breathlessly, giving me a hug, her canvas tote bag swinging wildly.

'No worries.' She's only five minutes late, and everyone is late here.

We start walking and chatting, cutting through the retail park opposite the station with its usual array of chain stores, a giant Staples, a Boots, a Burger King. Dull places where people spend huge parts of their lives. There must be stories in those experiences, in these places. I imagine the shadows and impressions left by the transient staff floating through these places. Non-people in non-places? No. People always have a story.

Exiting the retail park, we take a turn onto Markfield Road past the dodgy Irish pub where you can still see the bar staff cashing cheques for men in dusty overalls. Warehouses along this road are converted into artistic spaces, a boutique café whose outdoor seating spills out onto an uneven car park; diners dine in sight of rubbish trucks. We pass a speciality ice-cream-van repair garage, a noisy and chaotic waste disposal yard with lorries thundering constantly down the narrow road, a kosher-foods importer and numerous studios, units and warehouses whose functions remain opaque. This is a dirty and working piece of London and I like it for that, alongside the tendrils of gentrification – as always, some of it is welcome, decent, and some of it is absurd. There's always an odd, sweet smell of rubbish and decay here and I see Debbie wrinkling her nose.

'Odd, isn't it,' I say, laughing.

'Stinks,' she says, but she seems happy.

On Markfield Road is a brown and white sign directing the curious in the direction of pieces of cultural history. The Markfield Beam Engine.

'It sounds like something out of *Star Trek*,' says Debbie.

We follow the sign, passing crashing lorries and churning piles of rubbish in the waste disposal yard.

A man in a yellowing apron smeared with indefinable filth watches us from the shadow of a wooden doorway, surrounded by cigarette smoke.

At the end of the road we duck under a heavily graffitied railway bridge into a space entirely at odds to where we have just been. Markfield Park opens up in front of us. Ridges and clumps of concrete are colonised by wild grasses and flowers, smothered in graffiti. We feel as if we stand in the defaced fragments of a Neolithic civilisation. Two crusties sit on the painted concrete swigging from a cheap plastic bottle of cider.

Trees and picnic benches present a vivid contrast to the city's grime mere metres away. Debbie runs up to the metal silhouette of a cow, festooned with a bag of crumpled cider cans, standing atop a small mound.

This park is another one of the city's green spaces, used by local schools for their sports, home to a small café and a museum dedicated to the Beam Engine: 'A Masterpiece of Victorian Engineering.' How I would love to explore the imagined territories of Victorian London, the city of *From Hell* and Sherlock and sewer pigs and Spring Heel Jack. But I know it is only a fantasy. People go under chasing the impossible.

I wait while Debbie takes a few photos of the cow on her phone, no doubt soon to end up on Instagram.

'This is great here, I never even knew this park existed,' she says softly.

There's so much in the world we will never see. So much of London Incognita I will never know. I could walk its streets non-stop for eternity and I'd still never know it.

I tell her the ruined and grassy concrete was once the walls of settlement tanks and filter beds. This was the site of the Tottenham sewage works, in operation for a century, until 1964. I wonder if the crusties, drunk in the heat, know this.

I look at the tasteful café and the Grade II listed Engine House, cleaner and more striking than any of the working areas that surround it; it's hard to think of shit and sewage.

We decide to nip into in the café; there is a small exhibition dedicated to a punk history of Woodberry Down, commemorating the squatters of the past. Maybe it's what the two cider drinkers have been here for.

This exhibition brings together prints, illustrations, photographs and text created by a diaspora of squatters on the Woodberry Down Estate, near Manor House, in the eighties and nineties. This show was conceived in response to the estate's current redevelopment, which recognises only consenting voices in its gentrification process.

Daniel Eider saw the judderman peel itself from the shadows of Woodberry Down, didn't he?

The exhibition raises the question of London Incognita again. The politics of existence follow me around wherever I go. I don't consider myself a consenting voice, but I get tired of the questions, and sometimes just want to be left alone. Once I would have got annoyed that a piece of underground history was being displayed in one of London's new-breed cafés. But I'm doing the exact same thing myself, down in Peckham. Now I just look at the pictures and read the accompanying text and nod or shake my head. Debbie finds it interesting. It's relevant to what we'll be doing at TeXt after all, and the whole *Magnesium Burns* project is about exploring the voices of people who don't quite fit with the consenting narrative. I buy a cold bottle of water in the café before leaving.

The park's eastern boundary is the Lee Navigation. Friends of mine, recently returned from Australia, have taken to the waterways and now spend half of every month moored nearby at Tottenham Lock. On my first visit, rocking gently on the water and drinking cider, I realised how close the navigation is to Tottenham Hale station, the always-surprising juxtaposition between the shabby greenery and birdlife of the waterways with the grey concrete and depressing aspects of the retail park and heaving traffic. I see the appeal of boat-living. But now, even the waterways are clogging up with people who aren't willing or able to pay the rents but who can't bear to leave. There are stories of bad things in the water, grasping hands that will drag down the unwary or the miserable, crocodiles that take down Canada geese. PK lived on a boat for a while. A young woman suffering from depression drowned herself at Tottenham Lock.

We drift through Markfield Park like fleeting spirits of summer, passing screaming schoolboys kicking balls, picnickers and beer drinkers, a half-naked couple in a passionate embrace in a patch of shade.

'Shameless,' says Debbie, and seems almost genuinely affronted.

'We should be so lucky, Deb,' I say, and she blushes.

We step onto the navigation. The water is alive with life: large congregations of mute swans, families of Canada geese, reptilian herons standing motionless like the commare in the reeds. The oily water is clogged with the city's waste. Clouds of swifts are screaming and darting and catching insects by the mouthful when we reach the reservoirs that lie the other side of the water, opposite the park. I think of the swifts' journey, thousands of miles travelled, their useless feet, the pinpoint precision. The swifts are declining, dying out. Something still alive, depleted in the present reminding me hard of the past.

This walk is an essential reminder of what the city can be. Never one thing, always many.

I say, 'Another time we should visit the Walthamstow Wetlands. I can show you the tree of cormorants.'

Debbie says okay, and she doesn't ask what I'm going on about.

London never was like it was. I think hard about my own role in how all of this is changing. I am reluctantly part of the force that is changing Tottenham, and I'm a local. I have no answer to the question of London, of whether to stay or to go, or even if it's worth talking about anymore.

We drift along the water, flanking the Warwick Reservoir until we reach the café opposite the Springfield Marina. Debbie takes a photo of the amassed boats bobbing gently, sunlight glinting on the water.

Debbie and I have been chatting about the exhibition as we walk, going through all kinds of ideas for the launch event. We've decided on the following format:

Debbie will introduce the event, then I will talk for a while about the whole project, followed by a reading from *Magnesium Burns* – I'll be reading the new piece, *You're Already Dead* – and we've also got my brother along to do a few Scarp songs, acoustic. Debbie knows now about Gary and Daniel, the judderman story they clung to, the dark stories of a London long-gone and distantly past.

Then she asks me a question, one I think she's wanted to ask for a while.

'Melissa, this thing you write about, the commare? What actually is it?'

With the sunlight darting on the waters of the Lee Navigation and dying swifts soaring above us, it feels like a good time to talk. To try and explain a few things.

'Okay. You know about the judderman? The thing that Gary and Daniel, my cousins, seemed to believe in. I don't get bogged down in worrying about whether it was really, physically, real or not. And you understand the idea that negative energies of a place, the bad memories of events that took place in the shadows, can manifest somehow, that they can take on a life of their own. I think the commare is that; I think she is the same thing, in essence, as the judderman.

'Gary and Daniel were men, and they saw something male, could only imagine the sickness as masculine – the stories of child abuse, the brute force of police violence, the National Front, the war in Northern Ireland. They saw all of that as a male sickness. I suppose they had that toxic maleness in them, weirdos that they were by the standards of the time. It was a male world back then. One of them might have been homosexual. But I don't know if they ever considered the experience of the women of London. I don't think they did. But I do think about it, a lot. You do too, Debbie.'

She nods gently. A flock of green parakeets scream overhead.

I keep talking, flowing now like the river that passes by us on its way to the Thames. 'So I see the commare as a different facet of the same thing. She – or it – is something I like to imagine as the pain and sadness and suffering of the city, of London. To me she's, like, the indifferent goddess of London Incognita, and I think she works as a symbol, a metaphor or an allegory, or whatever you want really. She's as real as she needs to be.

'I think I have seen her, sometimes. Most likely my imagination getting away from me, I know. Once, and it sounds so silly, I was in Wood Green shopping centre with Cerise, and I swear I saw her. This thing I call the commare. Dumb, I know. I was shopping for a bra.'

Debbie seems to wince, or deflate slightly, at the mention of Cerise's name. 'I don't think it's dumb,' she says, 'it makes perfect sense to me.'

I'm a torrent now. 'And I just thought of something that could represent all of the unloved women, the ones battered and killed by their partners, the ones ignored and belittled and just not taken seriously, the women you see on the streets with the caved-in faces and all those tiny silent little girls whose home lives don't bear thinking about, the women left bereft and alone, the doddery old dears living decades after their husbands have snuffed it, all of us who have been catcalled and touched up and put in situations we never should have been in… Christ. Sorry, Debbie. That's the gist of it at least. Fucking hell, I need a cig.'

And I roll a cigarette for myself and one for Debbie and we sit on a bench in Springfield Park in the dappled shade of the trees talking more about the dark underbelly of the city and the uncomfortable truths we all try to brush away. Dirty secrets hidden in recesses. Bad things folded up and placed in locked drawers.

Debbie suggests the English reputation for stiff upper lips and the dignity of not airing dirty laundry in public was in fact a control mechanism, a way to stop people talking about the things that needed to be talked about. I agree with her.

'I think you're onto something there,' I say.

'But there has to be some hope, right? It's not all bad is it?' she asks, dragging on her roll up and coughing softly.

'Of course there is. This is life, right? Good and bad.' I spread my arms wide to encompass all of the park, the whole stretch of the Lee Navigation, the city entire.

She smiles.

Cigarettes spent, we walk further along the navigation, passing clusters of flats that cling to the riverside. There is an expanse of marsh opposite, a place where builders dug into Blitz rubble during the 2012 Olympics, releasing toxic asbestos into the environment. The past is never past.

At the far end of Millfields Park, by the bridge where the Lea Bridge Road, thick with cars, dips over the river, stands a woman looking directly at us. She is motionless, melancholy, weighed down by plastic shopping bags.

'What's she looking at?' asks Debbie.

'No idea,' I say. We head into The Princess of Wales pub for a drink and a sit down. We'll get the bus home later.

The Judderman and London, as Gary and Danny Understood it in the Nineteen Seventies

It was my mother, through her investigations of the family tree and the notion that, as she aged, she had to know more about her roots, that first made me aware of my relatives Gary and Daniel and this thing called the judderman that had come to dominate the last days of their lives. Not that any bodies were ever found. They disappeared, as people do in this city. In London, we know that disappeared means dead. Missing means gone.

You have to accept this; they are dead and gone and they are not coming back. Just as the Sky City skeleton is dead and Cerise is dead and my dad is dead and the carved-up Greek girl they fished out of the hut in Finsbury Park is dead.

But I am alive, and so is PK and Debbie and Andy.

We are here.

My mum was the beneficiary of her aunt Sarah's will – the kids were dead, missing, weren't they – and so she inherited a huge number of papers and other ephemera from Sarah, who had passed away in 2013. This was Gary and Daniel's mother, my great aunt Sarah, a nice old lady from around Bounds Green near the North Circular. A horrible bit of London if you ask me, but she stuck it out there most of her long life after her sons disappeared and she moved. Bad memories in the bricks of the old house, I suppose.

I only met her a few times in my life, and she had always struck me as ancient, almost eternally old. But everything ends, in the end.

Amongst all the detritus and ephemera of a whole life were a number of items that now, as I look at them and work out how I should incorporate them into the exhibition, I cannot believe ran the risk of being chucked out and ending up in landfill for the gulls to pick over, or in charity shops for hipsters like Debbie to sift through. It's too much to think about sometimes, the amount of information and history lost to house clearances, the unloved archives that went to waste. Invaluable records chucked for practical reasons. This new generation of renters flitting from property to property every eighteen months – what will their legacies be? They are fleeting ghosts soon forgotten, austerity wraiths.

Sarah held on to these things for over forty years. Perhaps she recognised their importance or perhaps she just couldn't let go. Either way, I am glad.

Of course, I'd heard about my cousins – we'll call them that for the sake of ease – through the whispered channels of family narrative. I knew that *something* had happened, but it was one of those things never really talked about and I wasn't that close to Sarah anyway. Whispered family secrets, hints, insinuations, nothing ever talked about openly. And what was I going to do? Ask this old lady I barely knew to open up about the pain of losing her two children? As if.

The most important thing that fell into my hands was Daniel Eider's journal. Reading it was an unsettling and comforting experience. So much of it chimed with a story called 'Notes on Pulling the Sky Down' I'd written in *Magnesium Burns*. I realise now I have to integrate it into the exhibition alongside extracts from the journal.

Daniel had written in his journal, *There is London Cognita, and London Incognita, and I know where I belong*. At that moment I felt a sense of communion across the decades and generations, a physical force surging through me. It was thrilling, electrifying like a drug. I was part of a continuum.

I flicked through his sketches and the unfinished book of London Incognita. I have framed *The Chthonic Tribes of the Tunnels that Wind and Writhe Beneath our Feet* to display at TeXt.

There were boxes of photographs to sift through, most from the first half of the twentieth century, images the brothers had hunted for in the bootfairs and markets of early-seventies London. Many references to a guy called Yaxley and his shop in Ladbroke Grove. Long gone of course; it's a Café Nero now. Andy and I took a long walk there from the South Bank a few months back, trying to recreate some of Gary's journey.

I attempted to hunt down Jenny Duro, to interview, or just to talk to. I found out she had been ill for many years, and presumably took things into her own hands, her body found floating in the Thames, overdose levels of pills in her bloodstream. I wonder if she had ever seen the commare.

There was all manner of other stuff that came into my possession, too. Gary's battered Malachite Press copies of Vincent Harrier novels, including an original edition of *Your Architect is Degenerate* that was worth a lot of money that I gifted to my brother.

And a black-and-white photo of the two brothers, dated 1970. It must be winter. They are duffel-jacketed, wearing monkey boots, skinny in that way people were fifty years ago. Andrew is staring up into the sky, Gary looks into the camera quizzically. Behind them flows the Thames. They're out near Wapping I think, when the river was still, in some sense, a working place.

I imagine myself taking the photo, can picture myself on that cold day so long ago asking them to pose properly and not move while I focus. I am there.

Notes on Pulling the Sky Down

[Collected in *Magnesium Burns: Two Decades in the Underground Capital 1999-2019*, Melissa Eider, Positive Press, 2019]

David and Matthew stride across London Bridge, dark rapidly engulfing the city. They zip their jackets high, buffeted by freezing squalls coming in off the river. An ugly monument to excess dominates the skyline. The Spike is nearing completion, a cyberpunk's dying dream punching an aggressive erection into the sky. Unsubstantiated reports suggest many of the palatial flats in the upper reaches have been snapped up by Qatari royals; Masonic forces use the temple for demonic blood rites; the tower is a temple to a blood god; it is a ship ready to launch into the heavens. So claim the street-drinkers. To earn the privilege of viewing the sprawl of the city from its upper reaches there is a fee of twenty pounds. Count yourself lucky. Strange beings with lifeless eyes are seen reflected in the obsidian windows. A man of shadows peels himself from the darkness and awakens as the city sickens once more. Rumour and hearsay hang like smog round The Spike's upper reaches.

It is November. The rain is incessant and pervasive.

Japanese tourists, two parents with small children in tow, cowled in plastic fluorescent waterproofs, run past the pair, heading toward London Bridge station for shelter. David vainly and obsessively attempts to light a cigarette. Andrew buries his hands further into his pockets. They've fortified themselves with lager, sturdied themselves for the journey across the water to The Balustrade. The building – what is it? An old factory, a warehouse? – lurked in a recess in Peckham, with vague directions that it was 'next to a petrol station.' Luckily, Matthew knows the way, just about; he remembers despite the time that's slipped by and he's happy to be back in his rhythm of revelries that can last days on end.

South of the river is not their natural territory though, and they feel rudderless, but the bands playing have been enough to lure them down.

'It better be fucking worth it,' Matthew says. David nods and sucks his damp cigarette. He hates south London.

Nearing the station, Matthew looks up to see crudely daubed graffiti masking a Clear Channel billboard. The defaced advert is of an airbrushed-beautiful woman, her teeth too white, promoting an indefinable and amorphous product. Thick burgundy paint spells out: THE JUDDERMAN'S COMING

Matthew frowns, then bursts out laughing. The absurdity of it all. Life is ridiculous, a bad joke.

'What are you laughing at?' snaps David. He throws his cigarette to the pavement. Beads of water fall from his hair.

'That graffiti. Up there.' He points.

David looks up, reads. He shakes his head.

'So, what is that supposed to mean?' He sounds tired.

'Don't know. Whatever.' Matthew is chuckling to himself.

David looks at his friend. Maybe he's drunk, he reasons, but he's fraying at the edges, a bit blurry.

Bedraggled, they push through the sodden crowds into the station. Travellers clutch supermarket sandwiches and stand in mute awe of the information board, their eyes frantically scanning in search of a train out of here. They are revenants waiting for their ticket home.

All is water outside. The smell of cheese and onion pasties floats in the air as bored fluorescent policemen stand watch. Somewhere, an infant screams its lungs out with all the effort it can muster. Matthew wishes he could do the same. The floor of the station is smeared with muddy fractal swirls.

'Filth,' mutters Matthew automatically. His heart isn't in it though.

Their train is due to leave from platform fourteen in two minutes. They half-run through the barriers, pausing to swipe Oysters, cursing TFL, and make the train with thirty seconds to spare. The unshaven pair, dripping wet and stinking of stale tobacco, raise a stern eyebrow from a man in a bespoke suit, who briefly looks up from his reading of *City A.M.*

Matthew scans the inhabitants of this busy carriage. He sees a woman he kinda knows, maybe she's Italian but he can't remember. Her head is stuck in a book, something called

Mujeres Libres. He decides against saying hello here; she must be headed to The Balustrade too. As the train departs, he imagines himself and this woman, adventurers on an arcane pilgrimage, canoeing through Hungary down the Danube, beset by preternatural forces they cannot hope to understand. Stark contrast to the pissing rain, the cold concrete and smoky darkness. South London closing in around them.

The train reaches Peckham Rye and they disembark. A group of moody teenagers sit on metal benches, ignoring the No Smoking signs, smoking. They are travelling nowhere.

The Italian woman, Francesca, disembarks also, heads for the exit, not noticing Matthew. He hopes, really hopes, they share the same destination.

He looks around as David strides ahead, and sees an old man, his face disfigured, in a multi-coloured jacket who sits alone at the far end of the station.

'Come on,' says David with a sigh.

All is water.

*

Francesca curses the weather as she exits Peckham Rye. Fuck this country. She pulls up her hood, decides against lighting a cigarette. That can wait until she arrives at The Balustrade. This awful rain is cold and insidious; it gets inside you, soaks right through the skin. Few people are on the streets. An old man huddles under the railway bridge, drinking strong cheap cider; beleaguered mothers with pushchairs brave the elements as they wait for a bus that will never come. A Turkish man leans out of his shop smoking, his eyes scanning the dark skies for hidden messages.

Francesca pounds up Peckham High Road, the party's dull thump first faintly audible, then a physical presence, bass shuddering the grey pavement, rippling through her sternum and ribcage. It's a good sign.

Soaked, she reaches the venue. Shifting dark-clad figures crowd outside, swigging cheap alcohol from plastic bottles, a fug of cigarette smoke mingling with the damp mist. A pair of black dogs dance in circles round each other, snapping at each other's heels. Caught in silhouette for a moment, a man and his dog resemble a hideous centaur, before the light shifts and reality is restored.

She scans the motley crowd for familiar faces.

A slap on her right shoulder.

'Francesca!'

She turns to see that hoped-for friendly face, Sofia, her dark red hair cropped short, ear-to-ear grin. They hug, move out of the damp and into The Balustrade, pay the modest entry fee that funds endeavours unknown into a sea of people, steaming leather jackets, body heat and cigarette smoke now a welcome change from the unforgiving London weather. Off in the crowd, Francesca thinks she sees someone, rigged lights gleaming off dyed-green hair, a familiar woman. Kerry Edwards. The crowd shifts, ripples, and she's gone. Kerry has been gone a long time. She is missing. Any number of women here have dyed hair, rose tattoos. It cannot be her.

A band takes to the ramshackle stage, heavy metallic grooves and dubby rhythms played by people with glinting teeth. Francesca allows herself to relax; she's reached her destination. Her body forgives the decision to brave the freezing damp, to run the gauntlet of dancing dogs and black centaurs.

'Let's get a drink,' shouts Sofia over the din.

They move into a quieter though still crowded room, better lit and warm with body heat. They buy cans of lager, the prices only mildly inflated from what you'd pay in the offy, light cigarettes, and revel in the joy of the moment. The Balustrade, they know, cannot last.

Eviction looms. Perhaps, Francesca thinks to herself grinning, this is a *pop-up*.

In one corner of this body-warm room, a young man slips into a ketamine coma, staring inside himself. A worried looking girl, no more than eighteen, tends to him. *He'll be okay in a while*, her manner says, her eyes suggesting this isn't the first time this scenario has played out. Men smoke, drain cans of cider, swap stories and slyly eye the women around them. The room is a room of dilated pupils, insect-eyed revellers, their minds flooding with light and colour. The low-level lighting and occasional candle creates a chiaroscuro for black-clad figures to wander through. Refugees from a world gone wrong, fleeing a land of billboards and boutiques.

More cans are drained, more cigarettes smoked. The night continues, loses its elasticity, becomes fluid, running through the two women's fingers as band after band take to the stage and the crowd swells, a multi-limbed polysexual gestalt. They dance, snort powder with minor acquaintances.

Somewhere throughout the night, she loses Sofia. Thinks she sees her chatting with that guy Matthew and a friend of his, but she is too high to care. Francesca feels she's tripping and is hit with images of the Crouch End spriggan and Sofia partying together among damp foliage and abandoned railway arches of Parkland Walk, near Finsbury Park. She feels Sofia is okay.

WALK 3: THE FUTURE

So, twenty years have passed. *Magnesium Burns* is a minor underground institution now and the anniversary is being marked with an exhibition at a small gallery in south London tracing its history over the years. I have loaned a number of my original copies of the early issues, some of which sell for not exorbitant but still ridiculous prices. Eighty quid for some stapled and photocopied pages – I suppose that's flattering.

What happened to Cerise only helped up the value of *In the Real World*. This is perverse, but I see why. Some authentic city grit. Proof of the intersection between the scene and reality. That issue goes for truly silly money.

The exhibition is nearly ready to go. But I want to take another walk beforehand, with my brother. Chasing the ghosts of ourselves, I like to think of it as.

It seems perverse, but he picks me up in his car so we can drive to where we want to begin our walk. In the car we belt out a playlist of London songs we love. A singalong to the Cockney Rejects and Booze & Glory, Conflict, The Clash of course, Hard Skin, Inner Terrestrials and The Skints.

We drive through clogged traffic towards Stratford, passing through Bruce Grove and Seven Sisters and into Hackney as the stereo belts out the classics. Andy drives and I watch the people of London, doing whatever it is they do, throng the streets. There are so many of them.

After an interminable time crawling in traffic we find a place to park. The idea is to walk from the new and gleaming East Village, pick up our beloved River Lea, then drift with the water through east London, following the water down to where it meets Mother Thames at Trinity Buoy Wharf.

Like Mike Skinner says, it was supposed to be so easy. Neither of us are novices at this stuff. A 'towpath closed' sign does not fill us with dread. Our plan is to see where the Lea hits the Thames, travelling through a part of east London with which we are both unfamiliar.

Just keep the water in sight. Easy, right? But we haven't bargained on the Olympic Park, on Crossrail, on the high rises, on the paths to nowhere, the cafés and sculptures that lurk in stasis, waiting for crowds to materialise. Inverted ghost towns, appearing before the occupants. Immediately we're thwarted by closed walkways and bridges at every turn.

'For fuck's sake,' says Andy, scratching his head and laughing.

We don't mind. This is all part of it, isn't it? Trying to work things through and navigate the terrain.

We're forced through the jumbled up and half-dreamt architecture of the Queen Elizabeth Park, with the giant West Ham United logo to our right. This is a place that doesn't know what it is, not yet. My brother and I are ancient beings transposed into the landscape of a future London.

Something for everyone, perhaps, and therefore for no one at all. What more can be said? There are so many competing ideas, developers, architectural preferences, the clashing desires of consumers, football fans, the drinkers in hipster bars. The comforting conspiracy I've always imagined must be at play. The truth is that the ship is rudderless, and there's no driver at the wheel. The car is on fire.

We know exactly where we are, yet somehow we are lost, and we've spent forty-five minutes since exiting the car attempting to get onto the Lea. Google Maps is begrudgingly consulted. We head down a short slope onto the City Mill River and past an inexplicable climbing wall. I pose for a photo halfway up a ladder making the V-sign at Andrew.

'You'll ruin your serious artistic reputation, Mel.' He winks.

Then it's across a small bridge and finally onto the Lea itself. Nearly an hour after we left the Timber Lodge, we have got nowhere.

We reach the *Big Breakfast* house, and I sigh. We should have just gone to Hackney Wick station and headed out from there. So much time in this city spent in delays, jams, walking in circles.

At the Greenway, we're thwarted again. Fucking hell. It's hard not to feel like the landscape is against us today, a corporate and concreted sentience messing around with us to alleviate its own boredom.

We hit a fence. There's a gate that foolishly opens, and yet another sign saying, 'towpath closed'. Crossrail. When I think of Crossrail, all I can think of is destruction. Inconvenience. Agendas other than those of my own.

'Shall we just keep going?' I say to Andy.

'I like it, sis. That's the spirit,' he says.

Bugger it. If we get kicked off the path for trespassing, it makes the whole thing more interesting.

'We'll just say we're visiting a friend on a houseboat,' I say.

Five minutes later, two orange-jacket men escort us off the towpath and onto the diversion. Sorry lads. Our feigned ignorance has clearly failed to convince. I'm pissing myself laughing and Andy has a grin plastered over his face.

The Crossrail site is a future postcard from the ruined London: grey mounds of building materials, asphalt, rubble and earth. Fluorescent men picking through the scene, dwarfed by the thing they're building. I imagine that one day this will all be finished, but as we head east, the skyline is full of cranes and buildings half-built, or maybe half-demolished.

London is never finished. London never was like it was. Build and destroy and repeat.

We find our way back to the river finally at a roundabout on the A12. New flats, a mouldy and decaying doll perched against an unlaid and mildewed paving slab. Photogenic detritus of the city.

I point at the doll, lichened skin and a missing eye, and say, 'That could be your new album cover, Andy.'

'Yes, very good,' he says, rolling his eyes.

At least we're on the river path now, something recognisable to stick to, but the surprises keep coming.

Next to offices for Amazon and Sainsbury's sits a welded sculpture made from supermarket trolleys. We try and decipher its meaning – a celebration of the weekly shop? A symbol of the redundancy of the high street? An altar to the god of supermarkets?

We reach Cody Dock. This is a kind of proto Hackney Wick, with a coffee shop, a Damien Hirst sculpture of an enlarged cross-section of an epidermis, and a small arts space with no one inside. Signs dotted around explain the things to come and the city we can all look forward to.

I am hit with images of things hiding beneath the skin, the layers of London, of emperor worms burrowing into flesh. I want the judderman to appear in its impotent male rage and rip this fucking place to the ground, put it to the torch. But he's a thing of the past.

Make a note, Mel: this will be the place you're complaining about but drinking in five years from now.

My brother and I stand in front of another padlocked barrier by Cody Dock in the winter light, the sky clouded and moody. I wonder if there truly is a conspiracy to stop people from travelling along the water.

In the distance, cable cars zip over the Thames from East India Dock to North Greenwich. I look at Balfron Tower and recall a decadent night I spent in its high rises, watching the blinking towers of commerce at Canary Wharf. We're heading in the direction of the Dome. We can't get onto the path, but we are in London, in its very veins.

I lean against the barrier and roll a cigarette, swig from my bottle of water. Andy crunches on an apple. It seems natural to stop here for a break.

'That was a great gig the other night, you know,' I say to him.

He smiles softly and says, 'Thanks sis. You shouldn't be smoking you know.'

I glare at him.

'It felt good to be doing it all again,' he continues. 'It's not like I want to relive the past or anything, you can't go back. But it just felt good to be up there and people still giving a shit. Or people getting into it for the first time, like your little mate Debbie. She single, by the way?' He winks as he says this. I let it pass without comment.

'And I was thinking about all this stuff when I was writing the intro to your book. I'm so proud of you, you do know that? It really hit me that we're the product of a specific time and place, and we aren't even that old, but that place has gone. I know we're London born and bred, but that place that made us has kinda gone. Just look at all of this around us. And think about Gary and Daniel, the world they're describing seems so close but so impossibly distant and far away, like it's another fucking planet.

'So, if I wanted to get Scarp back up and running then it couldn't just be about nostalgia and playing "Bilocation" to the same people every night on tour until I'm in my fifties. It's gotta be about connecting that past to this present and with room to expand into the future. Like how I know this exhibition isn't the end of *Magnesium Burns,* it's just a pause point.

'So, yeah, I'll do a new record. It's gonna be about all this stuff. I've got a title for it too – *What Never Was*.

'And I've already got a new song, and don't call me a soppy cunt but it's called "Melissa". I'm trying to write about Cerise too, I just don't know how to yet. But I'll get there. That's what I like about the two of us: we always get there in the end.'

My eyes prick with tears, and I move over to my brother and give him a hug as the river Lea flows behind us and darkening skies gather over the city.

The towpath has died. No access. We do not know why, and no information is offered, so we trudge off through the warehouses and industrial units of Canning Town, through a concrete badland of abandoned pubs that look straight out of a cockney gangster movie. I imagine myself as the protagonist of a Derek Raymond novel, alone and misunderstood rooting through the grubby underworld like a blind worm.

Approaching Canning Town underground station, the air is thick with pollutants, a rough smog that sits blackly on the tongue. Here the developments have gone into overdrive. We keep exploring, including a sad and dishevelled 'ecological park' that exists despite the choking fumes, and past the high rises that seem half-complete and only partially inhabited.

Through wire mesh we peer at an empty building, its grounds covered in pristine deck chairs next to a small swimming pool within spitting distance of the dirty Lea. Behind shining glass are rows of untouched and unused exercise bikes in rows like silent stormtroopers.

Finally we reach Trinity Buoy Wharf and see the river we have tried and failed to follow gush into the Thames. Threatening clouds gather over the Dome.

Here we find galleries and a small boutique café with moderately priced coffee. Monuments to London's maritime history are all around. The skyline is cranes and endless flats rising high into the sky.

'This is the future,' Andy says.

TeXt

There is London Cognita, and London Incognita, and I know where I belong.

This is the text that kicks off the stencilled explanation on a white wall in the TeXt gallery. It's all rendered in a font somehow taken and adapted from my scribbled and xeroxed early zines. It looks fantastic.

Tonight's the night then. Opening night, launch party, private view. Let's do it.

I've just walked in with Andy, and before I've barely been able to take in the place, Debbie has run up to us and given me a fierce hug and my brother too. She looks good tonight, a professional, and I'm grateful for all she has done. She's become a mate.

A table is lined with rows of full glasses of white and red wine. Amassed ranks of beer bottles. Two young people ready to pour drinks and crack open beer with the bottle opener. I hope they can get off early.

Another table has gleaming new editions of the book ready for sale and signing, recent editions of the zine that I still have copies of, and even a run of T-shirts. There are prints and posters of certain iconic images from the twenty-year run. Funny to think of people hanging parts of my life on their walls.

The walls are a gallery of *Magnesium Burns* covers, from the very early days right up until the present, with an enlarged print of the cover of *You're Already Dead.*

I added, in the end, a more hopeful subtitle, so it fully reads *You're Already Dead (so, Live Today)*. A reference to two of my favourite songs, but with a meaning way beyond that. The cover was something I thought long and hard about, discussed with Andy and PK and Debbie. In the end I selected a photograph of myself, Andy, PK and Cerise, aged about twenty-three, standing in front of The Balustrade, long before it was torn down. The photo has been degraded in proper zine fashion by being photocopied and converted into stark black and white before being incorporated into the cover. PK was using and drinking heavily at the time. Cerise was starting to get worn down by it all. Andy was touring a lot with Scarp; in fact, we're at The Balustrade because they're playing a benefit show inside for a cause long forgotten.

I've had a few glasses of white to fortify myself. Debbie has given her introduction to the crowd, for which I have to thank her effusively afterwards. She sounded like she meant the things she was saying.

Andy has performed his brief set of acoustic Scarp songs; he played 'Bilocation' of course and thankfully didn't play 'Melissa'. He also said a few words, essentially a live version of the intro he gave for the book. He's a charmer, and always has been.

So now it's my turn to get up on stage. I give a truncated history of the zine, what my inspirations were and why I started the thing in the first place. I give thanks to the people close to me in my life, and I thank Debbie and the TeXt gallery.

'And I just want to say how great it is to be here. To be honoured with this amount of attention given to something that I never thought would last more than a few months. I can't believe I'm at the twentieth anniversary of something I created. I was only nineteen when I started all of this – the time that has passed is now longer than the lifespan of the girl who started writing those early issues. Things like that blow my mind.

'I'm going to give a reading now. A long time ago I wrote a story called "A Monument to Nothing", which you can see plastered all over that wall over there, and the original issue in which it appeared. It's from my personal archive, so please don't nick it.'

Laughter. I sip my wine. My stomach is fizzy with nerves.

'It's probably the first issue I was really proud of. Definitely the first story I felt where things were gelling together. If you haven't read it, it was about a young woman called Melanie who gets stuck in the darkness beneath London, lost in the tunnels between Bank and Monument station with a strange feminine spirit or perhaps goddess. I was still feeling my way through my ideas in those days.'

I pause and look into the crowd. Shadows are gathering at the back where two men stand. Gary and Daniel, as they were in the photograph I keep in my possession, on the banks of the Thames near Wapping. Something flickering, manlike, sour and spent and angry hovers over them, behind them.

I blink the image away.

'After my best friend, Cerise, died, I realised it was possible to spend too long in the darkness. I spent many years fascinated with the grim, grimy stories of this city. They are endless. Spending too long with them can distort the world and how you look at it. The world, this city, isn't all poison and blackness. And it isn't all joy and light. It's both. I lost the balance for a long time.'

I scan the crowd. There's my mum, looking a bit doddery now but proud. PK, still clean and smiling wide in a Youth of Today T-shirt. Debbie and a few of her mates and co-workers at the gallery all done up expertly like edgy bohemians. Andy is in the crowd now, sipping from a bottle of lager. I'm wearing a new Scarp T-shirt under my jacket – a tour shirt for the upcoming album.

And at the back of the crowd, I squint and can see a flickering female form, the commare who follows me wherever I go in this city, and she assumes the form of old aunt Sarah, then a woman who must be Jenny Duro, slathered in the mud of the estuary. I hear rough cacophonous music in the distance, scorched and abrasive. She changes at high speed: a woman of Roman London, a Celtic princess smeared with burnt soil, a prostitute with a collapsed face, a makeup counter girl with a hole in the back of her skull, a woman with purple bruises circling her throat, a distraught woman in a long coat holding a speckled and mouldy photograph and, finally, Cerise. Cerise waves silently to me, gives a thumbs up and a wink.

I must be squiffy from the wine.

'So, I want to read something new for you, a new story that's in this exclusive edition of *Magnesium Burns*. It's about Melanie, a character I never stopped thinking about, and what happens when you choose to come back into the light.'

You're Already Dead

[From exhibition-only edition of
Magnesium Burns, Melissa Eider, 2020]

Melanie read once, in a book she cherished, that nothing sustains us when we fall. For a long time she was absent, deep down in the darkness of London trapped with a woman who gave her no solace. But she was young, knew she could not spend her whole life in the blackness, that there was still light above. She would not spend her life hiding from the man who peeled himself out from the shadows, or ducking out the way of the great worms that slithered beneath the city. She was never much of a team player and couldn't join the tribes in the disused tunnels. The commare would never help her, and the judderman was a pathetic father figure lost to rage and disappointment. As soon as you realised that, he became impotent. Mum and Dad could never help you in the long run.

Melanie realised too, that if you spend too long in the tunnels, you become a thing of darkness. Spend too long in shadow and you're already dead. She found a reason to come back up.

She's older now, and finally has made her way up into the light. She is back in the city and enjoying it for what it is – not what it was, what it never was, or what it could have been. She has found her way to the South Bank today. *Could people take me for a tourist?* she thinks.

The guy from the RSPB, young and eager, with thick glasses and a clipboard, guides her to the telescope. The Thames flows slowly and softly behind her. She had walked away from the information stand moments earlier, mildly disappointed. The female peregrine falcon was absent in that moment she decided to stop and chat, to look and to try to see something that was really there. The young man ran after her, excitedly brought her back to the viewing spot.

'There,' he said, 'she's back.'

There she was. A predator that gripped the imagination in sharp yellow talons, the falcon that reminded Melanie of everything you could lose and could perhaps regain. Bullet-fast and bullet-strong. She sat there, imperious, vicious, marble-still in the upper reaches of the Tate Modern.

Tourists flowed around them, the grey river calm. A busker played bad acoustic songs. A bubbler blew bubbles that burst soapily on the coats of workers hurrying to their sandwich shops. She kept her eye to the telescope and watched.

That morning Melanie had passed people covered in shiny sleeping bags with scrawny dogs as companions. She had to say no to a request for a cigarette; she had quit, and you can't share vapour. She wondered what the homeless would do in the cashless society some promised. In London, Melanie thought, nothing sustains us when we fall.

She left the falcon to soar above the galleries and museums.

She was heading now to the north-west of the city to visit a friend long laid low by drink and drugs but pulling out of it finally. They would catch up and listen to the music they once thrilled to and share memories of his deceased sister; her best friend.

The next morning, coming into the city on the Northern Line from Edgware, the line was bathed in sunlight as brooding slate-grey clouds loomed over north-west London, looking as if the suburbs of Burnt Oak and Hendon were walled in by majestic mountains. Melanie imagined peregrines catching diseased pigeons in the skies above the Brent Cross shopping centre, surviving in the choke of the North Circular.

She watched the looming mountains in the polluted sky for as long as she could. But after Golders Green, everything went black.

ACKNOWLEDEGMENTS

A huge thank you to Nathan, Amelia and Blue at Dead Ink for their continued faith in my work.

To the Influx Press team – Kit, Jordan, and Sanya.

Thanks to: Niall Griffiths, Timothy J. Jarvis, Matthew Hill, Paul Tremblay, Adam Nevill, Sarah Cleave, Nina Allan, Dan Coxon, Sean Preston, Fernando Sdrigotti, Adam Scovell, Vince Haig, Luke Bird, Gareth E. Rees.

To D.A. Northwood

VERSIONS OF THESE STORIES APPEARED IN THE FOLLOWING PUBLICATIONS:

Sinker (first published online in Reflex Fiction)

Judderman (first published as *Judderman,* Eden Book Society, 2018)

The Scorched Music of the Emperor Worm (first published in online in *Coffin Bell Journal*)

I Precede Myself (Longlisted for the 2019 London Short Story Prize)

We Pass Under (first published in *Uncertainties IV,* Swan River Press, 2020)

Where No Shadows Fall (first published in *The Shadow Booth*, Vol. 1)

A Constellation of Wondrous Places (first published in *City of Stories 2*, Spread the Word, 2018)

Staples Corner and How We Can Know It (first published in *An Unreliable Guide to London*, Influx Press, 2016)

What Never Was (first publishing in *Confingo* 13)

ABOUT THE AUTHOR

Gary Budden is a writer, editor and the co-founder of award-winning independent publisher, Influx Press.

He is the author of Hollow Shores (Dead Ink, 2017), the Shirley Jackson Award-Shortlisted Judderman (Eden Book Society, 2018), and The White Heron Beneath the Reactor w/ artist Maxim Griffin (2019).

He lives in London.

About Dead Ink

Supported by Arts Council England, we're focussed
on developing the careers of new and
emerging authors.

Our readers form an integral part of our team.
You don't simply buy a Dead Ink book,
you invest in the authors and the books you love.

You can keep up to date with the latest Dead
Ink events, workshops, releases and calls for
submissions by signing up to our mailing list.